When Walls Rise

K. Malady

"We do not suffer by accident."

Jane Austen, *Pride & Prejudice*

To everyone who wondered what happened when the curtain
fell and when the lights went up.
And as ever, for my favorites. You know who you are.

SEKAI
Last Light
The Four Fingers
Mana
Eoin
Calanyon
Egil
Danna
Railde
Cros
Caer Glen Forest
Outer Forest
Arail
Crumbling Spire
Main Gate
Helne
Solstice Sanctum
Ilsen
Riccter Peaks
Ghrad
Samian
Haddare's Pass
Dalmer
Breil
Archve
Nor
Kingswood
Lintom
The Wilds
Holland Wasteland
Wilder Frontier
Port Sarcan
Gunpath
The Wildlands
Howling Plains
Caern Ruins
Calas Swamps
Lone Menhir
Alacson
White Desert
Wilder Frontier
Aranvale

Contents

CHAPTER 1

*I*t's dark; a single window lights a small circular room. Wet tracks run down stone walls like sweat and the scent of sea salt tinges the air. There's a hazy quality to everything, more real than the many dreams I've had since defeating the Eósy and sealing the Gates, similar to how it felt when I experienced the swell of opponents' memories. But since that day, I've had no confrontations that would bring about memory magic, assuming it even still works with the wall as it is. And never was I able to move around without the dream's maker controlling me.

Something tinkles under my feet when I spin a half circle to better inspect the not-dreamscape. Glass litters the floor and I skitter backward to avoid piercing my bare feet. The back of my knees hit something hard, and I slip down with a thump, knocking a candle to the ground as my backside connects with a wooden bench behind me.

A thin sleeping bag sits beside the bench, with a person-shaped lump resting on it. The body slinks into a sitting position and turns to face me, revealing long blond hair glinting in the moonlight and a familiar, but pale, face. Leyden, no, the Voice's bright eyes widen in surprise.

"Grace?"

I wake with a gasp, a heaviness on my torso holding me down and unable to surge out of bed. I wriggle until the prison releases me.

Tans groans into my neck and snakes his arms around me again, pulling me to him and locking me back into the cage of his body. His fingers trail over the scars on my hips under my nightshirt.

"Was it the dragon or the sprite?" Even in almost-sleep, he speaks slowly and clearly, allowing me to understand the language I've spent the last six months learning.

I inhale and release the fear the nightmare left behind. Unlike the memory of my past sins, this dream didn't leave me feeling nauseous and guilty.

"Neither," I whisper into the dark of our shared bedroom, my voice shaky and broken. "Something different."

A fluttering at the back of my neck wakes me the next morning. I turn to trail my fingertips down Tans' biceps until I can embrace him. He caresses my jaw, tangling his fingers in my hair. I lean forward and capture his lips. He tries to deepen the kiss, but I pull away. His amber eyes are dark and there's a slight flush to his bronze skin.

"I do not have meetings until after lunch," he says, leaning forward to kiss me again. I avoid his mouth, which lands on my cheek. Undeterred, he drags his lips from my cheekbones to my jaw, down to the soft skin of my neck.

"I've got a study session," I remind him.

"You could be late," he tells my collarbones.

After a slight push, he lets me detach and slip from the bed. He leans on his elbow, our shared white sheets dipping to display his lean chest. There's still an undeniable quality about him that hints at a person who should be smirking at the professor and effortlessly charming his way out of missing homework with a playful wink. And yet, the Tans I know is the complete opposite: a man ready to work and be the best commander he can be, without feeling the need to prove his worth to others. It's something I hope to emulate. I lean back down and give him a smacking kiss.

"Morning breath," I say against his lips. He sighs audibly, directing more air into my face, and I laugh.

As I turn from the bed to dress, he snags my arm. "Be careful, Butterfly."

"Going to the library? I'll do my best not to trip and impale myself on one of those sharp books."

He doesn't laugh, instead his hand squeezes my hip, the one with a starburst scar and burn that took four months to close and heal. "Be careful," he repeats.

"I will."

He grins as the hand on my hip migrates to my buttocks. "Good," he says, squeezing lightly. I wince as dull pain blooms where his fingers connect. He recoils, an apologetic look on his face. "I'm terribly sorry," he begins.

"It's fine. I must have bruised myself training with Faburth and Eida yesterday."

Although yesterday was only endurance training, which left my muscles sore but not bruised. It was more likely I smacked into something on my walk up the stairs to our spire, but Tans didn't need to worry more about what happens to me when I leave the relative safety of our shared chambers.

The apology in his eyes doesn't fade but is joined by concern. "Perhaps you should—"

"No," I insist. Tans would be happiest if he wrapped me in metaphorical (or real) wool, safe from any danger and cocooned in our rooms. I understand his reasoning, given I tossed myself to my probable death six months ago, but I've outlived my usefulness here in Dalner. Being the false savior and then *true* savior came with consequences. I need to fix those consequences.

"There is no need for you to learn combat," he says. It isn't a new argument, but a discussion we've had repeatedly since before I could speak the language and we were communicating only through charades.

I shake my head. "I want to."

He sighs, his hands sliding up to his hair and pulling. The nervous habit has me lean back down to intertwine our fingers until the tension in his frame fades.

"Why don't we have lunch?" I suggest. "We can take a walk through the gardens."

He nods and presents his lips for another goodbye kiss. I kiss him again until he murmurs, "Morning breath."

With a laugh, I finish dressing while he watches me with assessing eyes. I don't let the muscle strain show until I leave the room and can hobble down the stairs. I don't mean to hide the fatigue from Tans, but the fear in his eyes adds an uncomfortable weight to my stomach. But he doesn't need to take care of me anymore.

By the time I reach the library, several spires and flights of stairs away, my hip pinches and burns. I've been told by multiple healers (slowly translated and pantomimed by Tans and Sáv at the time) that I'm lucky the wound didn't get infected. Non-magical health care developed over the past few decades as the magic in their blood dwindled, but it wasn't enough. Their medical capabilities had barely closed the wound. The raised scar looks like a red rippling root and is just as ugly.

I slip into my designated chair in the library with a wince. Rothàna is already present, sitting straight-backed into her seat across the table. She interlaces her fingers and rests them against her trim stomach. The thin lines at the corners of her russet lips show her mood.

"They've been going easy on you," she says, her cool topaz eyes inspecting the way I hold myself and the lean in my frame. "I've half a mind to visit those training grounds and see exactly what Eida and her unit are teaching you."

I uncurl my shoulders to mimic Rothàna's posture. "It's not just Eida, Faburth is there too, and they can't decide the best training—"

Rothàna huffs. "That's their excuse. What better way to appease their Lord Commander's worries than to train you sloppily? Then you remain incapable, and that boy of yours won't fear you'll run into another portal."

My cheeks heat, but I refuse to drop my gaze to the table. I can't shy away from what happened. That's the whole point of training, of these lessons: to have the skills to revisit the wall and fix what I broke. "Tans wouldn't do that." He knows it's more likely I'd 'run into another portal' half-trained instead of letting it hold me back.

Rothàna waves a wrinkled hand. "Perhaps he didn't request it outright, but they know better. Eida certainly, given her recent advance to Fourth Commander. If she wishes to follow me, she must think for herself."

"Is Eida from one of the noble families?" Fíl finished that lesson last month, as my vocabulary finally expanded enough to understand it. Rothàna was an only child and when the Council of her time refused to allow her to take her family seat, she enlisted in the army instead. After serving and earning the Second Commander title, the Council fell over itself to let her take her seat.

She scowls. "No. As you know, only twelve of us enjoy that brogchekres pleasure."

"Brogchekres," I repeat slowly.

The scowl turns to a sharklike grin. "Yes, do not think you can distract me from your lessons today."

I open my mouth to retort that she started it but swallow the impulse. That might only goad her into leaving, and then Tans and I will be stuck like this even longer.

Three hours later and I've added another two dozen words to my vocabulary and revisited my understanding of the adjective-noun order. My muscles tremble from the exertion of yesterday, the hard wooden seat digging into my bones. No matter what Rothàna believes, the disagreement about how to train me just means I'm training more. But there's still so much to do that I swallow the pain to start on the next dozen words.

"We shall stop here," Rothàna announces. She loosens her bun and long strands of white hair fall around the sharp planes of her cheekbones, the emerald bead describing her station tumbling towards her ear.

"Not yet." I clench my fingers around the parchment in case she tries to take it. "With the Council meeting tomorrow and training and history lessons, I won't be able to study with you for days."

"You must break, Grace, or you'll overtire and make mistakes."

I look out the floor-length windows. Though the openings are narrow, the view is clear. No clouds or mist block the landscape in the distance until the countryside halts up against a long opaque wall spanning up towards the sky.

That's the problem. Six months ago, when I closed the Gate that the Voice and his violent Eósy cronies attempted to breach,

I used my blood and electricity to shock the opening closed. The Gate shut permanently, and the invisible force field-like wall the original Eósy and Sàrkany erected turned visible and impenetrable. The invisible magical openings, the rifts, at dawn and dusk stopped too, leaving us with no animal visitors and no weather changes. Apparently, it was those twice daily openings that allowed enough magic to seep through the barriers for the Sàrkany's use, meaning with their disappearance, there's no more magic. Tans can no longer heal, he and Kórol no longer have control over their elements, Sáv can't shape shift, and Fíl can't do whatever it was Fíl did.

"I already made those mistakes," I grumble. "Resting just gives me more time to think about what I should have done instead."

She purses her lips.

"Is she complaining about her life of leisure again?" Fíl says from behind us. He squeezes my shoulder as he takes a seat beside me.

"None of that, young man," Rothàna says, glaring. "Like me, this young woman isn't made for leisure."

"That's not true." Fíl and I speak in tandem. My cheeks redden as Rothàna turns her scowl onto me.

"It isn't that I don't want to relax. I'd love to. But I can't, not while we're dealing with the consequences of the Gate," I explain, staring down at my hands. Only a few thin lines remain from the cuts I suffered at the Gate, pale crisscrosses spanning my palms to my elbows. "I can't rest until it's fixed."

Fíl bristles, his long hair swinging as he turns to face me. "You are the heroine of Dalner, Grace. There is nothing more you need to do."

Rothàna holds up a hand and Fíl closes his mouth, bemused. "Do not coddle her." She turns to stare me down. "Yes, Grace, you removed our magic. Yes, you have cut off our supply of meat. Yes, I may never see another thunderstorm. Yes—"

"Please get to a point, Rothàna." I cover my eyes with my palms.

Her callused fingers grab my wrists to reveal my face. Instead of the annoyance I expect at my interruption, as Rothàna suffers no attitude in her lessons, she smiles faintly. "I would give it all up to avoid being...prunreumchekm by some Eósy overlord."

I blink at the new unknown word. Rothàna releases my wrist and redoes her tight bun. "You can figure it out by context and roots," she says.

Prun means below, *reum* is choice, with *chek* making something negative. "A synonym to controlled," I blurt, before she leaves and I'm stuck with the mystery for three days.

"Close," Fíl says. "More like oppressed while under control. And we all accept the consequences of what you did to avoid being mastered and abused by...them."

Rothàna begins gathering her parchment of conjugations and linguistic patterns. "No wonder Grace feels she can laze about, with you feeding her the answers and not letting her learn on her own. Is this how you supervise your lessons?"

Fílga's mouth drops open before he bristles. "Lady Rothàna, you know I spent an entire month preparing my schedule, signed off by Tansr and Kórol, beginning with—"

"I just wish I knew what to do once I'm prepared enough to fix it," I say. My two tutors stop bickering and stare at me.

"Live your life, Grace, as it is now," Rothàna says. "That's all any of us can do."

"The Sàrkany have lived with so little magic for centuries," adds Fíl. "They managed once. They can all learn to be less dependent for the safety of those amongst us. Better we live with less magic than under the thumb of the monsters on the other side of the wall."

CHAPTER 2

Fíl escorts Rothàna from the library and jokingly kicks me out, but not before reminding me of my chaperone duties that evening. He and Sáven decided to court formally, which means they can no longer hang out without a neutral party. There's uproar over their pairing, not because of their genders (score one for Dalner) but because of their ages. It's only been whispered, but Sáv being under twenty and Fíl being over has left certain castle dwellers clutching their metaphorical pearls. It has the makings of a plot like books I've read and can never reread: the older experienced man and younger inexperienced love interest. Fíl hits the 'sugar daddy' trope too, as I accidentally saw piles of coins he had stored in an extra room in his chambers. But no one has explained the problem, just looking at me sadly and telling me I won't understand.

After we confirm the details for their date, I have just enough time to slip to the first floor garden that blooms outside the throne room, the one that reflects its three stained glass windows. They replaced the original and broken windows, even the one with Dalner's centuries' old motto, with the image of a dragon and a sword. It took months to gather enough materials and for the craftsmen to discover a non-magical way to manipulate the glass. Kórol made it a priority though, and just after my birthday, the designs were inlaid. The first and third window are simple patterns of black and red glass that look ominous and deadly when the light hits them, like the black stone of the castle itself is bleeding. The middle window displays a dismal motto in white surrounded by navy blue glass: 'Alone we stand, and alone we die.'

Tans sits on a metal bench, a cloth satchel beside him. He stands when he sees me, his face blooming into a smile, the deep creases of worry melting away.

He crosses the short distance and kisses my cheek before dragging me back to his seat. Again, when my body hits the metal, a pain bursts from my backside. Tans doesn't notice, too focused on pulling out various snacks. Thankfully, as it could start an argument.

The snacks look like Sáv's influence, a smorgasbord of new offerings and experiments. He's one who doesn't appear affected by the blocked walls. He can't shape shift, which he seems fine with, and can explore his own culinary creativity. Tans pulls out something that looks like vegan cheese, sniffing it dubiously. *Brogchekres*, as I just learned that day.

"How was your morning?" I ask as he hands me a hunk of bread and the mystery chunk of cheese.

He dips his own bread in jam before responding. "I spent it with Kórol. These are the remains of our breakfast. It is less than I expected, so I hope you aren't too hungry."

"I can handle less food if Kórol is eating."

Kórol hasn't taken a break since the walls solidified, working night and day to keep the Kingdom going. I'd say I expected this, given his love for his country, but Kórol does nothing else, not even sleep. Tans can only convince him to eat sporadically. *Health* care is something the Sàrkany developed because of the already-dwindling magic, but mental health care is another story. Their history with mental magic meant they never had to rely on non-magical cures. Until now.

"He watches the corners as if an Eósy stands there ready to attack," Tans murmurs, eyes downcast. "I had only just convinced him to release my troops to search for supplies. I fear he will withdraw his support soon."

"What happened?"

"You'll recall a group of six left from Port Sàrcàn."

I nod in recognition. The Sàrkany used to facilitate trade with the neighbors *somewhere*. One record called them the Barrens, but none of the others could confirm the truth. The remaining records couldn't explain who they traded with, if they were Eósy, a descendant of them, or another sentient species, like the sprites. "I remember you wanted to go with them."

Tans stares down at his hands. "I had hoped those relationships still existed, that someone was there. The ship returned, but the soldiers." He swallows audibly. "The soldiers were dead."

I drop the food and grab his hands, even as a vicious sense of relief—that Tans wasn't on that ship—grows. "I'm so sorry, Tans."

"They were...they were gray, as if the life had been sucked from them. There were no other signs of what occurred, not that our healers could even tell. We don't know what happened. If there was an illness, or if they made it to the Barrens and whoever they met harmed them and directed the ship back." He shutters and closes his eyes. "If I had been there, if I had healed—"

I squeeze his fingers until they crack. "The same thing would have happened to you. Unless there's magic out there, you'd have died too."

He slumps until his forehead hits my shoulder. "You're right," he says into the fabric of my shoulder. "Sometimes I simply hope..." His voice fades, but I can guess what he hopes, as it is the same desire rattling around my head too. He straightens and picks up his food. "We must move forward. We will try again to The Wilds or Alacson. There must be something out there."

"Isn't Alacson... empty? And in the opposite direction of where the food would be?" Fíl glossed over the history of those two areas, but he was clear that no inhabitants remained there, that the Sàrkany live, and had lived for centuries, in Dalner alone. With Alacson south of Dalner, it was unlikely other living creatures slipped through the Gates or the rifts and traveled the few hundred miles to Alacson.

Tans shrugs. "The Howling Plains exist. It must come from somewhere, a howling beast perhaps." The skepticism must show on my face because he continues with a smirk, "You aren't the only one who can read and theorize."

I huff out a laugh. "Mine was a bit more spelled out than this, though. I had an actual guidebook for one, and Kórol spouting poetry for two."

The laughter in his face dies, snuffed out like a candle. "When you see him tomorrow," he starts, as the corners of his eyes pinch with concern, "tell me if he seems different."

"But you see him every—"

"I see him as he is. I need to know if his mask is cracking in front of the Council, or if he behaves this way only with me." His eyes pin me in place. "We need to know."

I nod and busy myself eating. The garden is eerily still, the knowledge that no life will appear at sunset still jarring.

"You could take your seat tomorrow and see," I suggest after picking at my food and losing my appetite. "Instead of me as your proxy."

Tans' lips bloom into a half grin. "No, you're a better proxy than the man my father appointed. You deserve your own seat."

I barely restrain an eye roll. "Rothàna only gets a seat because she's the direct heir of her family. They won't add one for me." The hero worship is still present, but I swear I can see judgment in the male Council members' eyes when the subject of the Gates comes up.

Tans swallows down a hunk of cheese, his eye twitching. "Remind me to tell Sáv to avoid that spice for a time." He clears his throat and leans forward. "And I disagree. You deserve your own seat. But you are correct, you would need to be the heir or perhaps be connected to the heir."

"Sexism again," I groan. "How did a society with two female deities become so sexist?"

Tans tucks a lock of my unruly brown hair behind my ear. "As the deities were fake and attempted to control us all, perhaps the sexism has always been present."

"True. There was the attempted subjugation."

"A new word?" I nod and he beams. "That's quite advanced from what I saw in Rothàna's schedule."

I duck my head to hide a proud smile. "I'm trying."

He snakes his arms around my waist. "No, you're proceeding wonderfully. You've overcome such a deficiency. Not only with the language." His eyes darken. "For a time, I thought you might not walk."

"But I can. I even run sometime," I joke. His expression doesn't change. "Let's just get back to how wonderful I am."

He draws me to him until I can hook my chin over his slender shoulder. "Yes, yes. You are wonderful." He sighs, the proximity mingling our hair together. His pitch black almost eats my chocolate brown. "You are though. And you deserve a place on the Council."

"Maybe. But like you said, it's only for heirs."

"And spouses of heirs."

My heart drops into my stomach even as a shocked gasp slips past my lips. I pull back and Tans' expression is open, hopeful.

"Are you? I'm...I'm only eighteen, Tans."

"As am I. I expect nothing to change when I make it to twenty."

"But twenty-one is still a possibility?" I tease weakly. He looks at me like I'm missing something important, something more important than a future marriage proposal. "Let's—" I disengage from his grasp. "Let's stabilize the society before we talk about things like that."

He nods, his braids swinging around his bronze cheeks. "As long as you know that I'm serious."

My posture softens, and I lean back into him. "I do. I love you too, remember?"

Two men in black leather loiter at the edge of the garden. Tans catches their gaze and gestures to the wall, where they stand and wait. He turns back to me and grimaces. "I must leave you now. Shall we continue this at dinner?" He takes my hand and kisses from my palm to wrist, a devious expression on his face.

My stomach still flutters at his touch, and I swallow the impulse to giggle and blush. I try to channel Rothàna's serious countenance. "I can't tonight, remember? I'm chaperoning Sáv and Fíl."

His face falls for a moment before a smirk appears. "Have fun. Do tell me how many times they forget your presence and start engaging each other as if alone."

I slug him in the chest until he laughs, muttering "violent" under his breath. I kiss him goodbye, and he leaves me alone in the silent garden.

Zorin, a fifteen-year-old recruit who just transferred to Eida's unit after succeeding at his latest trainee test, escorts me to Fíl's chambers after the sun sets. Escorts have become a request of Tans' when I venture outside my usual areas. It hasn't been worth the emotions to fight about it, but my patience is running thin.

Fíl's chambers are on the opposite side of the castle from ours. Our spire is sparsely occupied and out of the way of the bustling area, but Fíl's are in the middle of the main residential block, with heavy foot traffic at all hours.

Whispers trail after us as we turn towards the stairs that ascend into Fíl's spire. Zorin shuffles closer to me. He can't hide the unease in his hazel eyes or the slight sheen of perspiration on his golden skin.

"It's fine, Zorin. No one will bother us." My hand shoots out to the stone wall handholds as I climb the stairs. The heights stretch the scar tissue on my hips uncomfortably.

Displeasure replaces his concern. He looks like a younger and dark-haired version of Fíl as his lips thin. "Bay told me what happened when you went into Ilsen proper, Lady."

"One time," I mutter. Two months ago, I convinced Tans to go into town to practice walking on an incline. It didn't go well. "No one in the castle will say anything. That was just a… frustrated citizen."

Frustrated is too mild a word, but my brainpower remains focused on staying upright on the climb to translate the Sàrkany word for shrill and panicked. The woman we came upon looked like she'd come up close with a dobhà, repeating "you did this," until Tans could usher us away. The story of how the Gates were permanently sealed is easy to explain to the populace, the *why* less so unless Bittállí physically spelled them, and they experienced the active betrayal in the castle on the Solstice. For most of Dalner, they can understand they should consider all the Eósy bad, but how that connects to their lack of magic just points fingers at the outsider. Me.

Zorin's hands flutter beside my waist before he finally hooks an arm around me. The damp of his fingers seeps through the thin material of my dress. "If you say so, Lady."

We trudge up the corkscrew stairs towards Fíl's chambers on the highest floor. I lean on Zorin when the stairs disappear, my muscles screaming. I refuse to show it on my face, but the still-concerned expression Zorin has means I'm doing a poor job at hiding it.

Sáven meets us outside the door to Fíl's chambers with a wide smile on his face. His green eyes gleam like emeralds in the candlelight, and happiness seems to leak from his skin. His shirt looks freshly pressed, and he's chosen the least stained clothing he owns. Even his wavy apple-red hair has been brushed until it gleams. This is the sixth chaperoned date I've been on, and the first where the two are having a meal in private.

"Thanks, Zorin," Sáv says as he replaces Zorin at my side. Zorin's cheeks pink and he dips his head twice before shuffling away backward. He trips on his own feet until he turns and scampers down the hallway, his guard-like stoicism gone in the place of his embarrassment.

Sáv watches him with an indulgent expression. "That boy," he says to himself.

"Do you know him well?"

Sáv releases my arm and raps on Fíl's door. "One of the castle children, like me. His parents work in the stables. All of us played together growing up." His explanation trickles off as Fíl opens the door.

Fíl changed from the cream tunic he wore that morning in the library, instead wearing a chestnut brown tunic so crisp it looks like it could stand up on its own, tucked into black pants and gleaming leather shoes. Even though Fíl never looks in disarray, today he's in perfect form. His dark beard is smooth and tidy, and not a strand is out of place in his long blond braid. But the icing on Fíl's appearance is the smile on his face, something warm that ticks up the corners of his mouth. Even the usual wrinkles framing his eyes look softer. Sáv stares back up at Fíl with a similar expression. They lean towards each other as if magnetized.

I clear my throat, making a mental note to tell Tans how early the 'forgetting me' began. "Gentlemen, let's get inside before this gets indecent."

Sáv turns almost as red as his hair as Fíl bristles, but neither denies my implication, their hands brushing against each other as they usher me inside.

Fíl directs us to the seating area. He's set up candles around the main room and a meal waits on a low wooden table. They kneel on two thick cushions on the floor as I shuffle to the bench on the opposite side of the table. I gingerly lower myself onto the wood, but still pain bursts at the connection. It feels as though I've re-hit the same spot I bruised earlier, but the only bench I've encountered recently was a nightmare version. I wheeze out a complaint at the memory.

"Are you in pain, Grace?" Fíl asks, tearing his eyes from Sáv. Only in private does he refer to me as Grace.

"Just bruised," I say, waving my hand. "Don't worry about me. You two do the courting thing."

"Thanks for chaperoning. Few would agree," Sáv says, reaching towards Fíl to interlock their fingers.

"Anytime, you're my friends. Though I still don't understand why you two are such a scandal. Fíl isn't that much older than you."

Fíl's eyes darken. "We certainly appear very little different in age."

Sáv squeezes their joined hands. "Distinguished," he says.

I inspect Fíl's face. "You look late twenties, thirty at most. At worst, you're a young sugar daddy."

Fíl straightens, his face contorting into a scowl. "As I've told you, I did not and have no plans to parent any lover, and whether I provide them with sugar should be irrelevant."

I slump into my bench seat. "Translation problem, remember? You're older and can take care of him with all your money, so Sáv doesn't need to work."

Sáv furrows his red brows. "I enjoy cooking."

"It's not... never mind." I muster up a smile. "You're perfect together, age or no."

Sáv's frown deepens as turns to Fíl. "Why's she—Hasn't this come up in culture lessons? Her age, it should be."

"Tans is revising the lesson plan now," Fíl says mildly.

I can't follow the conversation. "What should he add?"

Sáv blinks owlishly. "Tans shouldn't teach her. Not 'cause it's wrong. But in case of the worst, you need to tell her about soul—"

Fíl coughs, a hacking sound louder and more indelicate than he's ever made in my presence. Sáv places a callused hand on his back until Fíl quiets.

"What's the worst? What are you adding?" I ask, but they ignore me.

"If you—" Sáv starts. Fíl coughs again and something glosses over Sáv's eyes. He turns back to Fíl, cupping his bearded cheeks. "I don't care. That you passed twenty. Choices matter," he whispers. The two stare at each other, an entire private conversation taking place between them.

I lean back against the wall behind me, attempting to fade into the stone and give them as much privacy as I can while being only a few feet away. I tally my mental note to Tans at 'two' and let my mind wander.

CHAPTER 3

I'm back in that small circular room. It's dark again, night like where I'm sleeping in Dalner, but the Voice isn't asleep on his pallet. He sits cross legged on the bench.

"You're back," he says, laughing. I want to close my eyes and imagine the laugh is that childlike giggle, unsettling but not menacing, to remember the simpler times. But his voice remains as deep as the last time I saw him in person, standing on the threshold of the main Gate.

"Sit, sit." He gestures to the pallet beside his bench. He smiles wildly, as if we're old friends reuniting and not a dream manifestation of my enemy.

I stay in the center of the room, crossing my arms around my stomach. "What is this?"

"A dream. But not how you think," he says before I can interrupt and try to wake myself up. "We are speaking but through our dreams."

I spin in a slow circle, taking in the details. It isn't a setting I recognize, except from the dream of the night before. The circular room looks like a desolate prison in a tower, constructed of rough-hewn stone. The walls seem to absorb any warmth or light, wet and cold. Water drips steadily from a hole in the roof, forming a small puddle on the uneven stone floor. A single window allows a glimpse of the outside world, a night setting displaying a stormy sea. But the sea below us is closer than it is in Ilsen; I can hear the waves crash against the base of the tower. A thin sleeping mat is under my feet, next to the bench I'd bruised myself on earlier.

But the Voice no longer looks like a Bittálli rendition of himself. When I met him, he appeared slathered in gold paint, thick globs of color covering his skin with shots of gray peeking through. Now he's neither gray nor gold, but a milky porcelain, the same shade as Bittálli. At this distance, his eyes aren't the dark color I thought, but black, true black as dark as Tans' silky hair. He looks slightly less put together, given his dingy shirt and torn pants, but the effect doesn't detract from his otherworldly grace. His face remains manic, though.

"This is really happening?" I've learned not to take anything for granted. The bruise on my behind, in the exact shape of the edge of a wooden bench, coupled with the unknowns of Eósy magic, means it could be true.

He nods. At the confirmation, I shuffle towards the side of the circle farthest from him. "How? There's no magic in Dalner."

"That isn't quite true. But I am not in Dalner. As my magic strengthened here, the repeated connection with your mind had certain... unintended effects."

A dark scowl settles on my face. "You mean you stuck your fingers in my head for months, and now you're doing it again?"

He lifts his hands as if showing he's harmless, but I know better. "Not purposefully. Though I missed our banter."

"I thought you wanted out of my head on the first day," I say. It's petulant, but those words stuck with me. "That I was an annoying, unspecial human who you only spoke with because I was the perfect victim."

He smirks, the expression unfurling on his face. It looks handsome on him, like an old timey movie actor. I want to scratch it off. "Did my opinion wound you? Little Grace, I did not know I made such an impression."

The blush rises on my face against my will. Not because it's him, but because attractive people can have a magic that makes the rest of us forget anything but their sparkling charm. It's why 'enemies to lovers' works so well when the villains are handsome, their sharp focus on the protagonist irresistible as the plot throws them together. I drop my head and remember everything this man did to me until my cheeks cool. The handsome bad guy is still that: the bad guy. "How do we stop this? I have no interest in dreaming of your face again."

*He giggles. "If only humans could not lie like Eósy. Who knows what you might say then? But I've no idea. My time in Exile must have cured my magic to the point that the mental connection re-*connected. *It appears you're stuck with me." He leans back against the stone and pats the empty bench. "We might as well make the most of it."*

"You expect me to make small talk?" I roll my eyes. "After what you did?"

He sobers. "I wasn't in my right mind, Grace. Perhaps if I had the sanity Exile has provided me, I would have tried a better method."

"Don't think I'm going to feel sorry for you."

He shrugs. "I don't expect you to. But I expect you to engage me in conversation while you are inhabiting my tower. It is the polite thing to do."

"Like you're the best example of gentlemanly behavior," I mutter.

"I'll start then. Grace, you're looking...." He trails off and purses his full lips. His eyes dip down my body and over the short night-shirt that stops at my thighs. I drop my arms to my side and slump to lengthen it.

"You're looking worse, Grace. Scars on your arms, bruises under your eyes. You'd think you were the one in prison, not I."

"There's no magic for healing anymore," I snap. "And you're not looking that great either. Pasty and pale. And second-rate villainous," I add with a snarl.

He smooths a hand down his ratty shirt, the opening at the neck bulging and displaying the creamy skin of his collarbones and a toned chest. My eyes ricochet back to the wall behind him. If only he looked like that Eósy who almost tore out my hair.

"I look wonderful," he says. "All this space, and the gray has vanished. I no longer need the gold."

"You look less like that guy from that Austin Powers movie, sure," I grudgingly admit.

His blackening eyes narrow. "Ah yes. I remember you watching that on television while your father engaged his various paramours."

The reminder of what I'd learned after his defeat—that he'd watched me for years before stealing me from Earth, the perfect victim who'd never be missed—acts as an icy bucket of water tossed over me. "Let me out," I say, clenching my fists. The bite of my nails is further evidence that this is real, and this monster sits before me. "Voice, I swear, get me out of here or I will—"

"Leyden," he says. He smirks again, and he no longer looks like a handsome movie star but a predator whose appearance mesmerizes his prey until his jaws snap around their throat. "You know my name. You should use it."

I wake back in my room, back caged in Tans arms. I exhale shakily until my heart rate matches Tans' steady beat.

This is unacceptable.

I wake the second time to an empty bed, but with no dreams of Leyden or the guilt-ridden renditions of my past mistakes. The trophies from my clash with Leyden are stark in the morning light, the gnarled scar on my hip pale against my almond skin. My fingers run over it and its smaller spiral twin on my other side. Leyden's black eyes and devilish smirk play behind my closed lids, and I wish Tans had remained in our room to say goodbye and remind me of the good things I've done. But with the Council meeting and it being an open petition day, Tans left early to assign his soldiers to protection and crowd control duties. The glamorous life of a commander, he joked when he told me before his face fell in memory of the Sàrkany he'd commanded to their deaths at sea. Better than the life of a layabout with no requirements except acting as a figurehead, I'd teased back until the wince in his expression faded.

The shadows of my terrible memories trail me out of our spire—when I realized what the Sìnnách was, when I begged Tans for forgiveness after betraying him, when I'd stumbled into my room after killing the sprite. Zorin trails behind me too, stealth not being a skill he possesses. Although the trek to the throne room isn't new, the added people on the route must worry Tans enough to ask one of his younger guards to spy again.

When my feet touch down on the main floor, I stop and turn. "Come out, Zorin. This is just silly otherwise."

Zorin's fluffy hair peeks around the curve of the spiral staircase. "Good morning, Lady," he says in what I imagine he thinks is a normal tone of voice. Instead, he sounds shifty and offers an overly casual expression. "Were you intending to watch the petitioning?"

I cross my arms while a smile unfurls at Zorin's earnestness. Although not his aim, Tans can always distract me from my gloom. "Yes, as I'm sure you know. Unless you've moved to this spire instead of living with the other recruits?"

Zorin flushes and scurries down the rest of the stairs. "Will you not tell the Lord Commander you caught me?"

I hold out my elbow and he links our arms with a sheepish expression. "You can tell him I tripped on my dress, and you gave up your position to keep me from hitting the floor."

"Will that not make him likely to increase your guard, if clothes are your new enemies?"

I pretend to scowl. "Not if I have anything to say about it."

We don't make it around the next corner before hitting the crowd of people in line. There are more people in the castle than I've ever seen, even more than when Kórol made his damning announcements last fall. We slip through the side door to the throne room, near the back, Zorin using his gangly elbows to make space through the throng. The murmurs begin the moment I'm in view. Various accents color the words, but what I understand isn't as bad as I expected. The mutters that reach my ear are something about the magic and how it's gone. No one spits in my face or shouts invectives. No one blames me, at least to my face.

Relief mixed with a dash of confusion carry me from the door to the far corner of the throne room where several early Council member attendees stand. The Council members, none I speak to regularly, nod in recognition when Zorin and I shuffle beside them. Kórol doesn't acknowledge me, not that I expect him to. He sits on his throne like a mannequin put into position and not a real person with working limbs. He usually looks like a statue when in public, but not like this. His muscles tremble with the exertion of clenching them, his eyes twitch in time with his breathing, and the ghost of a frown remains on his lips, above his unruly beard. He threw himself into ruling and handling the lack of magic, leaving him little time for Tans, and almost none for the person Leyden spelled him to desire. The memory of Kórol's issues makes me want to kick Leyden in his handsome villainous face.

A young couple kneels before Kórol, in the front of the long line of petitioners.

"If there is some dried venison in storage," the man says. He squeezes the hand of the woman beside him. Both appear only a few years older than Kórol, but the gauntness to their faces didn't develop in the past six months. "The magazines in our province have run out. If you can spare a few racks, our-"

Kórol raises his hand, and the man slams his mouth shut. "I understand your plight. But we do not have the supplies to spare. We are seeking alternative sources, but we need all that remain in storage for the winter when our crops slumber and the emergent need arises."

"Perhaps slaughtering the horses?"

"No," Kórol says. If I didn't know the magic vanished, I'd swear ice burst from behind that stoic mask.

The man bows his head in defeat and backs them away until the woman notices me. Her eyes light up and she plants her feet. "It's, that's her, Gracel." She pronounces my name differently, sounding out the 'ce' and adding an el sound, like Gray-cell.

Zorin tenses behind me, grabbing my forearms as if preparing to drag me from the room. Kórol slowly stands, but the woman notices none of this.

"You did this," she says breathlessly, repeating the woman from Ilsen proper.

Now Kórol looks like the man I know, his scowl in place as he leaves the dais and stalks towards me. The statue disappeared and in its place is the man who first taught me to handle a knife, who stood by my side in front of Bittállí.

"Lady Grace is a credit to us, to all the Sàrkany," he says sharply. He clenches and unclenches his fists at his side.

The woman ignores him, leaning forward to keep her focus on me. Hunger and desperation color her expression. "You *saved* us from them. You can do it again, you can make it better."

Her partner stammers apologetically beside her, dragging her from the space in front of the dais. Kórol gestures to the guards nearby.

"You took their magic, you can give it to us," she says. "Gray-cel."

Finally, the guards and her partner direct her down the aisle and away from the petition line. Those remaining look confused and calculating, staring at me with intent.

Kórol's eyes close for a single moment, before they reopen, the ice-blue darker than I've seen it. "We must break momentarily before we hear the final petitions and begin our closed Council meeting," he announces. He spins on his heel and stalks towards the door behind his throne.

A guard holds the tapestry up while we slither through the door and away from the long line of whispering citizens.

"Can you get the magic back from where you put it?" Zorin whispers as he ushers us to a corner beside three stacked broken chairs. The room barely holds us all, and the light from the thin window snuffs out when one guard stands in front of it, leaving only a small gap of light reflecting above our heads. Two guards light candles and hold them aloft, giving the space an eerie energy.

Kórol remains in the middle of the room, staring down at the floor. I wonder if he remembers the last time we were in this room, when he realized what Leyden had done to him, what Leyden tried to do to me.

I blink away the memories. "Is that what they think happened?"

"Yes," Zorin says with a furrowed brow. "You took their magic to keep them from tearing down the Gate, sealing the walls."

Is that what that woman in Ilsen meant when she said I did it? "But how would me taking their magic affect the Sàrkany?"

Zorin looks at me like I'm a child who fell asleep in class. "We get our magic from the Eósy. Our ancestry is all that allows us to use it. That's why the Sìnnách was thought to be a boon for the King-it would allow him use of more magic that the rest of us can't access."

I'm almost sure that isn't true, except the shared ancestry part. But I don't have the energy to add 'audit Sàrkany education system' to my list of projects. "Where do they think the magic *went* then, if I somehow took it?"

Zorin shrugs, his hair skimming his shoulders with the movement. "The air, the earth, a secret enclave that needs royal blood to open, no one is sure."

"That should not happen," Kórol barks at his assistant Sethen. Fíl explained Sethen's formal title is Minister, but the duties seem more like a personal assistant. I'd joked once that a boss-employee relationship was a good trope, but that was before I fully understood Kórol's preferences, and before he got worse. "We must begin an information campaign at once. The Sàrkany must understand that magic is gone, and it will not return."

The room quiets.

"Is that true?" Óvag, the Council member from Undre asks, except he directs his question to me.

But Kórol doesn't let me respond. "It doesn't matter if it can return, it won't. We have no need for magic. Magic is something vile and vicious and our people will never have it again."

The room explodes with sound, guards only reacting through gasps, but the Council members and staff shoved into that tiny room are in uproar.

"We must have magic," Pirre says. He clutches the ties of his jeweled vest like a scandalized elderly woman would her pearls.

"No." Kórol's mask slides down his face, his expression as still as ice. "I have decreed it, and it will be so."

"We are your Council," Zovà from Gremeg starts but Kórol slashes his hand in the air again.

"And yet this is my father's and forefather's land. You all hold lordships at the Raddares' leisure." He beats his fist against his chest. "At my leisure. And I stand by the first of my line, who realized the need for the walls, and his sons who closed the Gates. I stand by the Eleventh of my line, who first saw the Eósy for the deceivers they are. I stand beside Lady Grace. She too saw the Eósy for what they were, and she rid us of the plague upon our people." The Council's shocked gazes slide towards me, but I can only offer them a wide-eyed stare.

"Magic has been a crutch of our people for too long," he continues, almost snarling. "We knew of its maliciousness when the walls rose. We felt it again before the Solstice." Kórol shutters, but only someone looking for it would notice. "I will not allow another one of my people to endure such evil again."

There would be less tension in that tiny room if Kórol had lit something on fire instead. But either Kórol doesn't notice the growing unease in his Council, or he actively ignores it.

"I am uninterested in hearing from additional petitioners, just as I'm uninterested in sitting through a Council meeting today. I will pass along my comments to my Lord Commander or my Minister. You are free to remain in your guest residences as long as you like, or you may return home." He stalks to the door leading to the hallway and leaves without another word.

As the door closes behind him, the entrance to the throne room opens. Rothàna glides inside before frowning.

"Why are we hiding in the closet?"

CHAPTER 4

I drag Zorin to the map room near the top of a small spire off the kitchen and down a long wooden hallway, an addition made to the castle within the last few generations. They sometimes refer to it as the war room, as dozens of kings and commanders have planned their protection of Dalner within those walls. When enemies aren't on the horizon, and when a solid wall and sealed Gates give more protection from enemies than Dalner has ever had, the room remains empty. But Tans likes the silence sometimes and will strategize alone in the compact room.

As expected, Tans is there, leaning over the large map. His lips are pursed, a deep frown on his face as he gazes down at the papers before him. With a wave, Zorin departs, and I slink inside the room. Tans hears the creak of my feet on the wooden floor, his braid swinging as he jumps to attention. The somber expression burns off his face as he beams in my direction. He crosses the room in three strides and takes me in his arms.

"I did not expect you for hours yet. Did you decide to skip the petitions before the meeting?"

I wrap my arms around Tans' slender waist and rest my head against his shoulder. Tans only stands a few inches taller than me, something I forget each time I'm not in his arms, simply because his personality is too big for his short frame. "Kórol canceled it," I say into the folds of his blue leather vest.

He pulls back, skimming his hands up to squeeze my shoulders. "He canceled the petitions or the meeting?"

"Both."

"Hurchá," he hisses, exclaiming a curse word no one will translate.

"There must be something we can do." The words drag from me before I know I'm saying them. But everything I've done has been preparing for this conversation and I can't hide from it anymore.

He releases me and collapses into a chair near the door. "Support him," he says, running his hands through his hair before spinning a braid between his fingers. "All we can do is be present and attempt to help him work through this."

"He threatened the Council," I say, leaning back against the wall and sliding to the ground. I look up at Tans' handsome profile. "He said something about everyone serving at his demand. I think he meant he could remove them."

Tans' eyes darken from amber to deep mahogany. "He's hurting. It isn't an excuse, but an explanation. People do and say odd things when they feel out of control." One hand leaves his hair and hangs below the side of the chair. I press the swinging palm to my cheek.

"It isn't an excuse," I agree. I could say the same of Tans and the daily shadow I've gained, but I still don't want to start a fight, not when I'm still trying to resolve the stress I caused when I leapt into the portal. I wet my lips, again preparing to make the proposal that's been stuck in my throat for the last few months. "I didn't mean for Kórol. There must be a solution, a *way* to fix this, get the magic back."

Tans laughs humorlessly. "Like reopen the Gates with all the magic we have now? Let ourselves be ensorcelled by some new ruling class."

"Not the ensorcelled part, no. But open then a little, just enough to reignite the magic here," I say. "Except it wasn't magic that closed them, but me. Maybe something with my blood will open them again."

He sobers immediately. "No."

"We need the magic, Tans, for supplies and healing at least."

He withdraws from my touch and vaults across the room. "No, Grace. We can't do that again."

I stand and fist my hands on my hips. "What do you think I've been training for? Why do you think I'm trying so hard?"

"That's why?" he asks, paling. "No. We'll be fine. We expected magic to disappear in a few generations, the timetable has simply shortened."

"You don't believe that, or you wouldn't send out scouting parties. People died when the Gates went up the first time. From poor nutrition and lacking food, Tans. It's that blow to their body that did it. They could die now, too."

He yanks on his hair as he spins away from me. "And so could you!" He slumps and stands over his map, pressing his palms into the parchment and staring down at the landscape. "You promised you'd be safe, that you'd not leap into danger with the Great—that Woman. You wanted an administrative position in the assassination, remember? And the next thing I know, you're joining us in the battle, with nothing but Kórol's dagger and a complete lack of understanding of what you were walking into." He lifts his head, and his gaze pins me in place. "Do you know what that did to me? You couldn't even understand what I screamed at you, I couldn't even say goodbye properly and...and..."

"Tans, this isn't the time for this."

He turns back, an agonized expression on his face. "This is the time. You never wish to discuss this," he says, twisting his lips. "But you can't bring up this lurnn-reckless plan and then hide away from why I can't agree to it."

I sigh and push into the wall behind me as if it will open and swallow me. "We need to fix the Gate, the magic, Tans. Not talk about what happened; that's not relevant."

He shakes his head. "You want to fix *your* mistakes, you say. But how can you do that if you won't acknowledge what happened, and whether there even *were* mistakes?"

My arms crisscross around my body, enfolding myself in a protective embrace from Tans' accusations. "There were. Are you happy now? I've always known I...made mistakes. That's why I'm learning the language and taking the lessons, so I can do something good to make up for it."

"I'd thought it was to better connect yourself to Dalner," he says without looking at me.

"It...it is." I curl into myself. "But how better to become a part of this place than by helping fix what I broke?"

"We don't know why the Gates sealed and the walls solidified. For all we know, your... actions in the portal," Tans bites his lower lip, unwilling to put words to it. "Your actions in the portal stopped the Voice, and kept him from tearing down the Gate, but perhaps he and his brethren sealed the Gates at his defeat."

That isn't what happened, I'm sure of it. But I lacked the language to explain it after the Gates first sealed, when the electric elements of my cell phone and my human blood connected with the magic of the Gates. When I gained the knowledge to explain it, everyone had moved on to reacting to the sealed Gates and lack of magic, so the *why* didn't seem to matter. Only I knew the truth.

But Tans isn't finished. "These things you're doing aren't to correct something that wasn't your fault, but a bandage on everything you're avoiding. You refuse to speak about what happened, how you killed that Woman and what happened with Kórol, so you bury that by overworking yourself now."

"That's not true." I have no guilt for Bittállí, at least.

His eyes are knowing, and I want to duck away from them. "Then why won't you talk about it?"

"This isn't the point, Tans. The point is the Gates. Whether I made a mistake or not, something must be done," I say, shaking my head in disagreement. "People died when the walls went up. Raddare the 2nd even, so it can't have just been the magic and the nutrition. Maybe something in the openings helped until everyone got used to it, I'm not sure." Fíl refused to indulge my theories on the subject, only sending me to deliver things or review my lessons so I don't have other theories. Leyden's pale face flashes through my mind, but I will the image away.

Tans looks back down at the map, defeated. "What else would you have me do? We are searching where we can. And no, I will not entertain your idea of opening the Gates or aiding in our search."

My mouth snaps shut as a sharp pin pricks my chest. He sighs again. "Things are not dire yet, Grace. The Wilds is our next destination. It is the most likely place for an added source of meat and produce."

Curiosity pushes my anger aside. "Why?"

He points to a spot on the map. "There is no wall here, only water separating the Wilds from Dànna. There may be no seal there, allowing some magic to come through. I will lead it, as I know the area well."

"I'll go with you," I offer. After the argument we're still having, I'm unsurprised when Tans' mouth pinches, but it doesn't stop the annoyance from churning in my gut.

"It isn't safe for you. You're unprepared for the trials of such a trek."

Just as quickly as it left, anger returns. "I did the trek, the Sìnnách trek."

Pity isn't an expression that looks good on Tans, something I didn't think I would say about him. "You could barely handle the trek, and it took us twice the normal time. The Wilds are another few hundred miles from the Solstice Sanctum."

I heave an aggravated breath. "Which is why I've been training. You can't use that against me, not after this entire conversation."

"Yes, but Sáven almost carried you to our rooms last night."

"Because I'm still *learning*."

He exhales as he closes his eyes. When he opens them, the fiery amber has vanished, and only muted mahogany remains. "I'm not trying to limit you, Grace. And I won't force you to discuss it if you don't wish to, but I cannot forget what happened then. I simply wish to protect you."

I cross the room to take his hands. "You aren't my—my keeper, Tans." I don't know how to translate the idea that he's 'robbing my agency,' but Dalner doesn't have the feminism classes my university did, so he might not understand even if I managed to. "You're my partner and I'm trying to work with you, not against you."

He pulls from me to sigh. "You're not ready."

I feel like stamping my feet but know it will do nothing but make this conversation more frustrating. "Come on, Tans. If I were one of your recruits, you wouldn't coddle me like this."

His face twists to something amused. "Coddle. Is that one of your new words?"

"Tans!"

He runs his fingers through his silken tresses, his eyes bright and burning. "You're right, you're something more important than my recruits. If you weren't you, you wouldn't train with my best commanders until you'd succeeded at the trainee tests."

"Fine," I say, crossing my arms about my middle. "I'll do that. Then you stop coddling me, you stop with the escorts, you stop underestimating me, and you'll support what needs to be done to fix the Gates. Whatever that may be."

He mirrors my pose, the leather of his armor creaking. "When you prove you can take care of yourself."

"No. I'm not a child," I say through clenched teeth. "I'm eighteen now, just like you."

"Yet I've been at the age of majority for two years and helping lead a country," he says under his breath. I smother the unkind thought that follows, about his age and Kórol's own deficiencies.

"Very well. If you pass the trainee tests when I return, we can discuss how to reopen the Gates."

"Tans, you can't put me off like that."

He frowns as if I've won something. "If you pass the trainee tests, which are for your protection and not any attempt at delay, whenever you pass them, we'll...attempt to reopen the Gates. Together."

"That's all I wanted," I say, sighing. With luck, I'll finish the important tests before he gets back, and finally take steps to prove my worth.

CHAPTER 5

Tans leaves that afternoon, before Kórol can revoke his approval for the trip because of the deaths of the first team. Luckily, the horses in Sekai are semi-domesticated. They can sprint hundreds of miles in a day, but only with healers on hand to rejuvenate their worn muscles. Without magic, the horses can only cover a fraction of that. Before the Gates sealed and the walls appeared, they needed to be tied with strong bindings to stop them from slipping back through the rifts at sunrise and sunset. That is one of the few benefits to the wall's solidification. We may not have magic, but at least the horses aren't trying to play a game of chase.

The Wilds are located just west of Bittállí's former temple and the town where I landed, meaning it will take Tans and his soldiers more than a week to arrive near the edge of the wall and investigate.

We don't revisit our bargain before he leaves, because I don't want destructive energy between us while he's gone. I've read too many books where the love interests fight, one goes off on a quest (to war, to ambush a rival gang member, to the country club for a billionaire's meeting), and they inevitably get hurt. I refuse to jinx us if I can help it.

The first week passes slowly, time only marked by the things to keep me busy- a history and culture lesson with Fíl, training with Faburth and Eida, trying to convince Kórol to speak with me and failing, a language lesson with Rothàna.

But my duties aren't the only thing helping distract me, I still involuntarily visit the Voice—Leyden—nightly.

"Welcome back, Grace. I trust you had a lovely day?"
"Shut up, Leyden."
"I missed your attitude."

"Your eyes are looking more bruised. Is dreaming of me not restful?"
"Shut up, Leyden."
"The first time it was charming, the third, bordering on rudeness."

"How was your day in Exile, Leyden? Surprisingly satisfying, Grace. Yes, no longer being imprisoned would be a boon, but one cannot underestimate the benefits of all this open land."

"Shut up, Leyden."

Grumbling is the only sound in response.

"Do you have any paper?"

Leyden jolts on his pallet. I'm seated cross legged on the floor across from him, as far away from him as I can be in the circular room. "Did you just engage me in conversation?" He presses a hand to his chest in mock shock.

"No," I say, not attempting to hide my irritation. "But if I'm stuck in this room every night, I can be productive. Instead of staring at my feet, I can study."

He frowns. "You want me to give you a good, something of which I only have limited amounts, and which is difficult to obtain, given my imprisonment?"

"I can just sit here silently and ignore you. Again."

"No," he practically shouts. "You are the only novel part of my day. I spend the rest staring at these walls and practicing what magic I can within them."

"Poor Leyden. His imprisonment is boring."

He blinks those unnerving eyes, the edges glowing neon. "I will give you paper if you let me write it for you."

I cross my arms and glare at him. "Fine."

Leyden shuffles upward and digs into a small box under his bench. He withdraws a single parchment carefully, followed by a pen nib no longer than my thumbnail. He drags the bench in front of him, laying the parchment on the seat and looks over at me expectantly. I refrain from rolling my eyes but only because I want the parchment.

"Gray-cel. Write that down. I'm trying to figure out what that means."

The nib scratches on the parchment. When he finishes, he lifts the sheet and displays it to me. Instead of "Grácel," the written version of the syllables I spoke in Sàrkany, he's written "Gracel."

I lean my head hard against the stone and groan. "Not my name with the letter 'el.' The Sàrkany way, with the accent."

He turns the parchment back to himself and makes a humming sound. "No need for the attitude. I assumed you were because we are speaking English, you desired it written in English."

The eye roll builds, and I don't stop it this time. "Why would it be in Eng—wait. Are we speaking English?"

He cocks a blond brow. "Of course."

"Why would it be 'of course?' You speak Sàrkany, we're in Sekai."

"Because it is polite to speak in your native tongue, particularly as I am the only being you know that speaks it," he drawls.

"Shut up, Leyden."

His mouth opens in shock, hurt blooming like a slap across his face. Something sympathetic rises within me, but I force it down.

"Just, write Grácel," I say with a sigh. "And if you know what it means, tell me."

He bends over the makeshift desk, hiding his face as he adds the accent. When he lifts his head, the hurt is gone. "It means nothing."

I slump then. It was a long shot, but I thought if I could find out why the petitioner called me that, it might tell me more about what people thought I did, and who they thought I was. I'm not the Sinnách, I can't be the savior. But maybe I could be whatever Grácel means—

"The 'el' could mean I, as in the pronoun. But if we add the 'cee' from your name, 'cel,' it could mean 'we'," Leyden says in an indifferent tone.

"Okay..."

"And the grá part could be a verb, as in 'I do something,' or 'we do something.'"

I turn my gaze skyward, the peak of the tower only a few feet above us. "So, what does grá mean?"

"It means nothing," he says again. "But..." he trails off.

I straighten to stare back at him, his own face pensive. "What?"

His focus shifts back to me. The moonlight gleaming on his pale skin, combined with the thin candle flickering over the sharp planes of his face and his black marble eyes, give him an ethereal quality. He looks like a demon, the tricksy kind that lure in women before killing them. I never read fantasies, or anything supernatural, but the romance lover in me didn't avoid the ubiquitous vampire romance movies when they played in the dorm's common room.

"You must tell me why you care to know," he says. "If I'm to waste my valuable supplies on you—"

"Not a waste, and you're the one who begged to write it for me," I mutter.

"Then I wish to know what you study and why," he finishes as if I didn't speak.

I consider it for several long minutes. There's no harm in it, so I tell him. Not of my plan to open the rifts at sunrise and sunset, but of my need to learn more of the language and progress, and to understand why that woman reacted that way to me.

His tone is smug when he explains his theory. "Grá means nothing but is a part of many verbs- to anger, clágrádh; to infuriate, clágrádmerh; to provoke, pegrálh; to incite, degráchh." He giggles. "It is also part of battle, braigrád, and war, braigrátrágge."

"Great, thanks. That's helpful," I say snidely.

He cocks his head. His blond hair is longer than I remember, and it grazes his neck as he moves. "Though, if we take the position that grá is part of a word, then perhaps cel should be too. And cel exists in the word today, tomorrow, and yesterday."

"It's also in 'day.' So, they think I provoke the day?" I huff an annoyed laugh. "That's you, not me. You're the one that's infuriating and provoking."

He pins me with his black gaze, his left eye twitching like a light about to burn out. "Perhaps the citizens believe you are the harbinger of something, something negative like war, or something that must be incited, or something coming in time, good or bad." That charming smile curls over his pale lips. "So, Grace, what is it you intend to do?"

"What are we studying tonight?"

I stay silent, keeping my eyes closed. If I try hard enough, I can pretend I'm alone and back in my room, sitting on the floor.

"Are you ignoring me? We had a deal, Grace. I didn't take you for an oath breaker."

"No," I hiss. "The deal was you would write for me if I wanted to study, and I don't want to study."

"Why not? I assumed that with your handsome boy gone, you'd need the distraction."

My eyes fly open. "Why do you think Tans is gone?"

He tosses me an unimpressed expression. "We're connected. While in this space, I get impressions of you, of what you felt, of your surroundings."

"Great. More violations." I visualize a brick wall, the same image I used when I first threw Leyden out of my mind. I hadn't

needed to block any mental intrusions with magic gone from Dalner. "Try now," I say through clenched teeth. "Can you get any impressions now?"

"Why would I tell you?" he asks, baffled.

"Because you want me to keep talking to you and entertain you so you don't start literally climbing the walls."

He pouts and leans back on his pallet. "Fine."

He inspects me again. He doesn't stop on one spot for too long, instead sweeping his glowing blue eyes up and down my figure. I'd taken to wearing clothes to bed. With Tans gone, no one would ask why, and it gives me an armor, meager notwithstanding, from Leyden's unnerving gaze.

"Yes, I can still feel you," he says grudgingly. "You're in your room, the sheets are silky but too hot on your skin with those pants." He inclines his head. "Is that frustration towards your King why you're poor company tonight?"

I press my palms to my eyes, though it's a useless act against Leyden's mental invasion. "Stop that. Let me try again." I tuck my thoughts about Kórol deep within me.

We had an impromptu Council meeting that afternoon, after my training session with the commanders. All Council members accepted Kórol's offer to remain in their assigned guest quarters, where they lived when visiting the castle, hoping Kórol would change his mind and reschedule the meeting he'd canceled the week prior. Only Rothàna lived here full time, leaving her son to handle her estate. When the Council found out through the castle's gossip pipeline that Tans and a few soldiers were out on a scouting mission after the last one ended badly, they all stuck around, eager for an update. Today, they held the meeting in secret. Rothàna convinced Bay and Zorin that she would escort me, and given her military history, they were content to leave me with her. She snuck us into the map room where the other Council members waited to discuss whether there was a way to depose Kórol.

I was one of the few dissenters. When the meeting ended, I tried speaking to Kórol, but he remained ensconced in his distant spire, Sethen and his personal guards refusing me entry at his request. I could almost feel his anguish and anger through the stone walls. Anguish and anger caused by the being now sitting in front of me, the being who violates minds and manipulates thoughts without considering morality or consequences. My scowl will stay a permanent fixture on my face that evening. If I'm stuck with Leyden, I won't indulge him anymore.

"It isn't like that, Grace," he whispers. I growl at the continued evidence of his intrusion, building another barrier in my mind, something thick and oily and full of electricity to violently shock any alien presence. At least, the sparking electrocution will be what I imagine happens each time Leyden drags his claws back through my mind. "Now?" I snarl.

"I only heard the last part, about the King. You felt it so strongly, it battered from yours to mine."

"Shut up, Leyden."

He purses his lips. "I probably deserved that this time. But I am not as callous as you claim."

"I don't care. Just tell me if you can't hear or feel anything again."

"I can't. You are silent again. Only my thoughts and feelings are within me now." Leyden ducks his head. "But I would like to explain."

"Why?" I explode. "Why does any of it matter? You clearly have no remorse. And even your own people must hate you to stick you in solitary confinement. You did it, it happened, you mentally raped and assaulted people I care about, ruined my life, nearly got everyone I know—"

"That's not true either," he breathes. "I didn't ruin your life."

I refuse to give him credit for any of my better circumstances. I have Tans, and Sáv, and Fíl and Kórol, and a half dozen other people that care about me, but how I got there nearly destroyed me. "You stole me from Earth, you said you only picked someone pathetic enough not to be missed, proving my father didn't care about me, something every girl wants to hear."

"You were estranged—"

I don't let him interrupt. "You lied and manipulated me every second I was here until I broke free. And that's just what you did to me. Thank God good can triumph in real life and not only in the pages of books. A world with you prevailing is no world I want to inhabit." My chest is heaving when I finish.

His chin lifts. "You have a faulty memory. Will you blame me for that too?"

"Go to hell."

"Do you know what it is like to have your sanity leave you, while your body kills itself?" He asks it idly, running one long fingered hand through his now shorn hair as he remains stretched out on his pallet like a monarch before his supplicants.

I slide back down the wall and wrap my arms around my bent legs. "I don't care," I mutter.

"That's why I did it," he says. "We needed the walls down to live."

"Now, Leda's twin sister held the title of the former Light faction when the walls arose. It must have been her who the Great Matron impersonated. Leda herself was a beacon of light for us on the Sàrkany of the wall. When Derul, Raddare the Second died, Leda—"

Fíl's droning voice won't pierce through my distraction, and I interrupt to ask, "Will you explain what happened when the walls went up? To the Sàrkany?"

Fíl drops the book in his hand and stares at me in alarm. "We discussed that months ago, before you lost your understanding of the language. We went through all the books on the subject, those that remained after the fire. Now, we must continue your education in the history of the royal family."

"No, you only skimmed it. I want to know everything about the wall, why it went up, and how it worked."

He blinks as if something doesn't compute. "But why? With the revision of your culture lessons, changing course now might put the entire lesson plan behind."

I stare back out the windows. Leyden's declaration burrowed under my skin. *If the Eósy 'needed the walls down to live,' did the Sàrkany need the Gates open, the rifts at sunrise and sunset?* They were Eósy descendants. But Fíl shares Tans' opinions on what I should do for Dalner, which is nothing. "What Kórol said about not needing magic," I say, offering a half-truth to appease him. "It got me curious, that's all."

His eyes bloom with understanding and a stilted smile appears. "There are no written accounts here, but perhaps I can locate something on the subject."

A sigh of relief bursts from me as I pull out a fresh piece of parchment for notes. Written language is still beyond me, but with help I can draft a few words. Notes saved me in the past, they may just save us now.

"But I need help with re-shelving first. Since you've not yet progressed to begin your recopying anew, you can provide more physical labor."

I can hear my goals plummeting hard to the ground. Fíl's legendary chores could keep me busy for days, leaving me without the information I desperately want. I clutch my hip. "But Fíl, I trained all yesterday afternoon. We should study first while I rest. After all, my hip—"

"Is fine. I saw you sprint to avoid that overeager escort of yours. Or should I report to Tans *and* Rothàna about your weariness? Both surely have opinions on how you should proceed, though I imagine they differ." He strokes his beard. "I'm not sure who would be more disconcerted to hear of your pain. Rothàna, at least, is here. I'm sure she has ideas on how to manage your hip."

Ideas that would probably kill me, considering she thinks my current training is too easy. Her version of training would knock me out for days, and then Tans would be smug about me not even being able to attempt the trainee tests. Grumbling, I stand and shuffle towards the pile of books he points to. "Tattletale," I hiss under my breath. "I should tell Sáv *all* about your—"

"What was that, Grace?"

"Nothing, Fíl. Just excited to learn more about your filing system."

"Can you read me?"

"No," Leyden says like a refrain, the call and response to the last few dreams.

"If you wanted the walls down so the Eósy could live, why were you punished? Seems like if you were doing something good, they'd praise you, not imprison you."

A tinge of desperation colored each memory he unwillingly showed me at his defeat, but I noticed no altruism. He focused on tearing down the wall, but there was no evidence it was for anyone but him. And Fíl had so far refused my request for information on the wall, leaving me unable to confirm what Leyden implied and learn whether the Sàrkany could be affected. I hadn't exaggerated to Tans that people died when the walls went up, Fíl told me that initially. But I didn't know why. Poor nutrition couldn't be the entire story.

Leyden shifts from sitting on his pallet to lying on his back and staring at the peak of the tower ceiling. "I believe I mentioned that lacking sanity was a symptom, yes? Bittállí had powerful friends, who believed everything was fine, and the slow death from the walls was nothing to be concerned about."

I huff out an incredulous laugh. "And you went the opposite direction? Your lacking sanity somehow made you the rational one who wanted the walls down?" I rub my palms against my eyes. "You're just manipulating me again."

"I cannot lie to you, Grace."

My hands fall, spots dancing in my vision making him look more otherworldly. He's not wearing a shirt today and seems pleased when I notice it. I snarl. "No, but you can play with words. You destroyed the belief system of thousands to remove your political rival, telling me she'd kill me if I didn't do something, when her attention only focused on me because you told me to. She'd never have even looked at me if you hadn't used your creative truth."

"That is only—"

"Let's see if I can parse it out," I say meanly, baring my teeth. "Something about the walls being down will help you live certainly, since you said that explicitly, but it doesn't mean you'll outright die. Maybe because you'll get Sàrkany slaves and have a better life. And the slow death isn't true death but death from boredom without getting to exploit your Sàrkany followers. Or you said 'needed' to live, not need, so maybe someone like you *was pushing them forward and would kill them if they didn't succeed."*

"We will die, Grace." His face is stony. "Actual, true, real death. As in we will exist on this plane of existence no longer. Not because we're bored, not from the idea that 'all things inevitably fade,' because time doesn't affect us, not because someone else forced us to tear it down. We will die with the walls up. And likely soon. I was trying to save us."

I gesture around his sparse cell. "Yes, you must be the hero of your people, bravely trying to bring the wall down. Do they exile everyone that fails, or are you just special?"

"If you must know, my exile is due to what I did before my attempt at the wall. Once they were freed from Bittálli's spells, I only had a few hours before it would catch up with me." He sighs and rests his chin on his pale hand, leaning over his crossed knees. "Had I been successful, they would have praised my name from the rooftops. Alas, that was not to be."

"Oh, poor Leyden. Sorry, your plight doesn't matter to me."

He tilts his head. "Yes, you wish to know about the Sàrkany."

"Why would you think that?" My tone is casual, but he isn't convinced.

He gives me a narrowed gaze. "Because they are your people now." I can almost hear him finish it with "idiot." But he says, "And I heard you."

My shoulders crack as I surge upward and cross the room in a breath. "You said you couldn't read me."

He displays the long line of his pale neck as he leans backward. "I can't now. I believe the term is 'zone out.' You did so while shelving books. I got a flash of your mind then." His brows furrow. "I also felt a flash of something magic near y—"

"No more. You can force me into this room, but I refuse to let you into my mind like that again."

His eyes cross as he stares up at the finger I've jabbed between them. "I didn't do it on purpose, Grace. I promised you I wouldn't read you unless necessary, and I cannot break my promises. Must you make me the villain in everything you do?"

I lose control; I slap him hard. The outline of my hand colors on his creamy skin and I hope it stays branded on him after I wake. "You are the villain."

His tongue probes the inside of his cheek, the appendage peeping from his lips and colored red. "To you. To me, you were the villain, the thing that kept me from succeeding and healing my people. It is only luck they placed me here in Exile and could reawaken the magic the walls kept me from."

"You killed people, you assaulted Kórol's mind, you—"

"As did you, Little Grace. You have lied, betrayed, and killed. It's only luck that keeps you walking free."

"What will happen to the Sàrkany with the Gates sealed?"

Leyden mulls over my question as we sit across from each other in his cell. Tonight, he's by the window, breathing deeply from the cracked opening. "I'm uninterested in telling you, after how rudely you treated me last time."

I voice a complaint, but he speaks again, his voice rising over mine. "If I needed to guess, I'd assume they could get sick, like we did, like what happened when the walls went up. They will die, like we did. Or perhaps, like we did, they will slowly lose their sanity until nothing remains but a hardened, lifeless shell." He gazes back at me blankly. "What a pity you sealed the walls."

"Kórol, I've brought dinner. Sáven came up with a new pie. It's... not bad. Will you let me in? We can talk about the Gates and what you said about magic?"

The door remains closed. As I press my ear hard against the wood, I hear movement behind it.

"We don't have to talk about that," I say, staring down at the offering in my arms. "We could talk about anything, books, music, your favorite childhood memory." *Or whether you're losing your sanity because of the magic, or this is a trauma response none of us are equipped to handle.*

A guard I've not met before gently touches my shoulder and directs me back down the stairs. I leave the pie at his door, placing it beside the three other untouched plates from days before. Zorin meets me at the stairs and silently walks me back to my room.

"Do you regret it? Any of it, at all?"
Leyden stares at me unblinking for too long. "No."

CHAPTER 6

We expect Tans and his team any day now. I've thrown myself into training to avoid remaining alone with my guilt or alone with Leyden. My sleeping hours shorten with every passing day Tans remains gone.

It's that fatigue that has me fumbling in my knife combat training. Faburth lunges for me and I parry to the side too slowly to avoid the wet red line he leaves on my skin. We're too close, within boxing range, and his weapon dodges and spins through the air as if compelled by magic. I slam my heel into his foot and use the short falter in Faburth's attack to slither away. Even in his old age, Faburth is better than that though. As his focus turned to the pain in his foot, his free hand grabs the hair at my neck and yanks me back towards him. Before I can connect with his chest, I wrench my elbow backward into his gut and make a play for the weapon. He doesn't release and before I can quite understand what he did, he has me pinned against him, weapon digging into my throat. He mutters out a three count before releasing me.

"You must be lighter on your feet, Lady," Faburth says. I bend over with my hands on my knees, breath catching in my chest. Red ink slashes dot my body where Faburth's practice weapon made contact. "Perhaps," he starts, sounding hesitant. I peer up at him through my sweaty hair. "Perhaps hand-to-hand combat isn't for you."

"Is it on the trainee tests?"

"One of them," he says between clenched teeth. That I'm skipping the training for the first few is an argument he lost.

He'd nearly begged, telling me how someone my age needed the fundamentals first, and he worried for my safety. It was a type of paternal care I didn't have experience with.

"Then we do it."

"If a knife-wielder attacks you, your best option is to run," Eida says from behind us. She tosses her long red braid over her shoulder. "We should focus on your endurance, not your footwork."

I stretch upward and lean my neck from side to side until the bones crack. "I'm not running anymore. I need to win my fights, not avoid them." *Physical fights,* I mentally add. Avoiding emotional turmoil is second nature by now.

She crosses her arms over her leathers, the embroidery signaling her newest station shining in the sun. "That is shortsighted. Avoiding the fight is just as important as engaging in it. Your goal should be survival at any cost, not victory."

A young blonde woman in red leather armor marches up to the edge of the training ring before I can answer. She bows low.

Eida calls her over. "Yes, Shivio?"

She stands and clasps her hands behind her back. "Commander Faburth, Commander Eida, Lady Grace. The scouting party has returned. Minister Sethen requested I find all present Council members to gather in the throne room for the report."

I barely let her finish before I'm limping out of the ring, ready to confirm Tans has returned whole and learn whether he's discovered the solution to the problems I caused.

The training grounds are just outside Ilsen, to the south right outside the mountain range that wanders from Dalner into Alacson. Shivio follows behind me as my silent shadow.

By the time I arrive in the throne room, I'm the last Council member present. The other eleven remained at Ilsen waiting impatiently for the update. Kórol hasn't arrived yet and the Council members and guards mill about the room. There are multiple soldiers in black leather armor with red stitching, but none that I recognize as the group that accompanied Tans to the Wilds.

Finally, Kórol strides through the side door. He perches on the throne and gazes over the assembled soldiers, his stoic mask falling over his face. The Council members quickly move to kneel before him as guards march behind us. When we're in the usual position for Council meetings, two soldiers who had remained hidden by the others step forward.

"Where is Tans?" Kórol asks. His ice-blue eyes narrow. "Where is Lord Commander Tansr?"

I crane my neck but can't find him in the room either. Something bitter grows in the pit of my stomach.

The soldiers kneel to the side of us, tilting their head in Kórol's direction. Worn spots decorate their leather armor, as if they sprinted through the dust and earth to get back. The older soldier bows his head low before speaking.

"Our Lord Commander was thrown from his horse after we arrived in the Wilds. We believe something spooked the animal."

The whimper burbles from me without my consent. I know what that means, I've read enough. People die when they're thrown from horses. And those are *normal* Earth horses, not these crossbreed deer monstrosities.

Kórol's fists clench until the skin of his knuckles pales. "What is his condition?"

The two soldiers look at each other before returning their gazes to the ground. "It did not originally seem dire. It appears he injured one of his legs."

I close my eyes in relief only to pop them back open as Kórol growls. "Then why did he not return home with you? A cracked bone should not deter him, so long as you properly splinted it."

"We splinted it," the younger one offers. "But he could not mount the horse. There is pain within him, other than the leg, something we cannot see."

That feeling in my stomach turns sour, curdling until it threatens to churn its way out of me. Tans is energy and movement, fire come to life. If he can't move again... "Can he still walk?" I ask from my place on the floor.

Kórol startles at the dais, as if he forgot there was an audience before him. He looks as though he wants to growl again at the interruption, but something passes over his expression when he stares down at me, understanding perhaps, recognizing that this is the man we both love.

The younger soldier looks up at Kórol, as if asking permission to answer me, but the older doesn't bother. "It appears painful, and he moves like a child, but he could walk when we left him in Samsen," he rumbles.

"Thank you for the report," Kórol says. "Please remain for a few minutes to provide any additional relevant details, after which you are on leave until you choose to return to any duties." He directs the rest of his speech to the Council members. "You are all dismissed."

But instead of the bustle of a dozen Council members and half dozen guards departing, the only sound the fabric of their finery rustling as they shift in place.

Only Rothàna stands. "Point of order. We should be present for the entire report. If the scouting party found something, if it startled Lord Commander Tansr's horse, it is imperative we be aware of it."

Kórol shakes his head almost violently. "Whether they found something is irrelevant. Whatever they may tell me will not change my decision."

Several heads turn. "And what is that, sire?" Plema asks, his brows raising.

"We will cull all travel until we can ensure our citizens have the medical care necessary to protect them from the circumstances our Lord Commander now finds himself in. We will turn our focus inward. No more meetings, no more scouting trips. Our citizenry must remain within their towns and cannot traverse more than a half-mile from their homesteads. Only the minimal guard will stand ready and patrolling at the walls." He turns to Sethen. "We must put a greater emphasis on our healers and their training. Contact the guild and have them call in their members for training and safety. We will also spare a single messenger to tell each province about this decree."

Eyes dart around the room as if confirming they truly heard what Kórol said.

Rothàna's lips thin. "Will Ilsen no longer provide goods and support to the cities?"

"Do you mean to keep us here?" Zovà asks, speaking over Rothàna and looking scandalized. Rothàna narrows her eyes at him, who wilts under the heat of her glare.

"If you leave, you do so at your own risk and under this court's immediate censure," Kórol says. "We cannot spare the soldiers needed to escort you."

"What of the farmers, those that till outside their home-steads?" Pirre asks. The population of his province is small, but the area isn't. His community is largely farmland.

"Their crops are failing regardless," Kórol says dismissively. "Better they concentrate on other activities as we navigate this new world."

"The goods, sire," Rothàna demands.

Kórol digs his fingernails into the sides of the throne as he leans forward. "We have moved beyond a time when our people rely on others. We are alone in this world and must remember that." He points to the window with its now-portentous slogan. "Alone we stand, alone we prosper, and alone we die. There is no savior to provide for us. If we cannot keep ourselves safe, perhaps we deserve the consequences."

Shock burbles through the room, even Kórol, whose breath bursts from him in a heavy exhale. He hunches over until his elbows rest on his knees.

"The messenger will carry that province's part of what remains in storage," he says through clenched teeth. "That should keep the cities subsisting until there is no longer a risk in engaging in intra-province trade."

With that last announcement, he gestures towards the door. This time, the Council members leave in unison. Part of me wants to join them, to hear what they'll say. I still know almost nothing of statecraft, but even I know if the government cuts off a state, the state is probably not interested in being part of the government again. But the other part holds me in place, with the men who will tell me more about Tans.

Kórol focuses on his lap. "Did the Lord Commander find anything?"

The two soldiers trade glances. "He couldn't remember after the fall," the older begins, "but he mentioned a butterfly just before."

My heart clenches. Kórol raises his head and meets my gaze.

"You said he was in Samsen?" he asks.

The older nods. "We created a cloth wagon and dragged him where he directed, to—"

"His family home, yes. At least he is safe and surrounded by his loved ones. That will be beneficial as he recovers." He stands. "Thank you again. Please excuse me."

He starts for the door, trailed by Sethen. I stand and scurry after him before he can clear the threshold.

"We're leaving him there? It could be months before he heals naturally, and that's ignoring whatever the other problem was keeping him from mounting a horse."

Kórol doesn't turn around, only turns his head to display his profile. "There can be no special treatment. We are all the same in this." And he stalks down the hallway.

Zorin appears beside me. "Would you like to return to the training grounds?"

I watch as Kórol's figure gets smaller until he turns the corner. "I need to go somewhere else. Can you not tell Eida and Faburth?" As an afterthought, I add, "And Rothàna?"

Zorin bites his lip lower lip before nodding.

Zorin follows me to the kitchens. It's midday and the next meal isn't scheduled for hours, but still the large room is bustling with activity. Sáven and another dozen people are all standing in a row along a deep countertop, each wrist deep in a pile of dough. Sáv's mother stands to the side, barking orders, her ruddy face flushed from the heat of the nearby ovens. When she notices me, her shout turns to a squeak.

All activity stops as the cooks focus on me. I wave awkwardly as Sáv brushes his hands on his tan tunic and slinks towards me. Sáven's mother claps his hands until the remaining cooks refocus on their work.

"Everything alright, Grace?"

I wet my lips. "Can you come with me?"

When we arrive in the hall, a heavy expression emerges under the flush and flour on Sáv's cheeks. "Is it about Tans?"

Zorin shifts between us, one arm reaching towards Sáv but aborting the gesture before it finishes.

I slump against the stone across from the door. "He broke his leg."

The color leaches from his face. "Can he—?"

"He can walk. Maybe."

A soft sigh bursts from his lips and he closes his eyes tight. When he reopens them, he crosses the hall and leans against me. "Could be worse."

I duck my head onto the arch of his shoulder. He smells like sugar and heat. It reminds me of Tans. "Kórol won't send medical aid. He'll be stuck there for months."

"I'm sorry, Grace." He slips his arm around me. "We'll manage."

I peer down the empty hallway and lower my voice. "It's worse though. Kórol is isolating the provinces- no travel in or out, no aid in or out. Even if—when Tans gets better, we'll be separated." *And the Gates will still be sealed.*

Sáv's bright brows raise. "Fílga's gone too. Left yesterday. On his annual walkabout."

I wince. Every year, Fíl took a horse and went south, somewhere around Kingswood, but he never explained the exact location. He could learn of Kórol's edict in Undre, Ovag's province, giving him a place to stay. But he might be near Ràur, Pirre's province, which doesn't have a town bigger than a handful of people each. He'll be stuck too. He's one of the few that might talk to Kórol with Tans gone. "And what if a larger province gets ambitious, with the lead commander bed bound miles away, is there any chance..." I trail off. Fíl could allay my fears on that count too, but my wild thoughts will run.

Sáv shakes his head. "Dunno. I'm not much for history but all the castle kids know enough. Not even a whisper of uprising since—"

"Since the Eleventh," I finish. And I just created the same circumstances that fomented the first one. "Could you talk to Kórol?"

"Me?" Sáv squeaks. "I wouldn't think of it!"

"But you're friends. He might listen to you."

"Not truly. He's my King, and I know him through Tans." He fixes me with a sheepish look. "Not like those stories of yours. No prince plays with the pauper's son. Tans' the best choice for speaking with Kórol. Fíl next maybe. They're friendlier than me and him, and everyone trusts Fíl. Never lied or made light of the risks. With them gone, you're all that's left to."

I snort. "He barely speaks to me. I remind him of..." I trail off again and gesture around my head. Zorin watches us with curious eyes and shuffles closer.

"What if..." I stare at Zorin until he stomps back. "What if we went to Gramad and got him?"

"Ignore Kórol's orders, sneak 'cross the countryside, traveling farther than we traveled on the trek without magical healing or any prep?"

I grimace but nod. I can't delay any longer: we need to get to Tans and figure out how to open the Gates, trainee tests be damned. Kórol's crown isn't the only thing on the line now, we could be looking at a war I accidentally started. Again.

Sáv shrugs. "Might as well."

CHAPTER 7

S áv's immediate agreement aside, it won't be as easy to leave the castle as it was the last time I snuck out and made for the wilderness. We need horses, which stable to the north of the castle. But we have time on our side. Kórol only told the Council an hour earlier, so it's possible the travel ban hasn't formally started yet and that the enforcers in Gramad won't know for a few weeks, depending on the direction the messenger travels. We also have Zorin.

"This way, Lady," he hisses from in front of me as we leave the castle and walk towards the training grounds. "Once we're out of sight of the entrance, we'll switch directions."

"Are you sure you're okay coming with us? You might get in trouble."

Zorin volunteered immediately, having overheard everything while he was pretending to study the hallway when Sáv and I spoke. "I signed up to protect the Kingdom. If I can do that by stopping a war instead, I will. My King needs Lord Commander by his side. What happened with the Succubus isn't something he can heal through alone," he explains.

My brows almost disappear into my hairline at both the name for Bittállí and the knowledge he's revealed, and I stumble. Zorin turns to keep me on my feet and glares at my expression.

"I'm young, not dense. Lady," he adds as an afterthought.

I walk beside him instead of behind. "I don't think you're dense. We're all young though." Kórol took over the Kingdom three years ago when his father died; Tansr commanded the entire army at seventeen. No matter the uncharitable thoughts I had during my argument with Tans, they seemed to have done well, the fallout from Bittállí notwithstanding. What Leyden said early on runs through my head, that experience ages you faster than time. The reminder pulls my lips into a frown.

"But you've done so much in your years, even if you've only gone around the sun three more times than I, Lady," he says earnestly. "I can only hope to prove myself as you have when I reach your age."

Discomfort burbles under my skin. "Is that part of your guard training? Watch, listen, learn dull facts about your assignments?"

He flushes. "Somewhat. But I know your age because you shared your celebration with Sáven."

Sáven has three weeks on me, born around the Sàrkany version of March 1. I ignore the implication under Zorin's explanation—one about Sáv that could make this trip awkward. "When is your birthday?" I ask instead.

"A week after the Summer Solstice."

So early July. And the Solstice is only days away. I twist my lips. "This trip will likely keep you until after that. It might not be as fun to celebrate with us rather than your friends. And isn't sixteen a big year for the Sàrkany?" They don't reach adulthood at eighteen or twenty-one like on Earth, but they are 'grown' by sixteen and able to decide for themselves and begin their formal careers. Twenty is the next important year, something to do with home life instead of work, but Fíl has avoided the subject when it's come up.

Zorin bites his lip before answering. Finally, he says, "This is where I want to be."

I hold in a groan. I'm seconds from politely asking Zorin to swap with Bay. Bay is quieter and would take some heavy convincing to do what Zorin volunteered for, but Bay also wouldn't moon over Sáven the entire trip. But before I can suggest the switch, Zorin grabs my arm and yanks me behind a fence pole that marks the start of the training grounds.

It's the width of my forearm, meaning all it does it bisect the view of our bodies in half. Zorin is better hidden merely because he stands behind me, his head popping out above mine like a second appendage. He peers around the pole almost comically, since three quarters of his face was already visible to the world. When he's surveyed whatever he's surveilling in the area, he spins me around. He presses one finger to his lips, the universal sign for 'quiet' and then points to the north. After swiveling his neck from side to side twice, he drops to the ground with a loud oomph. *So much for silence.*

Before I can laugh at the absurdity of it all, he clasps my wrist and yanks me down to a crouch. Then, we're crawling. Or *he's* army crawling and I'm on my hands and knees behind him attempting to avoid scratching my palms.

I half expect him to do a barrel roll behind one of the scraggly bushes that dot the trodden pathway. But he is surprisingly effi-cient, and quiet, as we make our way around the path. As soon as we crawl, or wriggle in my case, out of sight of the training grounds and path from the castle, he leaps up and helps me stand.

"I've been practicing my stealth," he says proudly.

"I can tell," I say with as much sincerity as I can muster.

Apparently not that much because he scowls, but I can see the smile in it.

Once we make it to the horses, we're able to find and tack three long antlered steeds quicker than I expected. It helps that Zorin knows what he's doing. All those horse ranch romances taught me the parts of the headgear, the bit and bridle mainly, but not how to do it. My own assigned horse, a butter yellow steed with spindly antlers who I name Sunflower as his antlers reach to the sky, patiently lets Zorin prepare his reins while giving me an impertinent side eye.

Sáv meets us just outside Ilsen, where the landscape opens into Raddare's Pass. I try to avoid thinking about the last time I took that Pass. With a hard shake of my head, I greet Sáv with a smile.

"I packed clothes for you," he says, gesturing to the packs at his feet. "And food for the journey."

"Where would I be without you, Sáv?"

"Naked and hungry," Zorin says from beside us.

If we could harness the speed at which Sáv and I turn our heads to gawk at Zorin, we'd make it to Tans in minutes. Zorin flushes but keeps his head held high.

"This'll be fun," Sáv says to me. Zorin beams.

Sáv hands him two of the packs to attach to the horses and does the same for his horse. When he finishes, he pulls something from one of them and offers it to me like a prize. "Thought you'd want to carry this around again."

It's the tote bag, the one I had when I was yanked into Dalner. It lives in one of my drawers with the remains of what else I brought with me from Earth, which at this point is almost nothing.

I reach for it, but he holds it back. "No condoms in this one, Grace. Must manage that yourself when we get to Gramad."

I pinch his arm and yank the tote bag from him, transferring in a few snacks to bribe Sunflower into liking me as I hold in a laugh.

Zorin comes up beside us. "What's a condom?"

As if we planned it, Sáv and I both say, in unison, "We'll tell you when you're older."

The jovial mood carries us the rest of the day. Kórol's edict hasn't made it far yet, so the roads aren't empty, but are sparse enough to avoid anyone asking why we've mounted the King's horses. We quickly leave Raddare's Pass behind us. Sáv and I agree we shouldn't stop in Nor, like I once demanded Kórol do, but should stay in the low hills instead of taking our chances with the horses in the Barrier Peaks.

We stop just outside Nor, after the horses ran almost all day. Sáv and Zorin handle the animals while I lay out our three sleeping pallets, tossing the tote bag on the middle one to mark my choice.

"I can do that tomorrow," I tell them when they finish and join me on their respective pallets. "So long as you teach me first."

"I don't mind, Lady. It's habit now."

"Passed that part of his exams earlier than any other recruit," Sáv says, ruffling Zorin's fluffy hair. Zorin's face can't decide whether to be bothered or pleased so it lands somewhere in the middle, like a puppet with an incorrectly attached mouth.

Once he's smoothed out his expression, he focuses on me with wide eyes. "Wait. Weren't you to take your first exam tomorrow, Lady? Tacking a horse is the first skill!"

I wave him off. "I skipped a few. I was going to complete the horse and earlier tests after I finished the more difficult ones. But it's fine. I don't *need* the tests."

Sáv and Zorin look skeptical, but my glower deters any further comments on the matter.

"If we're fast, we should get to Tans in about eight days," I tell them, pulling out a handmade copy of a map of Sekai. I drew it during one of my lessons with Fílga. Gramad is a straight shot from Raddare's Pass, almost recreating the path we'd taken on my first venture here.

"Better than the last time we made the trip," Sáv says. "At least we never need to walk that far again."

"I'd hoped to join those trips one day," Zorin says wistfully. His eyes widen and he continues, "Had the trek been true."

Sáv shrugs. "Could've taken my spot. You're not a poor cook. A guard with your skills? You're a great fourth."

Zorin flushes. "I'd rather have gone with you. We could show them the castle children are the best."

Sáv barks a laugh. "You, me, and Tans would've been a sight. Poor Fílga'd collapse."

"But he'd not go with us, if the three of us joined the King," Zorin says. "I never understood why he went anyway," he finishes sullenly.

I clear my throat. "All that riding made me hungry. Sáv, anything to share?"

Sáv takes the hint and rummages through one of his bags. He doles out bread and one of the kitchen's newest creations. It's firm and green and I hold in a wince when he hands it to me. I make encouraging noises when I take a bite until Sáv turns to light a fire. Then I discreetly spit it into my hand and toss it over my shoulder. After Zorin takes his turn with the mystery item, he isn't as controlled, coughing and almost losing the entire hunk to the dirt. But he keeps hold of it and swallows as tears leak from his watery hazel eyes.

"Good thing the kitchens make fire," Sáv says when he kneels back on his pallet. Good thing none of them lost fire magic, he meant, and they didn't have to learn that survival skill when the Gates sealed.

The unspoken reminder sobers us all. While Sáv and Zorin murmur to each other, I slip off to sleep.

"You're somewhere different tonight," Leyden says, inspecting me keenly from his place by the window.

I shuffle to the opposite wall beside the bench and slide down to sit as curiosity pushes a response from my lips. "What makes you think that?"

He gestures vaguely at my body. "You're dressed differently, there's dust in your hair, and the flesh of your arms is chilled."

"Maybe it's cold in the castle."

He tilts his head. "You'd add a blanket. You're not one to intentionally keep yourself from comfort."

I fist my hands on my hips hard enough to twinge the scars. "You don't know me all that well."

He graces me with his crooked smile. "Whatever you say, Grace."

I close my eyes to block out his presence.

"I could warm you," he drawls. My eyes fly open in offense but the predatory expression I expect to match the words is missing. Instead, he holds up one finger, a flicker of flame bursting from it like a human lighter. My stomach clenches at the gesture, something so very Tans-like. "I could build you a fire."

"We're fine." As soon as we get away from the Hallard Mountains and Barrier Peaks, the summer weather should kick in at the lower atmosphere. We won't need Sáv's fire, or anything Leyden could offer.

"I'm attempting to be helpful," he says, pouting. He extinguishes the flame.

"I don't need anything from you," I growl. "And if I were ever desperate enough to want your help, I'd never give you access to my mind to try."

"I wouldn't need into your mind; I could join you." Now, the predatory look is there, something dark and expectant.

"But you're in Exile, in Dànna," I counter.

He shrugs with one shoulder before loping to his pallet. "I've gathered enough magic out here alone, I'm sure I could make the trip."

"But there's no magic here."

He looks as though he's disappointed in my lacking understanding, and I bristle. "But I have the magic, Grace. There was no magic in your dorm when I took you."

"What happened to 'I can't directly interfere, Grace, I can only help you through riddles,'" I say nastily.

He sighs, something low and full of meaning. "I cannot and you needed the riddles. If not for them, you'd never have survived."

I cross my arms around my waist. "Whatever."

"I can help you now though. It isn't interference if I'm present. I simply need the invitation," he says, his black eyes focused on mine.

"That will never happen. I'm not letting you loose in Dalner and I'm not incurring the wrath of the rest of you monsters by breaking you out."

He laughs, but it's a bitter sound. "They'd thank you for the pleasure if you removed me and saved them the trouble of deciding what to do with me now."

"Poor Leyden, useful but unnecessary, on the edge of being important, but failing instead."

He blinks blankly before recognition blooms. "I said we were similar, Grace."

"Shut up, Leyden."

He laughs.

CHAPTER 8

"I'm not suggesting anything, Sáven. I only think you should consider it. In a year, you could wake up and suddenly realize the person for you wasn't who you thought, that maybe it was someone you've known for years." Zorin's quiet pleading voice pulls me from my nightly dream with Leyden.

"Doesn't work that way, I think. Ma said it was more like soup simmering. The flavors build over time, only the ingredients already work together because of it. Like flour and milk, not milk and meat."

My eyes blink open. Zorin and Sáv are brushing the horses. Sáv stands with raised shoulders, the skin at his neck red. Zorin leans against the other side of Sunflower and slants over his back as if trying to climb closer to Sáv.

We celebrated Zorin's birthday as best we could on the road a few days prior, Sáv baking bread over the fire and me trying to sing a poorly translated birthday song. The night was more fun than I'd expected, but since then Zorin took every opportunity to remind Sáv he was 'an adult' now.

"Morning," I call out before Sáv's entire body turns tomato colored.

They both spin and Sáv's expression bleeds relief. Sunflower stomps forward to dig into the emerald grass surrounding us.

"Morning, Grace! Ready to leave?" Sáv sounds like someone who is being held at gunpoint with the shooter hidden out of sight.

I shake the fatigue from my body before rolling up my pallet. "More than. Zorin, could you?"

Zorin takes the pallet from me with a ducked head. He shoves it into one of his packs and vaults onto his horse without speaking.

I raise my brows at Sáven in question, but he only shakes his head as the flushed color fades from his cheeks.

We're only hours from Samsen and Tans' family home. The trip has been uneventful, only marked by Leyden's nightly guessing what I'm doing, and Zorin's longing looks he can't camouflage.

"I'm sorry about all that," I tell Sáv after we've ridden for a few hours. Zorin allowed his horse to canter, taking him out of hearing range.

Sáv looks distracted but sighs. "Nothing to it. I love that boy, but like a brother." He stares into the distance where Zorin disappeared. "Feels familiar, like Fílga when we returned from the trek. Zorin can't change my mind but... makes me wonder if Fíl felt the same and only said yes to quiet me."

I want to leap out of my saddle and gather him into a hug. I settle for reaching out a hand and squeezing his arm. "No, I don't think so. He loves you. I don't know why he was hesitant at first, but-"

"His age," Sáv says, like it's obvious.

"I don't get it," I say, confused. "He isn't that much older, maybe 9 or 10 years? I mean, he never says his exact age, but it's not like an age difference should keep him from *loving* you."

Sáv furrows his brows. "No, 'course not. But people'll talk, with him over—"

The sound of hoofs on grass interrupts him as Zorin gets larger until he and his horse stop in front of us. He heaves frantic breaths and points in the direction we're supposed to riding.

"My King's proclamation has arrived in Gramad. I've tried to tell them who you are, and that unguarded travel is not to be a violation, but the wardens aren't listening. They demand to bring you to justice."

The sound of more clomping rises in the distance until it's close enough to vibrate the hooves of our horses. Six male wardens surround us, in varying ages, wearing clothes the colors of the forest. We've landed in a western, but instead of guns and wide brim hats, they have bows and deep-set scowls. Sunflower looks ready to puncture ribs with his antlers, snuffling at the interlopers.

"Hurchá," Sáv says under his breath.

If I knew what that meant, I bet I'd agree.

No matter that Zorin has his guard uniform on under his cloak, dusty but still displaying the embroidered dragon emblem; no matter that I explain I'm the proxy for their Council member and here to see Tans; no matter that Kórol *said* Council members could go home, they still drag us through the town like criminals.

Although, criminals *might* be a stretch. Half the wardens take our horses at the edge of Samsen while the remaining three march us down the street. With one in the front and two in the back, we could be a tiny procession of important guests. But the immediate demand that we 'follow them or else,' the long archers' bows on their backs, and the final oral reminder that 'all travel is forbidden' makes this more like a prison walk.

I can barely see over the stocky and broad shoulders of the first warden. He must be the leader of the group, based on the air of weathered authority he gives off. His chiseled face was framed by a close-cropped beard and two braids reminiscent of Tans. Deep-set blue eyes pin me in place when I attempt to peer around him as we journey through the town. I offer my most non-threatening smile, which is really what all my smiles look like, but he does nothing more than stare down at me with keen interest. After unsuccessfully peeking through the small window he made when he put his hands on his hips, he ends up grasping me by my forearm and walking me next to him. Zorin makes an irate sound, and I can barely hear Sáv attempt to calm him.

Samsen looks nothing like I remember it, if only because I remember little. That first morning felt like a dream, more reasonably dreamlike than the stubborn belief I maintained that the *entirety* of Dalner was a dream. I remember thinking it was like a small fair, and that feeling remains. There are still flags that wave at the edge of the buildings' gable roofs, and people still mill about in what I now know is traditional Sàrkany clothing. But the air is less charged with energy, a thick blanket of quiet during what should be a busy afternoon. I remember the hush that came over the town outside Ilsen, the shock at seeing me, a physical manifestation of what happened to the walls. At least empty roads mean no one will shriek at me.

The stomping escort brings a few faces outside the doors, but no one joins us on the street. We meander through several small side streets until we stop in front of an unobtrusive multi-story building. Dark wood forms exes along the sides, making the building look no different from any other we pass, except there's an inked design of a dragon on the heavy wooden door. The first warden opens it while the other two stand behind us with crossed arms. The implication that we must enter is clear.

The front room looks nothing like I expected—it isn't the first floor of a home, with a kitchen fire in the corner, nor is it a merchant's store, with goods displayed on the walls, or a clandestine prison, with stocks attached to the floor. Instead, it looks like a miniature auditorium. A podium stands in front of us, elevated on a dais, with a half wooden dozen benches splayed around the room like disorganized church pews.

A tall woman with wild black hair waits behind the podium. Sáv makes a gurgling sound to my left, but the woman's immediate glare silences any further outburst. Zorin angles himself in front of me in a protective, but probably useless, move (as they took his few weapons). The woman snaps her fingers and points to the benches directly in front of her podium. We shuffle towards them and sit as the front warden leans against a wall behind us.

"Not you," she shouts, crooking her finger in my direction. I squeeze Sáv's wrist before standing and moving before her. She's stunning up close, with high cheekbones that lend her an air of regality, and plump lips. Her wild hair looks even more untamed up close, as though it has a personality of its own. Her bronze skin is warm like she spends a lot of time outdoors and contrasts with the cherry red of her dress that flows around her like liquid silk. Her almond-shaped brown eyes twinkle, at odds with her angry expression.

"Hello," I say as brightly as I can muster. *This is all just a miscommunication*, I remind myself. I'm Tans' proxy and allowed to be here. But the glower on the woman's face, the full force of which is now directed at me, makes me almost forget.

"You," she says again, less like a shout but still too loud. "Trouble."

I stare back blankly. The lack of exact grammar keeps me from understanding what she means. The western montage I thought I was in has transformed into something like an expedition story, where the townspeople attempt to speak to the outsiders whose language isn't the same. I look to Sáv for a clue, but he stares hard at the wall behind her.

The woman's eyebrows furrow. "You understand?" she says slowly, dragging out the syllables and raising her voice even louder. At the proximity, it's almost deafening.

She looks behind me. "Sáven, Tans said she'd learned some of the language."

Before I can do more than open my mouth in shock, another slightly familiar voice yells down from the floor above. "She does, but you're talking to her like she's deaf. Honestly, Mara."

The woman—Mara—pouts. "You ruined the joke! How am I supposed to scare her now?" she shouts to the ceiling. Sáv bends over and covers his face with his hands. His shoulders shake. Zorin looks alarmed.

The first warden strolls to her side. "Subtlety, my love. You were missing subtlety."

Mara places her hands on his chest and runs her fingers over the rough green fabric of his tunic. "You like when I'm not subtle."

The man smirks and bends closer to her ear, a salacious grin on his chiseled face. Sáven's shoulders shake harder, and a gasping sound comes from him. A laugh, I'm now realizing.

My hands fist on my hips. "What the hurchá is going on?"

Mara and the warden stop gazing at each other like they want to eat the other's face and swivel their necks to refocus on me.

"Well, her education can't be too lacking if she knows how to swear," Mara says with an eyebrow waggle.

Sáv pulls himself together and gestures to Mara. "Grace, meet Mara, Tans' older sister."

"Youngest older sister," she adds, as though a necessary distinction.

"Youngest older sister," Sáv corrects. "And you must be her husband Breg."

The two men shake and begin a quick discussion on their mutual acquaintances in Ilsen.

I clap my hands to get their attention. "Hello, still confused. Where's Tans?"

Mara's expression falls but only briefly. "Upstairs. We'll take you to him."

Tans is in a small bedroom on the second floor, splayed on the white sheets like a dark shadow. He beams when I appear in the doorway and slowly shuffles to a seated position.

"This is a surprise," he says. Any lingering annoyance from our argument vanished the minute I learned he was hurt, and I drop my bag and fly to him. The bed is sized for a child, not a grown man and I barely fit beside him.

After I gingerly shuffle us until there's no longer a risk that I crush him, I inspect his expression for any trace of pain. But there is none. He looks tired, with bruises under his eyes, but otherwise unhurt. It feels like a memory—the white sheets, the single bed, the pale plaster walls, the smell of something clean but antiseptic. But in the memory, it's me on the bed and not Tans. I burst into tears.

His arms spread and he drags me down beside him. "What's wrong? Are you hurt?"

"No!" I wail. "But you are, and it's my fault."

He twists his lips. "Did you scare my horse?"

"No, but you wouldn't have been out here if you weren't looking for magic to fix the Gate," I explain as I wipe my sniffling nose. If I had taken an extra second, had charged at Leyden with intent to incapacitate him, instead of hiding from the actual fight and letting my blood do the dirty work for me, the risk Leyden posed would still be gone but Gates might be open.

Tans shuffles until we're laying side by side. Painted stars cover the ceiling in a rainbow of blues and whites. "Did you attempt to tear down the Gate and start a war with the Sàrkany?"

I cross my arms around my stomach and speak wetly. "I know what you're trying to do."

"Good," he says, angling his face to kiss my temple. "Then I can stop. I'd prefer to enjoy you in my arms for a few minutes without arguing that there are only three beings responsible for my current plight: me, my horse, and the Eósy. Mara will surely burst into the room with several inappropriate comments, and I'd like at least one of her accusations of what we're doing alone to be true."

Mischief fills his amber eyes, and he leans down to kiss my lips, even with my face moist and clogged. His breath is warm, and I can almost imagine the fire beneath his skin licking upward and drying the few tears that hadn't yet tracked down my face. Blinking them back, I roll until I'm half on top of him and deepen the kiss before he gasps sharply and grips my arms.

"Sorry, sorry," he breathes. "While I would enjoy nothing more than continuing, whatever ails me appears to be focused on my lower back."

I lift myself onto my forearms to remove any weight on him. "No, I'm sorry. I told you this was—"

"If you say this was all your fault, I will not protect you from whatever tricks Mara may still be planning."

"This is not what the healer meant when she said rest and relax," Mara says where she leans against the doorway.

I vault off Tans and slide to the floor.

"Dinner will be ready soon," she says with an impish grin, one normally seen on Tans' face.

Tans rolls his eyes. "We best leave now. It will take me time to get upstairs, and Mara will make unseemly comments if we arrive later than the rest." Before he stands, he tosses me a worried look. "And if she asks if you like swimming, run as far from her as you can."

CHAPTER 9

Dinner conversation flows as smoothly as the mead Tans' mother serves. Both Tans' parents join us, along with Mara and Breg. Zorin and Sáv look at ease sitting across the table from me, but the boisterousness still isn't something I'm used to. Though the clammy feeling covering my skin isn't because of the busy room, but that this is the first 'meet the parents' experience I've ever had. One of Tans' sisters, not Mara but Ridi, came to the castle a few times after the Winter Solstice, but the opportunity to meet his parents has never come up. I smother the discomfort in knowing that it's only arisen because of Tans' health.

Their family home showcases their status, reminding me that Tans grew up as something akin to a minor lord. As if him being heir to one of the twelve Council seats and having 'Lord' in his formal title didn't already.

The dining room is dominated by a long, sturdy wooden table, polished to a rich mahogany hue. Carved patterns adorn the edges, depicting tiny dragons and their curling smoke breath. Overhead, a series of wrought-iron chandeliers dangle from the ceiling, each holding simple candles that cast a warm glow across the room. The light plays on the wooden paneled walls, highlighting tapestries that depict the family's lineage. It looks as though they gained their power soon after the wall went up.

A single servant, clad in dark blue, moves discreetly about, ensuring the smooth operation of the dining experience. I swallow down my discomfort at my own attire and lacking status. I've certainly read this story before.

"Tansr tells us you came from another... world?" his mother, Elo, asks when Mara and Breg stop grandstanding. She glitters with maternal energy as she pours me another glass of mead. Her skin is the same shade as Tans', lighter than Mara's, but her hair looks like spun gold. It makes the bright amber of her eyes, the shape of which both siblings inherited, darker in contrast.

"Yes," I say after I've taken the obligatory sip and drop my hands into my lap, mimicking Fíl's table behavior. "It's very different from Dalner."

Tans' father Prieten, a trim older gentleman with hair as long as Tans' and a thick black beard, leans forward with his elbows on the table. "In what way?"

"More progressive." It comes out like a question. Sàrkany doesn't have a word for science or technology, so I can't explain it any other way. "The way of life here is like how it was for us hundreds of years ago, your medicine, jobs, hobbies." I pause. I'd like to say we're more progressive with women's rights and politics, but recent circumstances before I left would show that was a lie.

"But there is no magic," Tans explains.

"*We* don't have magic," Mara says from his other side. She grunts as if Tans elbowed her. "What? It's true. I don't know why we're acting as though it is a secret. Gracie *obviously* knows."

Elo's gaze sharpens and focuses on the two, who stiffen and stop their bickering. Her expression softens when she turns it back to me, but I can see pity in it. "And you have no magic at all?"

I shake my head. Tans' hand snakes to my thigh and he squeezes. The warmth of the room and conversation, joined with the need to prove myself to his magical, *important*, parents, pushes the next words from my lips, the ones I only teased out with Tans during our fight. "That's actually... that's why I think I could stop the Eósy."

Tans' grip tightens and if magic still existed, my thigh would have a burn mark in the shape of his hand. The soft sounds of flatware on plates and cups on wood fade as though someone muted them.

I clear my throat as the entire table focuses on me. "It's hard for mental spells to latch, so I couldn't be overtaken like...some others. And my blood could remove the mental spells on Kórol and Tans." My eyes dart towards him and he tensely nods in recognition. "In the Gate, my blood and..." There's no good way to describe electricity. "The sparking white fire, *electricity*, from a communication device I brought with me, a *phone*, combined and shocked the Gate closed."

Elo and Prieten share a glance I can't interpret while Breg eyes me with interest. "Would your blood be able to reopen it?"

"No," Tans almost snarls, overlapping with my reluctant, "Maybe."

"It seems unlikely. If the absence of magic closed it, wouldn't it need the addition of more magic to open it?" Zorin suggests, biting his lip when heads swivel towards him.

Sáv ruffles his hair. "Smart, Zorin."

Zorin ducks his head, pleased. The room stays quiet for a minute longer than is comfortable.

"Well, that's interesting," Prieten says gruffly. "What else is different where you came from?"

"Books," I say, exhaling as I interlace my fingers with Tans. "We have a lot more books."

I tuck the corners of Tans' bed with jerky movements while he watches me solemnly. Dinner ended with no more landmines before we shuffled him back downstairs and into bed.

"What changed your mind?" he asks. I sit beside his feet and don't pretend to misunderstand.

"Maybe you were right, and I need to acknowledge what happened and my role in it instead of keeping it buried."

He hums. "And you wanted to prove you were worthy without magic."

I slump. "And I wanted to prove I was worthy without magic."

His warm hand cups the underside of my leg. "You saved us," he insists. "You are worthy. And all this guilt you're carrying, all your demands to become better, none of it is necessary. You made a choice. That choice had consequences, but it doesn't mean they were bad ones, and it doesn't mean you need to fix anything."

I frown. "But they—"

"Acknowledge what happened so you can move on. So *we* can move on."

My frown deepens, and he runs his thumb over the bowed pout.

"Shall I tell you what I found in the Wilds?"

I smother the frustration, the clawing feeling that he doesn't understand. The worry over what might happen to him still sits heavy in my gut and fighting with him now won't solve the problem with magic. "You called out Butterfly," I say against his thumb.

His expression is soft. "I did. But I saw one too."

I rip my head backward in excitement. "There *was* something in there?"

"I felt something under us, that's what I believe scared the horse. And before I slipped from his back, an emerald butterfly flew over my vision." He doesn't sound as enthusiastic as he should, if he truly found wildlife.

"How sure are you that you saw one? It's not like we're lacking for anything green around here."

He grabs a lock of my hair and tugs. "How little faith you have in me. I can tell the difference between the surrounding grass and an insect in the sky. The horse didn't harm my eyesight."

I swallow the burst of shame the reminder gives me and take advantage of his teasing mood, leaning forward until our breath mingles. "Who knows, you could have lost your senses alone in the Wilds and started dreaming up butterflies because you missed me."

"The last part was true." He kisses me again, something soft and unhurried. It lacks any charge or need to go further, only the simple touch of two people. But even tender, Tans' touch lights a fire under my skin and I bury my hands in his long hair.

I pull away sooner than I'd like, sooner than he'd like by the look on his face, but there's pain there too and he needs the rest. I roll on my side to face him as he stares up at the stars on the ceiling.

I draw shapes on his stomach with my fingers. "What are you going to do about the butterfly?"

"Nothing," he says.

I keep my voice soft, my tone gentle. "Why not? There's a chance—"

"A butterfly isn't what we need." He covers my hand with his own.

"You felt something under you, you said." The gentleness seeps from my tone. "That could have been magic."

"And if it was? It doesn't mean there are foodstuffs there, merely a single butterfly. And if there was magic, I don't know how to bring it back to Dalner."

I lean over him and press as much persuasion as I can into my tone. "You can't give up. Every arrow in your quiver, remember?"

But he's undeterred, shifting until he can cross his arms over his chest mulishly. "With Kórol's edict, as I understand it, no one is going anywhere. He will not approve a search for something he's decided we no longer need. I've already sent off my correspondence with the messenger on what the units should do in my absence."

"We must do something, investigate, at least try. You can't let Kórol's poor decision keep you from trying to protect the people."

He scoffs. "You're explaining it as though I have only one valid choice. I must follow my King, but I must also protect my people."

"Exactly." My face flushes with intensity. "And he's not able to do that. Not with you here, him cutting off the provinces, and no magic fix."

"My men will keep order, of that I am sure."

My lips purse. "You're not thinking of the big picture. What if Plema or Mendeth decide to stir up trouble?" They are the most difficult of the Council members, and the look in Plema's eye tells me he wouldn't mind a little power change if the time was right.

"They wouldn't dare, no—"

"They could. Desperate people do desperate things," I interrupt stubbornly.

"Don't take this as an insult, but I know my people and the risks to, and from, them better than you."

I let out an irritated breath. "Then you know there is only one choice: find the magic, whatever you felt."

"*We* will do nothing, regardless of Kórol's plans. Me because of my leg, you because—" he trails off almost helplessly.

I sit up and he follows me, both at opposite ends of his bed. "What? Me because of what?" I demand.

He grips the hair by his scalp and pulls. "You—you haven't finished your trainee tests," he finishes triumphantly. "There is no way you completed them all in such a brief time."

I have taken none of them. Heat rushes to my cheeks but I push past it, hoping Tans won't notice. "I didn't need tests to travel with you on the trek last autumn."

"Did you—you took the first test before traveling here, didn't you?"

"That's not important."

His eyes pinch shut. "Grace, you promised."

"I said I would take them so you'd stop coddling me, not that I wouldn't do anything before them."

"The first test was about survival and safety, how to handle horses and start fires without magic." He sounds devastated, *disappointed*, and that bitter feeling I buried not minutes before threatens to claw out of me.

"Let's not talk about this now," I urge. "I'm here, I'm fine. No harm done."

He looks like he's going to disagree before his tense shoulders fall and he rests back against the bed. His eyes crack like shattered glass. "Did I mention Ridi's old room has a connecting bath?"

The sound of running water is soothing as I wait for the tub to fill with heated water. There's a large stove in the corner with a pipe running through it, the non-magical way they've discovered to heat the water. It's newly installed, only needed when Tans' family lost their fire magic.

I meander back to Tans' room to grab the bag I dropped on the floor when I first saw him, but quiet voices stop me in the hallway.

"All I'm saying is that she isn't magic," Elo is saying.

"That doesn't matter to me," comes Tans' immediate response.

"I know it doesn't, but I don't want you setting yourself up for heartbreak in two years."

"I won't," Tans says. I recognize his tone. It's one I use often, something stubborn and unyielding.

"You may not be meant, my love," Elo soothes.

I tiptoe back into the bathing room, unwilling to interrupt whatever argument they're having. I've read enough about families trying to pull relationships apart and it always has three outcomes: the couple either comes closer together, breaks up, or stays together while one of them resents the other.

I was right to remind them of what I'd done, and how I was the only one that could stop Leyden and his army, even if I did it the wrong way. Cleary, I *did* have something to prove to them.

I shake the thoughts from my mind as I slip into the water, drowning my restlessness. The liquid luxury eases the stress in my muscles and between my ears. I'll approach Tans tomorrow, not about the weird conversation I overheard but the butterfly.

What butterfly?

My eyes fly open and water spills to the ground as I seize upward. I'm alone in the bathroom, not asleep and in Leyden's loathsome presence in his moldy cell. My heart rate plummets back to a manageable speed as I sluice off the fear that Leyden saw me naked. I lean backward again but keep my eyes open, even as my muscles loosen under the pleasant heat of the water.

Loathsome seems strong.

I glare at the corners of the room, still the bathing room and still empty. "Get out of my head, Leyden," I hiss through clenched teeth. But there's no response. I wiggle back underwater, but all hope of relaxing vanishes. Now the heat only ignites a fire in my blood, one that wants Leyden to burn out of my life.

Again.

CHAPTER 10

S leep comes slowly that night. After the bath, I said good-night to Tans, mentioning the delay in heating the water. But he took it to be a complaint about the wall again. The hangdog expression he displayed, and the quiet "there is nothing for you to fix" he murmured when I turned away, created an oozing of something sour in my stomach that threatened to rekindle my annoyance. I refused to allow it to guzzle upward and spew out of me. Instead, I gave Tans a smacking kiss and let my frustration turn back to its original, and most worthy, source: Leyden.

"If you continue making that expression, your face will freeze that way," Leyden says from his place leaning against the wall beneath the window. "That is the expression, correct? I've forgotten much of your Earth sayings but—"

The sound cuts off as my hand arcs through the air towards his cheek. But his silence isn't because I connect with his skin but because I don't.

We both stare at my hand with almost equally comical expressions on our face. He attempts to poke at my wrist, but I wrench my hand back towards my chest. It doesn't matter, as the jarred motion has his finger going right through my forearm like a ghostly apparition.

"That's new." He scrutinizes my form as if it will tell him what's changed.

"Are you kidding me?" I growl the words as I pace the floor of his cell. "Now I can't even hit you? I should have slapped you

more. *Harder, and every godforsaken night we've dreamed of each other."*

"Do not take your frustration at that boy of yours out on me."

I stalk back towards him, my finger pointed like a blade at his chest, but the effect is meaningless now that we know we can't touch each other. "Don't mention him. Don't even think of him. I'd say don't think of me, but you can't help yourself."

His hand clutches at his pale throat. "I cannot imagine what I have done to inspire this level of anger in you."

I rear back in shock and a faint blush appears on those preternaturally pale cheeks.

"Today," he clarifies. "I cannot imagine what I did to anger you today."

My eyes narrow dangerously. "Are you forgetting the bath?"

A beaming smile bursts from his lips. "Is that what you were doing? I couldn't tell this time; I only knew you were relaxed." *The smile dims.* "Perhaps our connection is fading."

"Good," I snap, clenching my fists even though the action is futile.

"You don't mean that. You'd miss me."

The hysterical laugh burbles out involuntarily. "Miss you? After what you did?"

His expression flattens. "Yes, yes, that's getting old. But of the many individuals in your acquaintance, I am the only one who has always given you agency." *He holds up a hand to halt the beginning of my snarling response.* "Yes, I led *you to the correct decision, but it was always yours to make. I didn't hold the reins when you stabbed Bittállí and her creation. Nor did I force you to continue with any of the Sìnnách trials, or leap into the Gate."*

A gust of breath bursts from my stomach as if I've been punched. "Stop talking. You're spinning words again. 'I created you and pointed you at an unmoving target,' remember?"

"Pointed but did not force you to move. Each of them pushed you in the direction they chose but then wouldn't let you make your own choice—they forced you to endure the trials even when the

consequence was death, they tied you to your horse to keep you from battle—"

"I told you to stop talking."

He crosses his arms over his chest, leaning back against the wall. "I don't understand you, Grace," he murmurs. He studies the floor as if working out a difficult equation. "I received your memories as well; I know what occurred and what you thought. The girl who demanded she grow and finish this journey on her terms, who wanted to be the Fates' damned heroine, wouldn't sit idly by now. You wish to make up for your mistakes at the Gates and reactivate the rifts, but you wait for permission: permission from your teachers, permission from your lover, permission from your self-doubt. The Grace that faced me needed no permission." His head lifts and his dark eyes focus back on me. "That Grace was no bird, no net ensnared her. Where did she go?"

Leyden's a jerk, spouting tripe and quoting from Jane Eyre. I was too complacent and let him worm his way back into my head, assuming I was safe in that dreamscape and forgetting all that he did. I want to kick him in those charmingly crooked teeth.

Leyden may also be right, and for that maybe I'll kick him somewhere more sensitive. Not about him offering me 'choices.' After all, the illusion of choice isn't true choice; I've learned that much from books and my few classes. But about my fear: I can't keep waiting on someone to agree that I'm ready.

The morning after his embarrassingly accurate analysis found me hiding in my room. Not because of Leyden, but because of me. I let all that fear and guilt about what happened to the Gates keep me from doing anything about it. How long would it be before I felt *ready* to do something? When I could write treatises in Sàrkany? When I could beat Tans in battle? When someone laid out the plan for me? When Tans finally agreed to go with me and ended up doing the hard stuff himself? When the country was embroiled in war? I am a bird in a net of my own making.

I join the family at lunch, sliding into my seat next to Tans.

"Tell him," Zorin is almost pleading to Mara and Breg. "When you turn twenty, it is like a shot in the chest. You simply *know*."

"Who's to say it will even work now," Breg says as he brings a large vegetable to his mouth and tears out a bite like some would a turkey leg. His eyes twitch as he swallows the bite whole, and the vegetable tumbles to the table. "With the magic gone," he continues, wheezing slightly, "they may no longer exist."

Zorin sinks low into his seat while both Tans and Sáv look relieved.

"What may not exist?" I ask. All conversation stops and the others direct several pitying looks towards Tans.

He grabs one of the tiny braids by his collarbone. "Soulmates," he mumbles. It takes my head a moment to translate what he said, the words being more like 'life's match' and 'soul's pair' all at once.

I tilt my head. I know soulmates, the fake literary kind. But the tension building in the room implies I'm missing something serious. "Like, you're the one for me, my best friend, my love. Hopefully, we stay in love because our relationship seems to be going well. That kind of soulmate?"

Confusion sweeps into his expression. "No... like the person fated for you by magic, whose soul is bound to find yours in love."

The breath whooshes out of me and all my thoughts from this morning, from Leyden's accusations, vanish. "As in, actual soulmates, made for me, the other half of my soul?"

"It's a legacy from the Eósy still existing in our blood. They live forever with one match. We don't, but our souls are rebirthed,"

Breg adds, smirking at Mara. "And find each other across our many lives."

Something deadens in my chest, like a film of ice scurrying down my throat to my gut. I squeak out a question. "Why haven't I heard about it before?"

Tans, Sáven, and Zorin wear the same surprised expressions. "We've spoken about it in front of you many times," Tans says. "It was in your culture lesson with Fíl weeks ago, from the schedule I saw."

"You must've known, assumed that's why you stopped making jokes about his age," says Sáv. "Why *else* does Fílga's age matter?" Sáv adds sourly. Zorin perks up at his tone.

I blink. I'd stopped teasing him about Fíl being his sugar daddy because of Zorin. "Because he's older than you and people find that uncomfortable?"

Mara reaches around Tans and pats me on the wrist. "Because that man would have realized and found his soul's match when he was twenty. And for him to not admit it to Sáven…"

"Means it's someone else," Sáv finishes, rubbing his chin. "Doesn't bother me though," he says with false brightness. "Choice is important."

I nod, remembering all the stories with soulmates, how none of them seemed fraught with the tension and problems that real life soulmates would have. What if your soulmate died before you found them that time around? What if your soulmate was in love with someone else before that magical date arose? What if your soulmate was horrible and abusive and you didn't want to be reincarnated with them? What if you were asexual or aromantic, would you still get a romantic soulmate?

That was the benefit of fiction, and why I liked the subject in stories; it removed the messiness of real life. You find your fated match and, after escaping the inevitable madman who tried to break the bond, live happily ever after with the person who was perfect for you.

"I want Mara and Breg to tell us how it felt," Zorin says, almost whining. "Sáven said it was like cooking. The ingredients already work together but must simmer. But I thought it was immediate. That you'd know that second." He looks at Sáv almost pleadingly. "And things change."

Sáv's green eyes disappear upward with the force of him rolling them.

Mara gazes across the table at Breg as a smile blooms on her face. She looks as beautiful as Tans when she does, all passion and heat. "Simmering is a good word for it. It isn't as though I woke on my twentieth birthday and a mental messenger told me Breg was my soulmate. I'd seen him, knew him, but when I turned twenty, it was as though the possibility of him became real to me. I realized I could spend lifetimes with this man by my side, and my soul must have already done so."

Breg smiles back, an expression too intimate for the setting.

"That's why Fíl's soulmate doesn't matter," says Sáv. "Possibility's there already. And if I turn twenty and it's no longer him, that's life."

"Is that why you mentioned not thinking anything would change at twenty?" I ask Tans. The rest of the table pretends they can't overhear us, as Breg loudly brings up simmering soup and how Mara likes to hand feed him.

Tans interlaces our fingers and stares at our crossed wrists. "You're not magic, the opposite of magic as you said. It is unlikely there is a soulmate for you here, if the magic would still work in two years."

"And the souls are reborn," Zorin says. Apparently, the soup interlude didn't hold their attention from our business for long. "Your soul isn't from here."

Tans squeezes my fingers. "My soul from eons past didn't know yours was an option, or else it would know there is no other. I would choose you. I would choose us."

But can it be a choice when there is only one option, as all others are unknown? Can it be a choice if the outcome is already decided, if you're pointed in that direction with no ability to alter the course?

My eyes close. Leyden still deserves a kick in the stomach. I drag my hand back to my lap. "I want to go into the Wilds."

"Because Tans isn't your soulmate? That seems harsh, Gracie," Mara says, brows raised.

"No," I tell the table, wrapping my arms around my waist. "Because it's about choice, like Sáv says. If Tans has a soulmate out there, I want the magic back so he can choose me for me, not because he doesn't know of the other choice." I take a breath and risk looking back at Tans. There are so many reasons to do this, the soulmate argument is another drop in an overflowing bucket. "This is my best chance to find the answer. To see if I can fix it."

"What about the Eósy?" Zorin asks, his mouth pitched in a frown.

My breath catches. They can't know about Leyden and his nightly visits; they can't have heard me—

"They must not break through if the Gates reopen," Breg says, understanding what Zorin meant quicker than I did.

"The walls went up, what, two thousand years ago? The rifts existed and the Gates worked fine until some jerk decided he didn't like how things were going," I say.

Mara raises her cup. "I'd thank him. Not for the attempted slaughter or bringing down the Gates. Or for almost killing my little brother." She sweeps her gaze over me and the tightly coiled tension surrounding me. "Or scarring Gracie here. But that Great Matron business never sat right with me."

Breg snorts. "Because you wanted to be worshiped instead."

Mara sniffs but doesn't deny it.

I squeeze my side to urge myself forward. "I won't bring down the walls. Those monsters can suffocate on their side for all I care. But our side needs the rifts back and the Gates open."

"This is your excuse," Tans says, refusing to look at me. "The tests were a ploy, perhaps visiting me was a ploy, to get you closer to the wall. That this relates to soulmates is your justification. Fear for Kórol's reign is another. If not those, you would have come up with something else and done it anyway."

I shake my head fiercely. "No, it isn't an excuse. I came because it's you. And I want to fix things, you know that. I don't care if it is or isn't my fault. I've spent six months wallowing, waiting for—for permission." I give Leyden a mental middle finger for providing me the right words. "I need to do this. This just…" I wince before continuing, "seemed like the right time to tell you."

Tans stands, the bench below us sliding backward from the force. I wish the pain on his face was only from his unknown ailment, but it's clear that's not true. He can't make it downstairs alone, so Sáv vaults over from the other side and lets Tans lean on him. Together with Tans' crutch, they hobble from the room.

Mara picks up her fork and spins it casually in the air. "Gracie, do you enjoy swimming?"

Tans keeps his eyes downcast when I enter the room. Sáv sits next to him on the bed and gives me a strained smile before elbowing him hard. Tans looks up with a shamed and slightly pained expression.

"I shouldn't have said your visit was only a means to obtain your goals," he says, ducking his head again.

"I'm sorry for blurting it out like that," I murmur.

Tans shrugs but still won't look at me. "It isn't as though I am unaware of your rash decision-making skills." The words sound bitter, but there's no heat behind them. He releases a sharp breath and clasps Sáven on the shoulder as the two have some kind of mental conversation before he turns back to me. "I will support you. I cannot go with you, as you know, but Sáv-"

"No," I say firmly. "Sáven has his own things going on. He'll want to get back to the castle and see Fíl."

"Not sure we can make it back," says Sáv, his grass green eyes bright. "What with the travel ban."

Tans squeezes Sáv's shoulder. "Zorin would help. He's a good guard."

Both Sáv and I share a look and snort.

"What am I missing?" Tans says.

I pat Sáv's head. "Zorin would rather keep Sáven here and as far away from Fíl as possible. It seems he thinks he and Sáven are meant." I swallow the sudden burst of bitterness in my throat at the implication.

Tans' brows raise as a wide grin grows. "*Really?* My goodness, Sáven. A grave robber and a cradle robber."

I laugh, the sound only partly forced. The tension may have bled from the room but the wounds from upstairs are barely scabbed over. "Sure, grave robber translates, but when I try to call him a sugar daddy, you act like I'm speaking nonsense."

"I've no children, Butterfly, but I believe sugar isn't encouraged. Though perhaps our dear sweet Sáven has a different dessert in mind."

Sáv turns as red as his hair. "Don't encourage him," he says to me, shaking a callused finger in my face. That finger swivels to Tans. "And *you* don't encourage *him*." Then he stands, wipes down the wrinkles on his tunic, and strolls out the door with his head held high, leaving Tans and me alone.

Tans sighs and runs his fingers through his messy hair. He must have pulled the braids out while I was trying to evade Mara and whatever she intended to do to me. "Which should we cover first, the soulmate revelation or your foolhardy plan?"

I smile but it's all teeth. "My plans always work. Eventually."

"Soulmates it is." He braces himself as if expecting me to deliver a blow.

"It's not like it has to change anything," I explain, swallowing my inner romantic that knows 'soulmates' can trump all. "I'm annoyed no one told me but—"

He slumps. "We all assumed you knew. Fíl should have taught you the historical basis for it *weeks* ago."

I scowl, thinking of the lesson plan in my pack that says nothing on the topic. "Yes, and I'll be speaking with him about his choice to edit my studies when I come back."

"And," Tans continues bitterly, "why else was Kórol's immediate infatuation with you unsuspicious? He was twenty, and when we realized his feelings were less academic and politically tied to your status as a Sìnnách and consort but were instead amorous..." He trails off.

I slip to the bed beside him and begin plaiting his hair. My fingers aren't as dexterous as his, making the resulting braids uneven and lumpy. "I love you."

He smiles, but it's weak. "And I love you. Soulmate or not. I do not need to know all my options to choose you, because I would choose you in every lifetime. My soul simply didn't know what it was missing, spending centuries shackled to someone less perfect."

"I'm not perfect," I say, finishing the braids and resting my hands against his shoulders.

"I am aware. But you're perfect for me."

"Flatterer."

He laughs before sobering again. "I can't change your mind about this trip, can I?"

It's my turn to slump as I disappoint him again. "No."

He nods, as if he expected me to say that. "And you will not wait until I can come with you?"

I run my hands down his shoulders. "Did I ever tell you why I jumped into the Gate?"

His nose wrinkles as he stares at his lap. "I can imagine."

I grasp his chin and gently force him to face me. "The entire time you were saying how important I was, and that I could do anything. And I wanted to be that person and make up for what I did. I was going to prove it."

He blinks blankly. "You didn't do any—"

"I wanted to be worthy," I say.

He shakes his head as best he can with my hands holding him in place. "Utility is not a measure of worth, Butterfly."

"But you wouldn't even let me try. You tied me to my horse."

His cheeks flush. "Ah."

"And now won't let me go anywhere without a guard."

He pulls his chin from my fingers and drags me into his arms. "I've been overprotective, haven't I?"

I nod into his neck.

"It was—" He makes a frustrated sound, like he's not sure how to explain. "I knew you were important, and you still are important. But when that Eósy proved he could dig into your mind and manipulate everything, I feared for you. I feared for you after only just having you. I feared for you with the Sìnnách but that seemed controllable. You losing your speech, losing the luck that seemed to follow you, it scared me."

"It scared me too," I whisper to his skin. "I'm... I'm scared now. But I need to try. I can't keep waiting until I pass some undetermined 'readiness' marker."

He groans, but there's no anger in it. "At least let me show you how to tack your horse. I'd hate for you to open the Gates and then lose your steed."

"Sunflower," I mumble. "His name is Sunflower."

Tans huffs a strained laugh. "Maybe don't tell *him* that."

"You'll come back," Tans says as he leans on makeshift crutches outside his family home where Breg tacked Sunflower. It isn't a statement, but a question.

"Course," says Sáv, sounding wobbly. "Needs to kick Fíl for leaving out the soulmate stuff."

"I'll pick somewhere you won't mind bruising," I tell him as the blush rises over his ruddy face.

"This is a terrible idea," Tans says, ignoring our byplay, staring at Sunflower's sharp antlers.

I squeeze my arms around him. "My ideas are great. And maybe I'll finally see a butterfly."

Tans laughs wetly and kisses me goodbye. After Sáv helps me onto Sunflower's back, I kick off, alone.

CHAPTER 11

I take two days to get to the dividing line between Dalner and the Wilds. I went south to avoid the unnamed mountain ranges surrounding Bittállí's former temple. It meant I had to ford a river and walk alongside the massive lake and tributary leading into it for a day and a half. It's funny: had I turned south instead of north at Samsen, I'd have walked straight into the Wilds and gotten gobbled up by whatever lived in there. Lucky me then, I had Leyden forcing me to the Pack.

Lucky me now, the connection between us dimmed over the past two days. There was a film over his cell last night, hazy and milky, like I was staring through a foggy window instead of in the room with him. Leyden said unless I reconnect our minds, it's likely the dreams will fade completely.

Good. I don't need his distraction while I head into the Wilds, alone for the first time in almost a year. The Grace that Ley-den dragged here was always alone, even when surrounded by classmates or coworkers. The Grace that I am now has a support system and safety net, one with strings I cut by traveling here.

I only have a working knowledge of what the Wilds are. Fíl said they were once Eósy lands, but that was when five ruling families shared ownership of Sekai. The lands forming The Wilds were abandoned after the wall was erected and the Gates built. The Raddare family had its land and its people that now make up the Sàrkany of Dalner, and Alacson and The Wilds remained empty. But there's no wall between the Wilds and Dànna, only an inlet water source where the land forms a loch. Without a wall, it's possible the magic is still around, on the other side of that water or in the air surrounding the Wilds itself.

Except there's also no wall between it and Dalner. The delineation between the two is nothing specific, only a few trail markers, like those signs on the highway: "this side Illinois/this side Missouri." Nothing commemorates the signs on The Wilds, the markers blank and aged. If you ended up in the Wilds, I suppose they expected you knew what was on the other side, or you wouldn't live long enough for it to matter.

Those bleak thoughts drag Sunflower and me across the invisible barrier, though even they are better than remaining in my head and imagining Tans finding his perfect person while I end up alone, the only soulmateless being in Dalner.

My self-pity keeps me close to the river, remembering my past with the Pack when I realized their friendship was real. We follow it to the mouth where Dànna and the Wilds separate. But that isn't the only reason we stay near the water, as the landscape to the right is rocky and ominous. The mountain range covering the peninsula of the Wilds is ashy and tinted gray. Titan's Claw looks as sinister as it sounds, as if a massive creature will rise from the rocks and slash its long-nailed claws over any creature that gets too close. I blink away the fear that builds as I stare at those haunting peaks, ones that rise into the sky without a summit in sight.

An hour after we cross the barrier to the Wilds, Sunflower shakes his head from side to side and huffs. I feel nothing different, but I'm not a being of magic. His antlers point upward, but a sharp turn could imbed one of those prongs into my skin. To avoid the same situation Tans found himself in or worse, I slide off Sunflower's back and take the reins by hand, carrying my pack on my back.

His legs dance, as though he's avoiding something on the ground. Nevertheless, he marches forward with me by his side. Another hour later, the river turned sharply north, leading us away from the barbed peaks behind us and towards a thick body of water ahead, the beginning of the watery barrier between Dànna and the Wilds. Only now do I feel something, not through my feet, but a heaviness in the air, a cloying and thick scent of ash and dust.

Then, the sound changes, no longer only the gentle trickling of the river but a whistling, one that gets larger and louder by the second. My neck stretches to survey the sky, but the sound comes from behind us, from Titan's Claw. There's a flock of something like crows—no, bigger and getting larger as they swoop down closer to us. The large wings flap in time with my heaving heartbeat. I only spare a moment of terrified glee that my hunch was right and there *is* something in The Wilds. But if someone had asked me, I would have preferred something smaller, a fluffle of bunnies or flutter of butterflies. Funny the things your mind remembers when you're afraid. A group of crows is called a murder. *Is a group of dragons a rampage?*

Sunflower and I run in tandem towards the water, him outpacing me before leaping over the western river flow and heading back towards Dalner. *Traitor*, my mind shouts, but I'd do the same if I had the chance.

The mass behind me grows closer, covering the sky above me, and plunging towards the ground. Towards me. The swarm of monsters above me is something I'm intimately familiar with—

their whip thin wings and tar black skin a frequent nightmare visitor. Only Leyden's presence halted the frequent guilt-ridden dreams where I demanded Tans notch an arrow and shoot one of those imposing beasts.

The fluttering is closer now, within arm's reach. I toss myself to the ground and cover my head with my puny arms, using my backpack as a second shield. As the tandem wingbeats whip my hair and I feel phantom claws scratching my wrists, I try to recall what I know about dragons. Little comes to me while I wallow in the depths of my fear, cowering under the realization that they could snatch me from the ground and rip me into pieces, but I remember they don't attack unless provoked. *Does shooting one of them count as provoking?* Probably, but that was months ago! And none of the others cared at the time.

The rush of wind above me keeps coming, like massive bats bursting from a cave. I'm too out in the open. The sparse brush by the stream will do nothing to hide me from them should they decide to attack. I'm a beacon in the loamy green of the water's edge, an unnatural blue blob in my leathers, those styled like the Sàrkany guards, like Tans. *Would the dragons appreciate their image on my chest before or after they ripped it open?*

There's no other option and I army crawl towards the water. Not to the western river where Sunflower disappeared but towards the large loch between Dànna and The Wilds. The deep blue can hide me from their predatory gaze. I imagine telling Tans this tale when I return to Ilsen, when I've kept myself alive and opened the rifts, fixing my mistakes and putting the 'soulmate' problem to bed. He'll tease me for not taking the trainee tests and I'll laugh about the stupid ideas I used instead.

Like now.

The entire process from the dragons arriving to me dragging myself to the water takes under a minute, but it feels longer, each second marking one more that I've survived. I flop like a seal to the water's edge and towards the deeper depths. The wingbeats are still above me but stop with heavy thumps as they land on the ground. They're no bigger than I remember, still twice the size of horses, but anything wild is worthy of fear, no matter how big.

I gurgle and bobble my way deeper into the water until I can take a hard breath and push myself into the brine.

And then, I realize I'll never get to tell Tans anything. The dragons drink from the water but they also fly above it, arching their wings like banking swans and bubbling up waves and undercurrent that drags me deeper. My lungs ache and my limbs burn as I try to keep myself near the surface, the breath I'm holding bursting from me as one wingtip slices through the water and connects with my chest.

There's a hard thumping noise, one that rattles my brain. My heartbeat. Something that beats, and beats, and... slows.

In the distance, I hear someone yelling—*screaming*—demanding I let them help me, pleading that I permit them. It's inside my head, the deep buried part that knows I can't do anything alone, that mocks me. There's no help to come; I made sure of that. No Tans, or Sáv, not even Sunflower to drag me from what will be my watery grave.

The voice muddles, but the feeling within it is clear: **let me help**.

My last rational thought before my eyes close and I can't hear anything more—not my slowing heartbeat, not the pressured drumming in my ear, not my panicked conscience that doesn't want to die—is *of course you can help, when have I ever succeeded on my own?*

And then blackness overtakes me and there's nothing but icy silence.

Coughing water from my lungs wakes me. My eyes drift open as the world slowly comes into view. I'm on my back, Titan's Claw above me, soaking wet with a burning chest from almost drowning. But the fear that I almost drowned doesn't compare to the annoyance that pools in my chest when I see Leyden's frowning face beside me. He looks as damp as I feel, his short blond hair plastered to his head. He's no longer hazy like he was in my dreams, but in technicolor. At this distance, I can even see a small scar bisecting the edge of his right eyebrow.

"Is this where our enemies to lovers relationship takes its turn towards lovers, Little Grace?" He moves my wet hair from my face.

I bat his hand away, but miss, flapping it in between us. "Not even in *your* dreams," I say, turning to my side. "And stop calling me that."

He cocks his head like a pale bird. "What else would you have me call you?"

Anything that doesn't take me back to that day in the throne room, to each mental visit he made as he emotionally and physically manipulated me into doing his bidding. "Preferably nothing. Now go away so I can wake up."

The realization hits me slower than it should, but I'll blame the near-death experience and shock of seeing Leyden's unwelcome face in high definition. I *am* awake. I'm not in Leyden's tower, but on the shore of the loch. The sun descends above us, and my pack sits unmolested a few yards away. I've always unwillingly visited Leyden's location; he's never come to me. I scramble upward and away from him and the edge of the riverbank.

"What are you doing here?" I'm proud my voice is only slightly shrill.

He shakes the remaining water from his blond hair. It does nothing for his wet tunic and pants. He looks like popped out of a period piece, the shirt sticking to his muscular chest as the love interest rises from an impromptu lake swim. He has the pride for it, but if he so much as begins a phrase with 'in vain I have struggled,' I will clock him. And not only because it's another romance masquerading as a study in women's economic conditions and lack of choices. Real life shows enough of that, and I won't forget Leyden's continued weaponization of Jane Eyre. I drop my gaze to the ground.

"You called and invited me here. Truly, Grace, with your track record, you should avoid all bodies of water."

That he's right isn't comforting. I imagine the amended version of this I'll tell Tans. *Not only did I almost drown by trying to run from dragons into water, I pulled Dalner's most hated rival to me.* The embarrassment tumbles around my stomach, but I force it down in favor of annoyance. "Then I'm uninviting you."

"That's not how it works, dearest," Leyden says, smirking. "My, this feels even better than Exile. All the magic I can breathe in."

Annoyance reforms into anger: at myself for my accidental mistake, at Leyden's irritating face, at the situation we're in. I want to correct my mistakes, not make more. Shakily, I pull the knife from its leg holster and point it at Leyden. I'm surprised it didn't fall out during my thrashing, or that Leyden didn't take it.

His eyes narrow at the blade, though he doesn't appear afraid. "After I risked myself to save you from drowning, where is your courtesy?"

"With Bittállí's corpse," I snap. If I can't force him to return to Exile on his own, maybe I can force him to ford the water in the loch to the other side. Then, I'll formally withdraw permission. "And you risked nothing."

He holds his hands aloft. Instead of pale porcelain, the skin is red and rubbed raw, as if he's dipped them in acid. "I certainly didn't pull you from the water for *my* health."

I'm curious despite myself. After a quick survey of my own hands, no burns appeared on me. "What happened to you?"

"Wards, strong ones. Someone spelled them in the water," he says, his mouth twisting into a pout. "My hands are one of my best features. Of course, every feature is my best feature so—"

Ignoring his irritating vanity, I crane my neck to the peaks of Titan's Claw as if I can see the dragons there. "Then how can the dragons get in it?"

"The wards must be placed on Eósy specifically." He sniffs. "They were never my specialty."

No, his specialty is mind manipulation. I squeeze around the knife's handle until my knuckles turn white. If I can't send him back, I'll shove him through a rift when I get them open.

I release a shaky breath. And now I know I can. There must be magic nearby to power the wards. I refrain from doing a small happy dance in front of him. Now, I just need to get Tans into the Wilds to heal his legs, and then harness the magic and—

"It won't work," Leyden says, stretching backward to display the long line of his body. In the dimming light, it most certainly isn't to dry himself off and I let my eyes roll. "The magic here won't tear down the walls."

Anger blooms into fury. I leap on top of him, using the limited dexterity my training sessions gave me to press the tip of the knife under his jaw, where the bone meets his neck. "Stop reading my mind."

"So we *have* begun the lovers part of our relationship," he purrs.

I press the knife harder into his throat. Another millimeter forward and the skin will break. "Swear you will never read my mind again."

"I wasn't," he says mildly, unbothered by my threat. "It was reflected on your face. And it isn't hard to assume you want the walls down, not with everything the Sàrkany lost when the magic left."

"I don't want the walls down," I deny. "Stop trying to distract me. Swear you'll never read me again. None of this necessary stuff. If I'm stuck babysitting you until I get you tossed back to your side, you'll keep your mental hands to yourself."

The false flirtation falls from his expression, and he crosses his arms, almost pushing me off. The tip of the blade wobbles against his neck. "This isn't a kind way to speak to your savior. If I hadn't read your thoughts, you'd have drowned."

I dig the knife deeper. A single red drop appears and pools at the divot of his throat. I smother the shiver of discomfort seeing it brings, at the memory of Bittállí's bloody body.

His left eye twitches before he scoffs. "Very well, I promise to never read your thoughts again." He stands up, knocking me and the knife to the ground as if I'm no heavier than a feather. "*And I'll help you tear down the walls.*"

It's then I decide I hate his earnest face more than his smirk. "You'll do nothing. You'll promise to find your way back to your side of the wall. You don't have to go to Exile, but you can't stay here."

"No."

I move to stand and threaten him with the knife again, but he scowls.

"I will not, and I cannot. It took all my magic to cleave here to you. It will take me time to absorb enough magic from the land to travel such a distance, and I refuse to melt off my skin by traversing the water. In the meantime, you're stuck with me. Again. I might as well help you. You're welcome," he finishes with a flourishing bow.

I tuck the knife back in the holster. Reason number one-hundred-and-one why the rifts must be opened: to kick Leyden across the barrier. "I want the rifts open and the Gates back to normal, I couldn't care less about the walls."

He stares down at me, as if searching for something, before nodding. "I will help in reopening the rifts. You need magic and I'm your best option."

But skepticism won't let me simply believe him, no matter that he can only tell the truth. "How do I know you won't try to tear down the walls instead, while pretending to just help me with the rifts?"

"I *promise* I will not double cross you in this specific endeavor, in your goal to reopen the rifts. Once either the rifts are open, the Gates return, or you confirm your goal is met, I have no requirement to continue your goals at the expense of my own as it relates to the wall."

The promise isn't ironclad, and the exception about him betraying me otherwise isn't great. "That's a lot of wiggle room."

He licks his lips, and I feel I've missed something important. "Not in the important parts. I'm planning for all outcomes."

If I'm lucky, I can shove him in the water when he's not looking and deal with the rifts without his interference. He watches me consider his proposal with a small smile before offering me a hand up. "Partners then? As a start, in reopening the rifts."

I don't take his hand, sidewinding until I can stand on my own. The wet leather armor is heavy, and my body finally remembers it almost died a few minutes prior. "Reluctant allies. Until the rifts open or you have enough magic to return."

He flashes bright teeth. "We'll see."

CHAPTER 12

We spend the evening in a tense stalemate. The moon chased the sun away and we sit in darkness until he disappears to find logs for a fire. I don't allow myself to remember that I'd know how to do that myself had I listened to Tans and taken those survival tests. When he returns, he starts the fire with his fingers, and I try not to sniffle at the continued reminder of Tans. He must realize it as a self-satisfied smile decorates his face.

"How much magic will it take to cross the water?" I ask, staring into the flames to avoid looking at his smug expression.

He huffs. "You wish me gone so soon?"

My head pops up to glare at him, except he's not looking at me, but gazing deep into the fire as if it holds the answers to all his unasked questions. "I don't think I've been subtle about it," I grumble.

"It will take me several days to rest and gain the magic I need." Now he does glance at me, flashing a crooked smile. "But as I said, I will help you."

I throw a wet clump of grass into the fire and flickers flash upwards into the night sky. If I trusted him, it would be a nice offer, but there's no way I can take Leyden with me to the walls on the Dalner side and let him tinker with them. And I can't leave him unsupervised. The best thing for me is to get him back into Dànna and I'll work out the rifts on my own. "What if you ride a dragon across?"

I don't know how they're staying in Titan's Claw with the wall keeping the other reptilian visitors from coming elsewhere in Dalner, but maybe the lack of barrier in the Wilds keeps them around. Almost as if there is a blanket of 'non-magic' over Dalner but anything outside it is fine.

"Do you intend on shooting one again?"

Though Leyden's question sounds harmless, I still flinch. But I won't let Leyden wound me, not when my guilt is doing well enough on its own. I jut out my chin. "I healed it after."

"Erasing the pain you caused doesn't remove the scar," he says, leaning onto his back.

Pot meet kettle is on the tip of my tongue, but I swallow it. I have nothing to prove to him. "Do I need your magic, or could I get it from something else?"

I could gather a fluffle of bunnies or a swarm of butterflies, whatever they may look like. Even a rampage of dragons would be better than him. I wouldn't shoot any, but they seemed semi-sentient last time I worked with one. Perhaps I could explain my issue and they'd help. Then, they could fly anywhere in Dalner again.

He leans on his elbow as a slow grin forms on his full lips. "Clever question. Anyone's magic would do but only two beings alive know how to do it. You're quite lucky that I am one of them."

The plan to kick him back into Dànna and fix the Gates on my own dies a violent death. When it eeks out its swan song, I stubbornly ask, "Who is the other one?"

His eye twitches. "That is irrelevant. Just know that they will never help you." He points his finger at me to forestall my complaints about his word choice. It's unnerving how well he knows me. "This is not me spinning words either. If you seek their help, they would most certainly kill you."

I slump at the rigidity in his tone. I'm clearly stuck with him. "Fine. Once you gather enough magic to get back into Dànna, what next? How would you open the rifts?"

"Don't think you can sweet talk me into making you the third with my knowledge," he says teasingly.

I rear backward to gawk at his smirking face. "I would never—"

"All you need to know, dearest, is that I need to collect ample magic to apply it where we know the Gates were and prick holes. If we're lucky, the Gates will let enough magic through to mimic the rifts in that area and let the magic breathe again," he says.

The sound of that pet name continually coming from his lips feels like spiders crawling down my back and I restrain an uncomfortable shiver. "Stop calling me that."

"I've agreed not to refer to you as my little Grace, is that not enough?"

I scowl. "Considering *that* charming nickname gives me flashbacks to your mental assault, no."

He has the decency to look chagrined, but I ignore the remorse building in his dark eyes. Instead, I focus on the plan. My lack of magic is more of a liability than a benefit now. I could let him hop back into Dànna and rot, but then I'll be stuck without the magic or information needed to open the Gates and reactivate the rifts. It's like Zorin said, I need magic. Which means I'm stuck with Leyden even longer, as long as it takes him to gather enough magic to put it into the Gates.

I release a frustrated breath. The sacrifice will be worth it. "Alright. A few days together, then you do whatever it is you're going to do with your magic, and I walk back into Dalner at sunset." Like the hero does at the end of any good story. The animals will return, healing magic will be available again, Tans won't be half bed bound, Kórol can stop his irrationality, the risk of war will be gone. And, that new blooming desire to know whether Tans has a soulmate will be quenched too.

"If only it were that easy. If one of us could affect the walls, I would have attempted it ages ago. This is not a solo endeavor. I will need at least one comrade-in-arms to share their magic, more if you want a larger opening," he says, as if it's obvious.

My neck snaps to stare at him. "If you're some kind of vampire Eósy and you need to suck the magic outside of someone else—"

He jolts upward across the fire, the speed reminding me he's the predator here, no matter I'd like to imagine I'm not prey. "Are you pretending to care? Would it matter to you if I needed to bleed the magic from every Eósy I meet, that they would suffer and die, to reopen the rift?"

The quiet question stops my thoughts in their tracks. But he's not finished.

"Would our plight be worth it, so long as you succeed in your wants, damn the rest of us? Would you condemn us all to die to get the magic back as it was?"

"I—" My voice fades and I flinch.

"That's what having the walls up does, dearest. Condemns us all."

Anger licks at my skin like lava, ready to erupt. He's chastising me for my 'callous' actions to prepare for fighting Bittállí, actions that still give me nightmares, while he was unconcerned sacrificing his supposed kin. "Is that what *you* were doing when you were tearing those holes, bleeding them dry to get what you wanted?"

He folds his hands in his lap, the dimming light catching his rough burns. "Had I gotten the walls down, they would have crossed over and replenished their magic before death took them. If not, it was their choice."

The anger ebbs and I'm just tired. "You're such a hypocrite," I whisper.

He doesn't answer.

He sits across from me by the fire, just as he did when my eyes first closed. Pulling him to me must have strengthened our mental connection and given strength to our shared evening dreams. Had it not saved me from drowning, I'd berate myself for affixing myself tighter to him.

Leyden doesn't speak to me, nor I to him. He remains silent, fingers steepled against his knees in contemplation. He's taken the first shift of the evening and will wake me in four hours for mine.

I roll away to stare up at the trailing rubble from Titan's Claw. The dreamy haze makes it less ominous, even though it's dark. That I'm not alone to face off enemies might also help that impression.

I pinch my eyes closed tight at the guilt that thought creates. I can't keep doing this to myself. I'm stuck with Leyden. I don't need to forgive him for what he did to me and mine, but maintaining the bitterness will choke me before any bile lands on him. If I must spend twenty-four hours a day with him—in life and in dreams—there has to be a way to keep myself from drowning in anger at what he did and in guilt for when I forget it.

Leyden makes a soft sound from behind me.

A truce. We're already accomplices in solidifying the walls, and allies in pricking holes in them. A truce won't kill me.

With that settled, I stare back at Titan's Claw and wonder what Tans is doing now.

The dragons return to the water at sunrise. We both wake with a gasp and run for cover behind the boulders at the base of Titan's Claw, what I should have done the day before.

Leyden looks better than he did yesterday, his pale skin almost luminescent in the early morning light. The only mar to his allure, besides his existence—*no, we have a truce*—are the burns on his hands.

As the dragons complete their morning jaunt to the loch, I pull out a tiny tin of salve from my pack and hold it out to him, a physical manifestation of my ceasefire. There can be no aggressive friendship between us to avoid further irritation, but aggressive politeness is a viable plan. "For your hands."

He takes it silently and works the aloe-like cream onto his skin. "This is made with the distilled poison from dart-snakes," he whispers.

Which haven't been seen since I sealed the Gates. The reminder churns something uncomfortable in my stomach and I clear my throat as if to force it down. "I have enough to spare."

He shakes his head. "You misunderstand me. We hunt these creatures, to leech their poison for our tinctures and to eat their flesh."

"Yes, and we honor their sacrifice." Like Sáven says.

Leyden smiles faintly as he taps his thumb against the lid of the container. "Exactly. They are a sacrifice for the rest of us. Something necessary to improve our lives- sustenance and health."

Red blooms at the edges of my vision. It isn't the same. Killing the dart-snakes is on a different level than sacrificing his people, my people, for some supposed lofty goal.

"Stop trying to make me feel bad for the...subjugators."

"Only one subjugated the Sàrkany people," he mumbles.

"But all of you benefited from—" I close my eyes and count to ten. If I can't make it through one conversation without abandoning the truce, I may as well give up and go home. When I look back at Leyden, he's staring off in the distance.

I plaster a pleasant smile on my lips. "You never answered me last night. How long until you have the strength to cross the water?"

"A few days but—" He cocks his head as if listening and drops to the ground, digging his fingers into the trampled grass beneath the pebbles from the mountain. "We may not need to cross. I sense another Eósy nearby."

That still leaves the problem of him remaining on the Dalner side, but one step at a time. "Where? How?"

His fingers drag through the dirt. "I can feel it. The magic is thick here like syrup, finally awakening and cracking out of its amber casing. I feel where the syrup flows. From me." He turns, craning his neck over the rocks and trailing towards the edge of the loch. "To there."

I shiver involuntarily. So far, the only Eósy I've met are Leyden and Bittállí. No matter that Fílga claims there were once 'good' Eósy that lean towards the Light, my experience with them says otherwise. "Are they dangerous?"

He hums. "Who isn't?"

"So, you're like mosquitos not vampires," I say, grasping for a foothold in the conversation to level out the roller coaster we've been on since I woke on the shore.

"In that we can suck out magic from the land, yes." He smiles as his fingers continue petting the grass. "Fates, I cannot recall when I felt this good. My 200s, perhaps."

The dragons have begun their flight back to the peaks of the mountain. I shuffle to lean against a rock, moving farther away from the gentle touches he's giving the earth. "How old are you?"

There's humor in his voice when he answers. "I am eight hundred and thirteen."

I grimace. I knew he had lived for centuries, the memories told me as much, but seeing him still looking eighteen when he's forty times older is a shock. "How do I compare that to the human lifespan?"

"We're effectively immortal," he whispers. In our little nook, we're hidden from the deafening flapping of their wings. "In a perfect world, we could live forever. Like elves, or the Scottish sidhe."

My brows furrow in his direction. He's no longer touching the ground but staring up at the dragons overhead. Leyden catches my gaze and raises his brows. "Your adamant vehemence against fantasy stories is laughable, given you're living in one."

"It's not like Sàrkany has a library of fiction novels," I say, crossing my arms around my waist.

He concedes my point with a lazy nod. "We could live forever, but I've not heard of anyone older than 4,500."

A gust of surprise bursts from me. "But that's *common*?"

"It used to be more common, but with more of us and less magic in the land because of the walls, we die sooner." He huffs a laugh, but it's bitter. "Even without the walls, at some point there will be too many taps in the barrel."

The energy around our hideout wilts. I drag my pack towards me and leaf through it while Leyden stares upward. When I find parchment and a pen nib, I sketch out a quick equation. I don't restrain the giggle that bubbles out of my throat at what I've discovered.

"Hot damn, in human years, you're not even fifteen yet!"

Quicker than any human, he snatches the notes I'm brandishing, pouting when he sees the conclusion. "I'm *centuries* old."

I point to the equation. "But, assuming you mature at the same rate as humans and we live until 75-80, you're barely more than a preteen."

The pale skin of his cheeks flush. "Experience ages you—"

"Yeah, yeah, I remember." I clutch my neck and offer him an expression filled with mock horror. "Does this mean I'm some kind of child kidnapper, or predator? Dragging you along with me on a dangerous quest without your parents' knowledge? Should I have gotten a permission slip?"

"I'm suddenly remembering how annoying you can be," he says, slinking back to his side of the nook.

"Shut up, Leyden." But I'm laughing. It's a forced thing, as I swallow my true feelings with every second in his presence, but I'm still laughing.

And so is he.

CHAPTER 13

B ehind Titan's Claw, a metal structure juts into the sky, a spiraling tower of glinting steel. 'The Crumbling Spire,' Leyden called it, the former stronghold of one of the last Eósy factions in the time before the wall. Fílga mentioned the other four that made up Dànna and Dalner, but shied away from discussing the former inhabitants of what's now known as the Wilds.

A woman in white wails at the base like a specter. She starts near the staircase leading into the spire and makes a winding circle to the edge of the land, teetering precariously at the cliff, before tumbling back towards the tower. With each circle, her bellows ebb and flow in pitch and volume as she tears through her black hair like I imagined banshees might.

We watch the circuit six times from our vantage point behind the trailing rocks from Titan's Claw until I finally ask, "If that's the Eósy we need, why are we sitting here?"

Leyden's attention hasn't left the woman since she first appeared from the spire when we started our trip at sunrise. He leans close to whisper in my ear, "That is Bittállí's mother, Carn."

Chills run down my spine, whether from Leyden's nearness or the identity of that woman. "Is she anything like Bittállí?"

Leyden doesn't look at me, his blue eyes glowing neon. "No. But from the memories Bittállí gave me, she wasn't altogether rational before the walls went up, and it doesn't appear she's gotten any better since."

I wince. A more agitated version of the Great Matron is not what I had in mind today. "What are the odds she'll help us with the rift?"

He cocks his head from side to side as if weighing the options. "That depends. Carn has spent centuries alone. If she set the wards on the loch, which is seeming more likely with each swipe I take of her mind, then she has the magic I need. And either she'll help us out of boredom, or she'll try to cut out our eyes for bothering her solitude." He sounds oddly cheery at the prospect.

I thump my head on the rock. "Odds on the latter?"

He purses his lips. "There's a bit of a block on her mind, but we can't ascribe rationality to her. If she knows what you did to Bittállí, high. If she doesn't, still quite high. "

"I liked you better when you were being cryptic and giving me silly puzzles," I mutter under my breath.

"You humans and your lies again." He stands and brushes the dust from his stained tunic. "Off we go. Keep up, dearest." And he saunters towards the woman whose daughter we jointly murdered.

"What's her magic?" I hiss as she grows more life-sized.

"Fire. Though she has no talent for it." He glances at me from his periphery. "We're related, you know."

That stops me in my tracks and his lips curl.

"She's my something-something fifth removed aunt," he says as he picks up the pace while I gawk. "Don't look surprised. There aren't *that* many of us. We're all distantly related. One of her sisters married a child from the Launna family. Generations later, here I am."

I wonder how soulmates work, if they're all related. What if you house the same soul as your dead twice removed cousin, whose soulmate is still living: do you suddenly hook up with them when you finally hit twenty? Do your third cousins become your stepchildren? A shiver runs through me at the incestuous thought, and I refocus on the task at hand. "Did you know you were intending to kill your distant cousin or was that just a lucky coincidence when the bodies fell?"

His gait falters, only noticeable because I'm hiding behind him. A screaming, possibly vengeful woman who might discover we killed her daughter and can turn her fingers into flamethrowers? Leyden can be my hum—Eósy shield.

"Both," he finally says. "But had I not known, seeing her wield fire would have told me." He rotates his neck to waggle his brows in my direction, one corner of his mouth ticking up. "Anyone who can manipulate fire is related somehow."

I blanch and his tiny smirk blooms into a wide grin.

"Yes, Grace, I'm related to your boy too." He holds up a hand as if to forestall any outbursts. "I didn't read that, yet again you're giving away your secrets on your face."

I grumble various uncharitable thoughts about Leyden under my breath, but they're milder than they've been in the recent past as I attempt to keep the truce active.

Whether or not it was his goal, his revelation distracts me from our final approach towards Carn. As she curves around the spire and towards the steps where we wait, she stares right at us with eyes I've seen in my nightmares. They aren't the same neon purple as Bittállí's, but close enough to feel as though someone poured ice water down my back.

Though she's seen us, the woman's wailing doesn't stop. Instead, she makes two more circuits before quieting so fast, it wouldn't shock me to discover that her vocal cords had been cut. Then, she pads inside the spire at a steady pace. We follow her at a distance as she winds up the spiral staircase to the top of the tower. Leyden doesn't appear concerned, so I try not to be, ignoring that he's 'effectively immortal' and I'm not.

The room at the top of the spire looks similar enough to what I saw of Bittállí's that I choke on my tongue. Everywhere I've been in Dalner has been an homage to medieval and gothic interior design- walls and floors made of stone and rich wood accents with carved imprints, oversized hearths, and solid wood furnishings with thick brocade embellishments. But this woman's home, like Bittálli's from memory, is a walk through the Victorian era. The stone walls are covered in rich purple paint interspersed with white iris illustrations. The furniture is what I'm used to, heavy dark wood, but more decoratively carved with swirls and loops. Glass light fixtures dot the various tables, and an iron candelabra as tall as my shoulders stands beside a forest green chaise lounge covered in tufted buttons. There appear to be two windows, only evident by the floor-to-ceiling mahogany brown curtains. It's as elegant as the sad woman who lives there.

Carn doesn't speak when we enter behind her, instead sitting in one of the overstuffed chairs.

Leyden motions me forward and I jab him in the elbow as I stand in front of her. She stares through me, as if I'm not present.

"Good morning, ma'am," I begin in Sàrkany. Only when I speak do I realize that Leyden and I had been conversing in English again.

Carn doesn't react, looking more like a porcelain doll than a person. Only the spiderwebbed lines near her eyes and across her forehead show her as someone who has lived, rather than sitting abandoned on a shelf. Though, after another look at the stunning but lonely tower room, perhaps this place is her shelf.

Leyden squints as he surveys her still form. "Carn hasn't spoken since her last child was born," he says. "Outside of shrieking, she hasn't made a sound."

But I'm undeterred. "We were hoping you could help us with the walls. Not tear them down," I blurt before she thinks otherwise. An immortal being who puts wards on water to subdue other immortals from crossing doesn't seem like someone interested in more Eósy visitors. "We just want the rifts back, allowing a little magic to seep through."

Leyden scoffs, mumbling something that sounds like, "Not all *I* want."

I ignore him. "Things changed six months ago. You may not have noticed, but it would really—"

"'Things changed,' she says," Leyden interrupts as if scandalized. "A month ago, you acted as though I'd destroyed the *world* after Bittállí—"

The moment the first syllable fell from his mouth, Carn turned to him with wounded eyes.

"Bittállí?" she says, her voice like a shard of glass against my brain.

He squints, his eyes blazing an electric blue. "That broke a block of some kind. She loves her daughter. Her disappearance cast her into this state."

Carn doesn't react again, returning to her doll-like condition. An uncomfortable guilt shifts within me: I've killed this woman's child. I exhale shakily, reminding myself all that Bittállí did. Leyden pushed me forward, but Bittállí was a horror.

"Even monsters have mothers, I suppose," I say from the side of my mouth in English. Not that Bittállí's monstrous state means I was justified in killing her. But I don't have time to let that thought carry forth more guilt as Carn hisses, baring her teeth. Leyden and I trade glances as we both slink back towards the door, both deciding she won't be offering 'help' anytime soon.

"Yes, and thus, I would caution you," Leyden responds in English, "to not mention that you murdered her."

Carn roars, not the mournful wail from before, but the thunderous howl of rage.

"You understand English!" Leyden sounds delighted.

"You couldn't figure that out from her mind?" I snap back, guilt ebbing and joining with sheer panic.

"It isn't as though there is a table of contents," Leyden says unapologetically.

Carn flies from her chair like a hawk with a mouse in her sights. Leyden disappears from beside me, but I have no time to shout complaints at his gutlessness as she tackles me. The scream surprised me, Leyden's epiphany distracted me, and we tumble to the ground before I can jump from her path. I can only imagine what Faburth and Eida would say at my poor reaction. I won't even *consider* what Rothàna would.

Her forehead knocks into my nose, and a flash of pain blooms from the contact. I manage to twist us before she regains her senses and crawl away from her on hands and knees. My backpack saved my head from injury, but I abandon it on my search for cover. I find it behind the chaise lounge, hiding against the seatback and pressing my hand hard against my burning hip. I'd curse Leyden if only I could see him.

She screams again, not like the sound she made when circling the tower, but a wild keening that echoes through the tower. Her agony gathers under my skin. It isn't a magical feeling, not that I can tell. The raw pain within her would have even the most merciless person feel her suffering in their bones. But empathy can't sacrifice survival, and pain doesn't excuse consequences.

I remember my training, swallowing the nerves that bubble up at the knowledge that this is my first *proper* fight since Leyden, since killing Bittállí. But I think of Tans, of Kórol, of why I need to survive this encounter and open the rifts. My reasons for hesitation die and I can't let guilt and fear keep me from acting. I drag my knife from its holster, my fingers trembling around the handle.

The backrest of the chaise melts as flames burst from above my head. I spare a second to close my eyes in resignation. She may be terrible at magic, but her torment would light the entire building on fire.

I roll away from the next burst of flame and crawl under the desk. It's there I can see Leyden standing in front of one of the tall bookshelves, running his fingers over the spines. Her next aim barely misses me, rippling against the top of the desk and into the drawer above my head, shattering the stained glass lamp.

Flecks of flame and shards of glass fall into my hair, but I hold my ground, crouching until the hem of her dress comes into view. I leap for her legs, slashing at her ankles and knocking her over. Blood splashes over me and I heave. Carn hits the burning chaise, stopping her flamethrower fingers from erupting again as she howls louder. But I've lost my knife after slicing her skin.

"Stop browsing and start helping," I screech at Leyden's back, letting anger rise instead of cowering.

"But books, Grace," he calls behind him. "If you were in my position, you'd take a moment to peruse the offerings."

Carn rolls off the chaise and crawls back towards me as blood pours from her ankles. Her hands on the ground are my only protection from being burned to death.

"No, I'd definitely keep my ally from melting her skin off!" That I can still speak, that I can still berate Leyden for being a jerk instead of freezing, tells me I have a chance at succeeding here. But bringing a knife to a firefight already meant I was outmatched, bringing nothing to it almost suicide.

I inch backward, frantically searching for my knife on the ground, but I can't find it anywhere. Suddenly, she stands, the knife in her hands as it catches fire. It's special steel, Fíl told me when Kórol gave me the blade, something Eósy-made so it won't melt. Instead, it protrudes from the flame like a barbeque skewer ready to run me through.

"Yes," Leyden says absently. "She is better than I expected. Overwhelming emotions and all that rot."

I growl. She's no longer attempting to light me on fire by throwing flames but trying to stab me. It's like a high stakes version of my training with Faburth, and that thought does *nothing* to comfort me with my odds. "Will you help me!" I shriek, each word interspersed with gasping breaths.

"I am helping. There could be something in one of these books about the rift."

I shove the iron candelabra over as I skitter behind the remains of the desk. "How—how likely is that?"

The candelabra slows Carn's shuffling progression but not for long, as she kicks it from her path, no matter the blood from her ankles pool below us. I leap backward as she swipes the blade at my chest. She misses, but flickers catch on my tunic above where the leather armor ends, burning little holes into the fabric and searing my skin.

"Not, given the tower was abandoned before the wall's erection," Leyden says, squinting at a text. *Jerk*.

"I was just the tool," I gasp as Carn surges for me again. She stops mid movement, like a puppet with her strings cut. "He made me do it, spending centuries planning it. He manipulated me and used me as his human blade. *He's* the one that killed Bittállí. *He* got her memories."

Leyden makes an offended sound. But Carn turns mechanically and shuffles towards Leyden, flaming blade still aloft. It looks like a preview for a horror film, red rivers below her feet, scorched fabric fluttering around her legs and a deadly expression on her face.

"Carn," he says placatingly in Sàrkany, holding out his hands. "Let us discuss this. I haven't even introduced myself."

She surges towards him, blade arching. Leyden ducks and slides towards the brocade covered windows. I dart to the bookcase to avoid getting in her way.

"Carn—" Leyden starts before squealing.

I grab a random book from the bookcase and pretend to skim it, letting my heaving breaths die down and my fingers stop shaking. "You know, you're right. These are some int—interesting books. It's been forever since I had time to read for pleasure."

Leyden looses his fire, catching the edges of Carn's dress and spiraling upward, displaying the pale skin of her ankles, her knees, her thighs. She drops the knife and curls her hands, flames erupting from each finger. She doesn't appear to notice she's on fire.

"Hilarious, Grace," Leyden huffs, ducking Carn's questing claws. "Allies, remember?"

I drop the book with more care than the situation probably calls for and grab the long iron candelabra. Wielding it like a baseball bat, I take a deep breath and thwack into the back of her head. She stutters and falls into a gangling heap on the stone floor. Only the remaining adrenaline coursing through my veins keeps me from falling beside her.

Leyden straightens his back and brushes ash from his chest. "Thank you. We're a good team."

I refrain from grumbling my denials or grousing about his blame in the situation. After blowing the loose locks of hair from my face and letting my heart return to its normal speed, I gently poke Carn with the feet of the candelabra. "Is she dead?" My voice is flat.

"Would it matter?" But the words aren't biting, more teasing. "She lives. She will even walk again."

Together we lay her on the remains of the smoldering chaise lounge and bind the wounds on her feet. I can't explain why I do, knowing she tried to kill us, knowing what she is, but we did technically murder her daughter and the pain she exuded wasn't fake. I still have nightmares about Bittállí. Carn will be another recurring star, but there can be no guilt from what I did.

Leyden gives me smug glances as we gently position her and I can almost imagine what he's saying, attempting to humanize the Eósy as not the villains. As if Carn didn't raise a violent daughter, as if she doesn't act like a living ghoul to scare people away and place burning wards on the water to isolate herself from her own kind. I can't even *think* of Leyden's sins, or the hours-old truce might die along with Bittállí.

I replace the candelabra beside the chaise lounge and find my backpack under the nearby wreckage. "You know, you three are not giving me a good impression of the Eósy."

He hums, clearly unable to deny it, and stalks away from Carn's body.

"Are there any helpful books?" I ask as I follow him to the bookshelves, eager to be distracted from the pain in my hip and cheeks. And chest. And—

"For this? No," he says as he idly flips through a few and then tosses them to the ground.

I huff and place them in stacks. Three slim volumes look interesting, so I quietly slip them in my backpack. I can only read a word of two of the titles, but they could be useful someday. The pack's strings are tied when he turns around. He raises one eyebrow at me kneeling on the floor, but I offer him a guileless expression.

"What now?"

He sighs, glaring down at the discarded books. "I'd hoped to find something in these tomes or in her mind to break the wards and swim, but I see no other option now than waiting until I regain enough magic to cleave back to Dànna and finding an accomplice there. Though it is probably best we not put you in water again."

"Waiting, waiting here?" I gesture to the scorched room. A few flames still lick the edges of the once brown curtains.

"It is infinitely better than remaining outside. No sleeping shifts, for a start. The rooms may be dusty, but surely we can find suitable accommodations indoors."

I peek back at the woman looking as though she wants to beckon death. "What about Carn?"

He waves a soot covered hand, the fading burns hidden beneath the grime. "I will manipulate her into remaining asleep or in her tower until we leave. She'll be fine and can haunt the loch when we leave."

"Depending on how long tendons take to—*excuse* me?" My voice is hard as I stand and pivot towards him. "Did you just say we could have avoided getting burned to death?"

Leyden blinks. "Indeed. I must have forgotten to attempt it during the excitement."

"You forgot your most overused trick."

"Yes. But no one is blameless here, dearest. I thought you were against my mental meddling."

I winced at the memory of Kórol. But Carn is different. "Had *you* manipulated her mind instead of leaving me to handle her while you skittered off like a rat, we'd—"

"It was a strategic retreat. You can't meet every foe head on." Leyden attempts a winning smile. "And we're fine, we didn't burn to death. You kept yourself safe."

"You didn't burn to death, you have fire magic. I'm a mortal who had her blade stolen by the mourning mother with flamethrower hands!" I punch him hard in the shoulder. He doesn't even move. But it jostles the tender skin of my chest where embers from my blade fell. I rub the spots as Leyden's face falls.

"It wasn't intentional, Grace," he says quietly. "Had I known you were in genuine danger, I would have interceded."

My lips flatten. This is one of those times when 'truths' seem as malleable as lies. "Keep telling yourself that, but I've gotten enough scars from you already."

CHAPTER 14

I take refuge in what was once the youngest child's room, evident by the size of the musty clothing and slightness of the bed. I don't think too long about why that child is no longer here: dead or across the wall, from what my lessons taught.

As a peace offering, Leyden explains the spire was something like a summer home for the Caern family, one of the five ruling families before the wall went up. Fílga never spoke about them. He mentioned them once and then said anything else I needed to learn would be in the books. But no books from that time period remain, meaning my knowledge is limited.

The furnishings in the main part of the tower appear futuristic, if only because they are made of metal and not wood. That's apparently because of the Caern family magic, a dominance over minerals and metals. One of the lower floors holds the remains of two forges. I could only wonder how metallic their primary home was.

But the child's room is unique, more like Dalner's style, full of dark furnishings and heavy fabrics, not a rod of steel in sight. Dozens of history books rest on the surfaces and even through the layers of dust, it's clear their owner loved and took great care of them. Had I had a better grasp on the written word, I would have spent my afternoon holed up inside reading each one. It's similarity to my room at Ilsen is why I chose it.

It's right after I rub cream into my burns that Carn's memories flood my mind.

I've never received memories from someone who didn't engage me first. Then, knowing how they plotted or were coerced into fighting me had a natural beginning: what brought us to the event for the former and when someone else demanded it of them for the latter. Like the first bandit, the kidnapper, the Brute, even the eel monster. And Leyden in his own former category alone. *I'm* the aggressor now.

So, when I fall into Carn's memories, I don't know what to expect. There is no one moment that led her to me, it's Bittállí that led me to her.

Two thousand years earlier, when my ancestors' ancestors were not yet born, Carn has a girl child, her first in the many she's birthed over her centuries. She's proud this girl may follow in her footsteps, to birth regimes and spread their family's blood across the nation. Bittállí shows early interest in expanding her knowledge of magic, in living beyond her place and taking power that doesn't belong to her. She's six when Carn's Lord physically reprimands her. Though Carn agrees with her Lord's actions—she must, in all things—Carn stops speaking. She's not sure why. It coincides with the birth of her last child, though she doesn't know he's her last. No one questions her silence.

The scene shifts. Nearly two thousand years ago, when my great great great et cetera grandparents aren't yet specks in their parents' eyes, Bittállí is nearing her majority and Carn waits for her to fulfill her birthright. But something happens, something one of her living sons did, and there's talk of a wall. Since Carn refuses to speak, no one notices whether she listens. The story is told—family against family; Light versus Dark. Her remaining sons die, her husband is slaughtered, and Bittállí disappears. Her daughter, the mastermind of the Dark, due to be slaughtered by the husband of one of Carn's many times removed nieces. Carn wasn't even aware Bittállí could do magic but the feeling blossoming in Carn's chest when she thinks of Bittállí, her last remaining child, is pride.

The scene shifts. No one remembers Carn. She waits for half a century for someone to take her—to prison or across the wall, she's not sure—but no one arrives. One day, she realizes no one is coming, and no one cares what she does. She slips from their abandoned castle and starts walking. She passes the place where her fifth son was killed by her sixth. She wanders beyond where her Lord killed the fourteenth and fifteenth, her only twins. When she arrives at the death place of her first and fourth sons, she stops walking. Not out of sentimentality, but because there's no land left. That's when the screaming begins.

She takes two centuries to realize her screams aren't of pain but of freedom. Bittálli gave her that, by her actions with the wall. Carn's only regret was not thanking her when she had the chance.

The scene shifts. While my ancestors form and reform societies, she has only one regular visitor, a wild boy child who comes once every century to stare up at the spire. He doesn't speak to her, nor she to him, but she sees the same freedom in his eyes that appear in her mirror. She wonders what he escaped from. As he ages, faster than he should if Carn's own dead children are the measurement, he stops coming and Carn resumes her screaming without interruption. She didn't mind the boy, but his presence made no difference to her when she had her own desires to fulfill, simple though they were. Perhaps Bittálli taught her that as well.

The scene shifts. Centuries ago, when my family has yet to branch from our tree, desperate men attempt to ford the loch. They are unlike the boy-now-man who used to visit. They greedily pull from the magic and attempt to take the life Carn has found in the spire. When they cross back over to bring more men, she learns how to ward. It isn't through study, but something instinctual. Her fear at losing her freedom boils the water with her fire until no man can cross it.

There was a benefit to their interruption, however. Although those interlopers nearly ruined her refuge, they brought rumblings of a great and powerful lady across the wall. She wonders what

Bittállí would think of that, of a woman in power. Did Bittállí's sacrifice herald that woman too, much like she gave Carn her freedom?

The scene shifts. When Leyden and I appear, she cares not. We've come from the opposite direction of the loch, not the water, and she knows who we must be—the children of her former blood. Weak, like her, with little magic, though our lack is not our fault. We were given little choice as the magic dwindled, having been born after the walls arose. She doesn't pity us, but she understands us. She understands enough to allow the handsome boy-almost-man into her home, one who looks so like her deceased family, one who is tied up in expectation and demands that no child should experience. Though her tolerance of us doesn't mean she'll change her patterns. She screams her freedom each day, then she returns to her tower each night. It would begin tomorrow as it has almost every day, whether we're there or not.

Until she hears a name she hasn't said or heard outside her mind for centuries. Her daughter, her joy.

Tears track down my cheeks when I leave Carn's memories. The dozens of memories show a reserved but painful life. She lived without power or opportunity, just like the characters in the regency stories I complain about, just like the reality I'd rather not revisit in stories. I realize that the anguish she felt when she realized Bittállí was dead more than mirrored my own when Mom died. The depth of her emotion is humanlike, Sàrkany-like, which shoots an arrow into my heart.

She's no different from me.

Minus the lack of rationality, that is.

And flame fingers.

And trying to kill me immediately upon meeting me. Something every Eósy I've met has as "step one" in their plans.

I roughly wipe the tears from my eyes. When my empathy returns to more manageable levels and I place the Eósy back in their "other" box in my brain, I curl onto the child's bed and try to sleep.

It's all a bit macabre, staying in the abandoned home of a living ghost who Leyden has caged upstairs. I don't revisit Carn's tower during our stay, but Leyden does, to drop off food and gather more books. I try not to think about it, or the memories I received from her.

On our second morning there, we're both sitting in the dusty kitchen. We found dried meat in the larder, but only took what's necessary to avoid inconveniencing Carn more. That she's a hostage in her own tower already weighs on me, requiring me to remind myself of who she is and what she is to keep the guilt from burying me.

Leyden sits across from me at the metal table, two stacks of books beside him and another in front of him. He pages through the top book, stopping only to take a bit of food and wipe his hands before plunging back into the text. I have my book, not including the three I've squirreled away in my pack, a short introductory piece that the child most likely studied when he or she first learned to read.

"Anything interesting?" I ask Leyden as I painstakingly flip through my book. It's a history, of course, of the consolidation of power in Sekai that led to the five ruling families. Fílga would probably salivate to see it, since Dalner has no books on the subject, only an oral tradition, which, comparing it to the book, has been distorted. Reasonable, given the Raddares were the victors and only preserved what they felt mattered. Even though the book was written at a child's reading level, it's dry. What I wouldn't give for something fictional to read, romantic or no.

"Possibly," Leyden says, his focus on the book unwavering.

"Anything I should be worried about you learning?"

His lips quirk. "Probably."

I stare down at my duller-than-a-box-of-rocks book, which fails to distract me. Since I left Tans a week ago, I've done nothing useful, save getting Leyden's help, and I don't know that I can count him in my 'win' column yet.

After fidgeting in my uncomfortable metal chair for the rest of breakfast, I turn my attention to my reluctant ally. His promises may make him a benefit for me, but he's unpredictable otherwise. He seems more rational than before, but how do I measure that? I thought he was clever and helpful, if still aggravating, when he was playing his 'childlike guide' role. Seeing him now paints a fuller picture, but his motivations are yet unknown to me. Centuries worth of planning, poor planning if I'm honest, went down the drain, and without me he'd still be stashed in his distant cell. Did he honestly intend on waiting out his never-ending sentence? Or does he have another risky plan up his sleeve?

Although, knowing he's centuries old but should be mentally considered a teenager improves my impression of his poor judgment and planning too. I let my mind give him a little credit. A poor plan, but successful overall. That's how my plans end, too. He got the despot killed and made a run for the wall. Even if it didn't work, he still got that far. If their side had won, it would be the Eósy editing their historical accounts, and not Kórol's ancestors.

Leyden's lips thin as he reads over what must be a disagreeable paragraph. No wrinkles appear even as he squints at his studies. He looks barely older than me.

I rest my chin on my hands, my elbows on the table. "Did I tell you I got Carn's memories?"

"No, but when I didn't, it was an easy assumption to make," he says, dragging another book to the top of his pile.

"She looks almost the same as she did thousands of years ago. Bittállí too."

"Yes, they would." He finally pulls his focus from the words and flashes his bright blue eyes at me. "That shouldn't be surprising."

"But how? How *do* you age? You're 800 years old but look maybe 18. Bittállí was two-thousand-ish and she looked early twenties at the oldest. Carn didn't look a day over thirty, and that's mainly because of the crow's feet."

He blinks. "The magic."

I give him my most dramatic eye roll, one only a good night's sleep and a lack of imminent danger can create. "No kidding! Magic keeps the immortal people immortal. But how?"

"Through the *land*," he says with just as much snark as I did. "How else can I explain it?"

I clench my teeth, and hiss, the movement jarring my bruised cheeks where Carn head butted me. "By *explaining* it? You talked about syrup and amber, which did not change my 'mosquito' impression, by the way, but how does *land* do anything for you? "

He closes the top book with more force than necessary. "We are beings of magic, and gain life from our magic, magic that lives in the earth." He raises his brows expectantly, as if confirming I understand. I nod while imagining kicking him under the table. "But our connection to the land...what is the word for what bats do? We have nothing similar in the Sàrkany language."

"Echolocation." The shortness of my tone could be from pain in my jaw or that Leyden's existence still irritates me.

"Echolocation, yes." He steeples his hands together. "We project our magic to the ground, which echoes it back to us and bounces inward, like a jug filling with water. When one jug fills, it moves to the next."

"How many analogies do you have? Mosquitoes, bats, water jugs..."

But he's not listening; the lecturing voice is gone and his eyes turn haunted. "With the walls, there was only so much space, only so much earth. We projected but the surrounding earth couldn't fill up our jugs. There were too many of us. It was over-stretched, over capacity. That feeling, it eats at you. Literally, the magic has nowhere to go and nowhere to return, and simply existing demands we use magic. And our body wastes away as the magic dwindles. We end up aging faster than we should. Doing any form of magic makes the eating faster, killing us. But we are magic, so how can we stop?"

"That's why you were gray," I say in stunned realization.

"Yes, except *Bittálli*," he spits her name like a curse. My eyes fly to the ceiling as if Carn will come storming through. Leyden doesn't notice. "Bittálli was the only one who could cross the wall and could use the magic on the other side. Which is why she was twelve hundred years older than me but appeared my contemporary."

"And Carn?"

"She was the sole Eósy here, she had the land," he explains. Meaning she didn't have to compete with other users.

"What about the Sàrkany? They were Eósy once. Or still are, unless a new species intermarried. None of them are that long lived."

He sighs, his eyes cast downward. "They were, at first. There weren't that many of them on this side of the wall and they had the entire southern half of Sekai to fill their jugs, cutting off the magic to the north entirely. Many died or became ill, not because they couldn't access the magic in the land but because they *promised* the Raddare King they wouldn't, that they would limit their magic use. But others who made those promises learned to adapt overtime. They evolved through the generations."

I furrow my brow, bursting out a comment before I can stop myself. "But there's no science in Dalner."

"That's only partly true. We have no scientific study like you do, but the phenomenon exists. Magic happens to be the cause for it. Like gravity, and mineral compounds. And the Sàrkany's evolution from Eósy. The magic within the Sàrkany learned how little they used and adjusted accordingly. Their children were born with the need for less magic. And then their children were born with even less, lowering their lifespans, with each generation living for fewer years and with less magical ability."

He presses his lips together until they turn white from the pressure, before shaking his head sharply. "They needed less magic but could have accessed it before their children lost the ability. Those generations made no promises to the original King, they were under no obligation *not* to take it. They'd even evolved away from the power of promises affecting them. And they let the magic that the Eósy would have died for, remain hidden underground."

I lean back against my metal chair. But if the Sàrkany use and need so little magic, then will the rifts even matter? They'll get healing back, yes, but how long until-

Leyden scoffs, interrupting my spiraling thoughts about my usefulness. "Don't worry, you single minded menace. They still need magic; you still need me."

My cheeks heat. "I didn't—"

But he doesn't let me offer any false denials. "While they used so little that the earth slumbered and its magic grew dormant—that is the amber analogy," he says as an aside in a snide mock whisper. "They still used magic. They don't have the strength or knowledge to pull it from the earth, and our scholars believed the evolved Sàrkany used the magic powering the rifts instead. It is a paltry amount to us, but enough for them. Though they are nearly human, normal that is, they aren't fully. No matter how small, their bodies used the magic to live, like us.

We didn't have enough, and it is killing us. And with the wall no longer leaking magic, they have none and no instinct to take it from the earth, which could kill them."

He stands with a force that screeches his chair against the stone like a wailing bird. "Fates forbid you act in a way that will help *us*. You'll get your rifts and need not consider the 'monsters' on the other side. No matter that without the wall, we could wake the dormant magic and spread it amongst the earth again. *We* can all rot."

Then, he storms from the room, and I'm left feeling as though I failed some test I wasn't aware of. But Leyden's overdramatics on this topic isn't new; he has no reason to keep trying to make me feel poorly about his failure.

He knows my opinion on the Eósy. He's the one that said there was no light or dark. *They have a twisted morality*, Fíl once told me. They expect to be treated as gods merely because they're immortal. They're the bad guys. Good people don't go out of their way to save the bad guys.

I drop my head into my hands and heave an exhausted groan. Life seemed so much simpler when someone was telling me what to do.

CHAPTER 15

Our last day is tense but quiet. Leyden pretends he didn't imply I was a hypocrite; I pretend Leyden's censure hit harder than it should. I wish Tans or another from the Pack were here to help me work through my uncertainty.

We agree to leave right after lunch, avoiding the next dragon flight and sparing enough time to clear our presence from the tower.

"Do you intend on joining me upstairs?" He stands at the last winding staircase to Carn's tower. The question is free of expectation, and I want to refuse, but I've promised not to run away from uncomfortable situations anymore. I nod and we creep up the tower.

Carn sits ramrod straight on the chaise, where I last saw her. Guilt steadily burbles in my gut until I see her clothes are new, even if the fabric isn't as nice as the burned dress, and her feet are well bandaged with thick white cloth. At the confirmation of her polite treatment, the guilt wanes, but doesn't disappear. I can't tell myself the guilt is unnecessary, no matter that she started the fight, and I did nothing wrong by Bittállí, because I still hear Sáv's voice in my head, reminding me that I can't shy away from consequences, no matter how right the act was.

Leyden kneels at Carn's feet while I slip to the bookcase and reshelve the books Leyden sped through. I keep my back to them to avoid seeing whatever Leyden will do to her and her mind.

"You won't remember Grace or myself," Leyden tells her. "You'll assume you tripped on the rocks and cut your ankles."

I wince as I spread out the books to hide the missing three volumes in my pack, which I've joined with the history book from the child's room. The guilt rises like a wave when the tide comes in.

"But when we leave, you'll think of Bittállí." He pitches his voice low, making me strain to hear it. I twist my neck to catch Leyden holding Carn's hands. "You'll remember how much you love her and how proud she made you, even if you never got to tell her. You know your daughter better than you think, and you'll realize how strong she was, how wonderful and how dedicated. How she let no one stop her from getting what she wanted."

Carn sighs almost inaudibly and Leyden withdraws. I turn back to the bookshelves, but not before seeing a flash of something complicated on Leyden's face.

"That was kind," I tell him when we trail down the stairs. Kinder than I expected given how he orchestrated Bittállí's death so callously. I want to say 'kinder than Carn deserves' but my mouth won't form the words. I stare down at the burns on my inner arms and attempt to remind myself of what she's done.

His lips thin. "She needed it."

"But it had to be true for you to say it."

"It was, once. But things change." And he elbows past me outside.

Leyden spends the rest of the morning outside kneeling on the grass and staring out past the cliff to the ocean below. I'd like to think he's only soaking up as much magic as he can, but I'm not sure if that's true. Leyden is a more complicated being than I imagined. It was easier when he was the simple villain, and not this multifaceted antagonist. This isn't the story I signed up for when I immersed myself in Dalner.

And I still want to kick him.

Lunch comes and goes, but Leyden continues to sit unmoving by the cliff side. Carn's memories confirm that at least two of her children died in this place, though she doesn't know how. From behind, Leyden could be one of her children, blond and beautiful.

"Are you ready?"

Leyden startles, the first and only time he's been hesitant in my presence. He plasters on a winsome smile before it falls, as though he didn't have the heart to keep it up. "As I can be." He looks back past the loch and silence descends again.

"Dreading the return?" I say, offering a verbal olive branch.

He takes it. "I am a wanted criminal," he says dryly. "It may be a long while before I can feel the magic this way again."

I frown. "Will you be able to bring us back if something happens?"

He drags his fingers through the grass beneath him. "I can open a window for you to return, but once I cross the perimeter, I cannot return without another invitation from you."

So, the invitations have expiration clauses. Helpful, but not what I meant. "I meant your amount of magic, the jar of syrup." One of his many mixed metaphors.

He huffs and stands, brushing his palms on his knobby looking tunic, a different one than he arrived with. Perhaps I wasn't the only visitor in the spire that helped myself to some of its possessions. "Coming to you required me to cleave cross country and slip in between an area with fully dormant magic that I can't wake without touching. Unless you demand we return to Ilsen, I'll be fine for several cleaves and opening the rifts in Dànna."

Appeased, I nod, and he holds out his hand. I take it gingerly as Leyden closes his eyes and straightens one finger to point at the space in front of us. It looks like he's scratching the air, and then he *is*. He rips a seam in the air, the two edges of the tear flapping just like torn fabric would. It's almost nauseating to see pieces of reality folded that way. My knees buckle, but Leyden's firm grip keeps me from sinking to the ground. When the tear is large enough, Leyden steps through, dragging me with him.

One would think the trip would be instantaneous, given we're walking through a thin window in reality. But as Leyden drags me from one place in the world to the next, it feels longer as my entire body gets squeezed through space and reformed on the other side. Perhaps I should thank Leyden for letting me sleep the first time I experienced this.

When we land on the opposite side of the window, the rip in reality neatly zips back up as if it was never there. I barely notice this as I sink to the ground with a ringing in my ear, a roiling in my stomach, and a heaviness pulling at my extremities. A nauseous groan pulls from my throat.

"Now you see why I kept you unconscious the first time we did this," Leyden says, squeezing my shoulders.

I jerk away from his touch. "How kind of you." It sounds sarcastic, but I mean it as the world continues to spin.

"Don't worry," he adds blithely, clearly enjoying my discomfort. "It gets easier each time."

Finally, I can sit up comfortably, and I brush off the wet dirt stuck to my knees and palms. "I don't plan on doing that again. Next time I'll just walk through the opening we make from the rifts."

He stands above me and offers a hand up, his eye twitching. When I just stare at it, he drops his neck to his chest and groans. "You've inflicted enough violence upon my person that I know touching me doesn't truly bother you. Indeed, you had no issue touching my skin a moment ago."

I toss my wild hair back mockingly. "Maybe hitting you is how I act towards allies. And touching you as a necessary step in walking through a portal is different." There's something shifty in his expression and my playfulness wanes. "Was it *not* necessary?"

He sniffs. "I don't care to say."

I let him pull me up so I can jab him in the shoulder when we get close enough.

It's then that I get the first look at Dànna, the Eósy realm. I should have expected that it would look no different from anywhere else in Sekai, as the wall didn't change the land, only the people. The shoreline where we arrived is as green as it was near Carn's tower, leading into a forest of trees as large as the redwoods I've seen in pictures. I've not seen the massive forests of Dalner before, only small pockets of woodland thickets. Likely those woods look the same.

Leyden marches into the trees without waiting for me.

"Where are we going?" My voice trembles as we slip past the first line of trees. The foliage is too dense for the light to penetrate, only the scattered reflection of the sun flickers above as we move.

But it's not the half-light that makes the hair on my arms stand on end, it's the sound. In Dalner, I got accustomed to only hearing wildlife at sunrise and sunset and then not at all. But here in Dànna, it's almost a cacophony within the forest. Shrill birds call overhead, rustling the leaves but remaining hidden for my gaze. Something chirps near my feet, but the thick underbrush doesn't reveal what. Leyden's voice pulls me from the thoughts that will no doubt devolve into panic as I remember the horror-show animals Sekai created.

"There's a large city nearby, a day or two's walk but we will cleave through as soon as your stomach settles."

"Don't you have to avoid being seen?" I hop over an overturned branch, pointedly ignoring the skittering sound coming from inside it. "The hardened criminal you're supposed to be."

He offers me a flat look. In the low light, his blue eyes look like a neon sign in the dark advertising something dangerous. "After we cleave to the city on the other side of this forest, I will remain in the trees while you enter and work your magic to convince one of them to follow you in the woods."

I plant my feet. "You're making me sound like a predator again. *Luring* someone into the woods to possibly die at the wall?"

"You don't need to mention that part," Leyden says, waving his hand as if unimportant. "And I'd assumed you'd not care if they lived or died, so long as your goal was met."

"And even if I *were* persuasive," I say as we start walking again, pointedly ignoring his accusation of my callousness. "Who would follow someone into the woods?"

"Have you forgotten how you persuaded that merchant in Chead?"

I squint in thought. "When I pretended to be a simpering ingenue?" He nods and raises his brows expectantly, as if waiting for me to connect the dots. When I do, I jab him on the other shoulder. "Come on! You can't use me as some kind of escort luring men into the dark with the promise of something salacious."

"Is that not what would happen in one of your novels?"

I jut out my chin. "Not any of the ones I've read."

He looks at me through his long lashes. "What about that erotic one you found—"

I quickly interrupt as my cheeks heat. I don't need the reminder that Leyden was there when I discovered smut. "And anyway, life's not a book. It doesn't work that way. There's personal safety to worry about, not to mention I have no charm."

He shrugs, unrepentant. "I'll be there to stop anything untoward. I don't see why you wouldn't at least attempt it. Charm or no, you have the beauty to summon them."

"Right, like I'd—" My voice tapers off as I register what he's said. I'm surely tomato red now, a full splotch of color covering my almond skin. He must notice as something teases the edge of his lips, and they slowly curl into a wide grin. I wrap my arms around my chest. "We'll think of something else."

"As you say," he says slyly. When the humor from my embarrassment leaches from his expression, he adds, "How is your stomach?"

"Better." Though I'd be lying if I said my stomach's current discomfort was from the trip and not the recent conversation. "Why didn't we cleave to the city instead of making two jumps?"

"The farther the distance, the longer you'll experience that stifling sensation. Given how you reacted on your first cleave, I assumed shorter trips would avoid any...uncomfortable consequences."

"What consequences?"

Now it's his turn to flush. We've stopped again, deep in the trees and a single ray of light illuminates the red on his cheeks. "When I first pulled you here, I needed to do it in two parts. I could not cleave a portal directly between your realm and Dalner as I was not in Dalner, but Bittállí described the area near her temple well enough that I knew I could send you there. Once I knocked you out, I dragged you into Dànna first, at which point you mumbled something about a blue door and vomited on me. Then I pushed you through to Dalner."

I'm about to laugh, or offer an unwarranted apology, given he kidnapped me. But then, something rumbles the earth beneath us.

"Hurchá," Leyden mutters. "Are you prepared?"

At my nod, he closes his eyes and stretches his finger outward. The thumping continues, like heavy footsteps from a massive creature, shaking us almost off our feet. Chittering animals skitter from the underbrush, away from whatever being shakes the earth. Leyden cuts two in parallel lines as he trips. On the second try, the tremors are so intense that he can't even create a tear. He growls and grabs my hand, dragging us to the closest tree. Fear has me squeezing his hand. He quickly pulls away and kneels at the base of the tree, cupping his hands.

"Up," he says between the rumbles.

The thumping steps are closer now and I stare wide-eyed at the branches that seem miles above us. Once I step into Leyden's hands, he thrusts me upward and my fingers scramble for purchase along the rough bark of the tree. I spare a single second to curse myself again for not taking those training tests. Then, flashbacks of fighting the Brute play in my head like a terrible movie but I use the memory to propel myself higher. I reach the nearest branch right as whatever makes those thumps sounds as though it is directly beneath us. Leyden is at my heels and gracefully swings himself beside me. In silence, we stare at the creature below.

Its body is muscular and leonine, covered in red copper feathers with a whip thin black tail that whistles as it moves. Its paws are larger than my head and tipped in red claws. Sprouting from where its neck should be are three long tubes resembling ostriches' necks that end in vulture-like naked skulls. Each neck protrudes in a separate direction—forward, left, right—with a single bulbous eye in the center capping sharp beaks. The eye attached to the center stares up at us unblinking.

"Can we cleave away?" I'm proud my voice only trembles once.

Leyden leans against the tree trunk. "We need to be on solid ground, or the trip is... unpleasant."

"Unpleasant is better than being ripped to pieces."

"She didn't see us," he says, unconcerned.

"But one of its heads is looking at us."

"One isn't an issue." His eyes fall shut as he answers my next, unasked, question. "If all three heads saw the same prey, then we would have problems. She would not stop hunting us until either she or we were dead."

The being remains below us. Leyden can't lie, but he isn't all-knowing. For something that hasn't seen us, it's spending a long while stopping our escape. I clench my fingers hard into the bark beneath me.

Two spindly appendages appear on the creature's back, rising from somewhere under its feathers. They're wings, leathery like a bat's and just as long. "Can it fly?"

Leyden peers over the edge of our branch. It squawks in anger and ruffles its coppery plumage. "Not to my knowledge. They're vestigial."

"Thank God. That thing is terrifying."

It moves again, circling around our tree, shaking the branch. We both clamber to keep our hold, wrapping our arms around the branch as we lay flat upon it. One of the three heads keeps a snake-slitted eye on our branch, and I'd swear its expression was anticipatory.

"*She* is a sàchenda, a being of violence and destruction. And the mascot of Dànna," Leyden says with a sniff, as though offended on the beast's behalf. Though he's certainly not showing his patriotism by hopping down to hang out with it.

"Why am I not surprised you chose a horrifying female as your symbol?" My whispered question is rhetorical, but Leyden hears.

"It was originally of the Launna family, who birthed more girl children than any other noble family combined. Sàchendas self-reproduce and only create females." He does something that looks like a shrug, but uncoordinated since he can't release the branch. "It fit. The symbol was co-opted when they formed Dànna. Each head was supposed to signify the new ruling family, the heirs of the joint houses: Ellen, Mashan." He pauses and swallows. "And Pender."

Something pained crawls over his expression, so I don't pry into why he seems affected by the name. We watch the sàchenda for another minute before Leyden collects himself and sniffs.

"It isn't as though Dalner's mascot is all that better, Grace. A *dragon*. How gauche."

"What's wrong with a dragon?"

"Nothing," he says, scoffing. "Except the Raddare house is known for ice. Choosing a symbol of fire seems like you're trying to compensate for something. Trying to exude the fiery power of war when you can only make snowmen."

I bristle, protective of Kórol, especially after all that's occurred. "Watch it."

He smirks. "I make no insult, dearest. The Raddares weren't the only noble family to pick mismatched symbols. The Menhirs, Bittállí's family, chose a wolf, which is supposed to symbolize loyalty. The Caerns used to flaunt a horse, the symbol of freedom, independence, and valor, and yet they were first to surrender at the War of the Separation when the Caern heir ran away."

"And the last family, the Dandres?" I ask despite myself.

"A manticore." He laughs a little. "They could not decide what form to take, so they took all of them. The nature of the sàchenda is probably the only reason Mashan didn't revolt at using a Launna symbol."

The sàchenda releases a snarling squawk from its middle head and sprints away from us. We remain in the tree until its footsteps no longer haunt the forest.

"What happened to the power structure here?" I ask after regaining my balance on the ground. Leyden takes hold of my elbow as if to keep me upright. "You said Bittállí's death got you the support to attack the wall. Who put you in prison?"

"We were a larger contingent than I expected. Many of the Eósy I manipulated for her put aside their hatred of me and agreed to attempt the breach, along with several like-minded families. When I failed, the support vanished, though the like-minded are no doubt still willing to bring about a coup if the circumstances arose again. Those that never promised allegiance to the new ruler."

"But who took over?"

"Pender." His eyes get that haunted look again. "My brother."

CHAPTER 16

I don't have time to ask more, as the sàchenda lets out an ear-piercing shriek. The ground doesn't quake, meaning she's far enough away that we can escape, but not so far that we shouldn't hurry. Leyden has the same thought as he immediately begins a rip in reality.

Something sprints past us, disturbing the underbrush. Leyden finishes the rip and holds out his hand. But the thing stops only a few yards away and squeaks out harsh gusts of air.

It looks like a child, a three or four-year-old. They are little and wearing a long overshirt, their bare feet peeking out from the hem. When they turn to stare back where they came, they reveal gray tinged skin and a terrified expression.

The sàchenda's steps get closer. Leyden yanks hard on my arm, almost pulling it from my socket.

"Grace, we've no time for this. We need to go."

My eyes don't stray from the child. "She'll hunt her prey until death?"

Leyden finally sees what holds my focus. "She's an Eósy child." I glance back at him, and something ripples over his expression. "Would you risk yourself against a sàchenda to save one of the so-called monsters, even one as innocent as her?"

My head rears back as if struck. But it's a rhetorical question, as he zips up the tear and begins barking instructions. "You must replace the child as the sàchenda's prey, or she will never turn focus from the child. Act as bait and distract the sàchenda and I'll get her somewhere safe."

I nod and we leap from the tree. My hip screams as I hobble as fast as I can towards the sàchenda while Leyden runs the opposite directions. A small part of me wonders if he'll come back or leave me to the sàchenda's red-tipped claws.

My heart slams in my chest, but still I race in the direction the child came from. Fear overtakes the pain in my legs and I push it forward, letting it color my voice too. I start shouting and waving my arms wildly, alerting everything in that forest to my presence. The squawking roar gets louder, the thumping closing in and almost knocking me off my feet. I freeze, scanning the surrounding woods until it finally comes into view.

The sàchenda doesn't move that quickly, but still faster than you'd want a three-headed lion monster to run. All three heads twist and converge in one direction: focused on me. A shudder goes through it, as though selecting me as prey made it reset somehow. I jog again, away from Leyden and the child and in a different direction than the sàchenda. Six months of training has done little to make me a great fighter, but I *am* more agile.

The sàchenda closes in as I weave around trees, running it in circles and figure eights. Each step is a chore as the sàchenda's heavy tread nearly knocks me down, but I use my unsteady gait to better delude her into realizing my ultimate direction. Its large body can't turn as quickly as I can and more than once its heads knock together. I zoom between trunks, seeking the smallest openings in hopes it will get caught. But somehow it wedges its car sized body through the gaps I force us through.

Finally, a whooshing sounds behind me and the squawking turns into a howl. I don't turn around to check what happened, weaving in and out of trees and underbrush, until I realize the thumping is getting softer, turning away from me. Only then do I double back. Leyden arrived and created a wall of flame keeping the sàchenda from advancing towards me. She shrieks in rage. Leyden turns the fire into a circle, igniting the thick tree trunks surrounding the sàchenda until he cages it.

Tans can manipulate fire, but it's a child's version of the skill Leyden possesses. Even Carn didn't display the artistry Leyden does. He spins around the circle on nimble feet, letting loose fire that glows almost blue when it leaves his fingers. He fires flame after flame at the circle, keeping the heat stoked and raging, pirouetting and leaping like a dancer.

She continues shrieking and withdraws the leathery bat-like wings I saw earlier, flapping them with fervor. Twice her wings beat hard enough into the base of the flames that it creates a small opening, but she's not positioned right to hop through it. But that could change.

"We need to kill her," Leyden shouts from the other side of the fiery enclosure.

The dragon Tans shot with an arrow runs through my mind. It was sentient enough to help us when we needed it. *Is she just as sentient?* Am I adding another nightmare to my tally?

"Grace," he screams. "There is no other option!"

He's given me the magic words to overcome my rising guilt, and we both know I won't run from fights anymore. But with only my short blade, I either need perfect aim or a much longer sword. "Damn those trainee tests," I hiss. The first one I'd intended to take focused on close-combat *and* aim. But there's nothing to be done, chastising my short-sightedness will do nothing. Leyden looks to be tiring. Even in the dim light, I can see his skin turning gray.

Her screeching almost covers my shouted question. "Does she have a weak spot?" I see none, but there must be something. Surely, whoever created these monsters wouldn't make them invincible.

Leyden struggles to answer; he sounds exhausted and on the verge of collapsing. "You need to sever the connection between her spine and neck, right at the place where her necks protrude from her back."

Easier said than done, since her three heads are laser focused on me and will surely rip my skin off the moment I approach her. But I have an idea. Another one that might make Tans faint.

But Tans isn't here.

I race around the sàchenda and her prison to Leyden's side. Her body follows me in a slow circle, her three eyes never straying from my form. "Can you maintain the flames without continuously firing them?"

Leyden licks his lips but nods. "Whatever you intend to do, you must be quick. She may extinguish them if I'm away from them too long."

"I need you to give me a boost up a tree again."

On three, he releases the flames from his fingers, and we bolt to a tree with a low hanging branch. Flames lick the base of the truck, but it hasn't caught fire yet. Only the trees directly surrounding the sàchenda are ablaze. He hoists me up and I scramble to the nearest branch, scraping open my palms and ripping a hole in my pants. Leyden's back in position feeding the flames by the time I land on my chosen branch and scoot towards where it nearly hangs over the sàchenda, hugging the branch to keep my balance. She stops squawking, all three heads twisting from one side to the other as if in confusion. Then, they converge again, pulled together like magnets and she jumps.

She can't jump high, as her body is made for leaping forwards not upwards, and each lunge pushes her close to the flames until she shuffles backward and does it again. I crouch on the branch, and mentally recite every curse word I've ever heard. Even though I've tried to turn myself into one of those protagonists who is somewhat competent, I'm still me underneath. A little bit braver than I was nine months ago, but that doesn't pair well with my usual amount of recklessness. I'm still the girl with unorthodox plans, hoping the successes that always happen in books will happen for me.

"Aim for her eyes," I shout down to Leyden. He sways for a second but complies quickly. The flames from his fingers burst forth and blind her, causing her three heads to wobble and scream until she beats them against the ground to extinguish the fire. And then I jump.

I'd like to say my landing is graceful, that I skillfully settle on her back like a limber cowgirl. Instead, I land sideways and nearly slip off her back. Her feathers are coarse, more like wiry terrier fur and I grab handfuls of it to keep from dropping to the ground as my legs slip off her body to the side. Before she can buck me off, I plunge the knife into the top of her spine.

"Don't let her blood touch you!"

I can barely hear Leyden's screamed warning as she roars, knocking me to the ground. Blood whips off the wound, arching to the air and landing with a hiss. One speck lands on my inner arm and I join her in howling, the liquid burning just as hot as fire. Leyden drops the flames and skitters to my side to drag me away before she tramples or tosses more of her blood on me. It takes less time than I thought; we've only just cleared the charred area when she falls with a thud.

Together we kick nearby underbrush and leaves over the remaining flames until they burn out, wafting smoke into the air.

"You realize that when I teased you about always running from your fights," he starts, each word punctuated by a heaving breath. "It didn't mean you should literally *leap* into every battle you find."

My voice is just as winded. "You realize you need more experience with teasing, if you think that's what you were doing back then. Besides, you said we needed to kill her."

He doesn't respond, pursing his lips and snatching my arm as he crowds me. I haven't forgotten the pain that droplet caused, but it all combined into the enormous ball of pain I've been in since Leyden pulled me from the loch. He runs his fingers over the spot, but it's already cool and sealed. It looks like a burn, but it is just one of many that now litter my forearms. A small part of me aches at the continued scarring of my skin, but even I'm not so vain as to think pristine and dead is better than mottled and alive.

The bigger problem is that I may have pulled something in the muscles above my elbow when I landed. I twist my arm in his grip before he releases me. "Should I be worried?"

He blinks and puts more distance between us. "It doesn't appear to have seeped under your skin. You should be fine."

Now it's time for my inspection of him. He's still pale, but there might be a gray undertone the shadows hide. "Are you okay?"

He nods, tossing his hair from his eyes. "Well enough."

"Do you still have enough magic to open the rifts?"

"I should be fine. With another person's help, I believe I can open the rifts and still manage a cleave or two without dying." He smiles, but it's shaky. "A pity, Grace, you won't be rid of me that easily."

"Well, drat." But I inject enough humor into my voice to let him know I'm not actively rooting for his death at this moment. Too quickly, my lips turn down as a stare at the body of the monster only following her instincts, no matter the possible consequences to us as her prey. "Is there anything we need to do with her?"

"There is nothing to be done," he says, staring at me with a peculiar expression. "Nature will take its course."

He slowly leads us back through the trees and away from the corpse until we arrive at the base of the tree where he left the child. She stares down at us with wide eyes, full of innocence and recognition.

"Hold out your arms so you can catch her," he says.

I blink. "Me? I'm more likely to drop her. I'm all woozy from that jump and probably sprained my wrist. You're the stronger one here."

His expression pinches like he's sucked a lemon. "You'll spring onto the back of a sàchenda, but carrying a child scares you," he mutters under his breath. She leaps into his arms without him requesting it.

She looks smaller than she did when she first ran past us, except the terror has leached from her expression. Her skin is a sickly gray, but she's otherwise no different from other kids I've seen. Pin straight black hair frames her face, curling under her chin, and her eyes are a warm brown reminiscent of Tans' family. Leyden attempts to release her to the ground, but she clings to his arms. He huffs but makes no other outward complaints.

"Hello, I'm Grace. This is Leyden. Are you hurt?" The switch back to Sàrkany isn't seamless and I stutter the first few words.

The child blinks but stays silent.

"Do you live around here?"

She still says nothing. Leyden sighs and shifts her onto his hip, like I've seen moms do.

"Her name is Mittio. She's not hurt but may be in shock. Her parents live in a tent near the wall. It's a five day walk."

My gaze slides from her sweet little face to Leyden. "You need to be careful doing that."

"I've been reading minds since before you were born. I know what I'm doing."

"Yes, but—"

Mittio buries her face in Leyden's neck and snuffles into his skin. He raises his brows as if to say 'see?'

I refrain from making a snide remark, instead asking, "Do you know where her tent is?"

He points deeper into the trees, towards the water. "We should move quickly, in case another sàchenda appears."

And we're off, with a child in tow. I can't say I haven't read this story before. But the universe has another thing coming if they expect Leyden and I to become the adoptive parents of an orphan while we share opposite wings of some mansion.

Although, I wouldn't mind a bed and indoor plumbing again.

CHAPTER 17

We walk until after sunset, as it seems to be my lot in Sekai to constantly sleep outside. There wasn't even a question that we would return Mittio to her parents. The fate of the Sàrkany can't wait too long, but we can't abandon a child to another sàchenda or worse. We stop where the trees thin, scattered sparsely in a small grove. Mittio has remained silent, only snuffling periodically. After the first hour, she let me carry her, but I could tell she seemed put out about it. What I've done to annoy a toddler is a mystery.

I wait with Mittio as Leyden gathers sticks. The sounds of the forest quieted the farther south we went. We've done our best to straddle the edge of the forest and the shoreline of the loch to avoid catching the eye of another sàchenda and using the moonlight as a guide. The few stuttering memories I gleaned from the sàchenda confirmed there were a few others with territory in the northern part of the forest.

Only when Mittio finally sleeps do I place her on the ground. With her speed, we'd never find her again if she ran off. Her gray pallor lessened a little over the day, but not enough. In certain lights, she looks how Leyden did during the memories when he covered his skin with gold powder—sickly and weak. I cover her with one of my tunics and slip closer to where we've prepared a campfire.

"Should we worry about a fire?" I survey the small grove. No longer do any mysterious birds caw from above, and the underbrush has remained scamper and chitter free since the sun went down. But something more terrifying than a Sekai-version of a squirrel might be attracted to the flames.

Leyden dumps the sticks at my feet. "I'd worry more about frostbite. We're more north than you're used to." He leans forward and unfurls a salacious smile. "Unless you'd prefer we warm each other in other ways."

I try to kick him, but he grabs my foot before I can connect. "First, there is a child present—"

"You would agree if there wasn't a child present?" He giggles and squeezes my ankle. "Is *this* the first step in our enemies to lovers game?"

I yank my leg from his grip, irritation speckled with guilt bubbling in my stomach. "*Second*, never in a million years." I pile the sticks with more force than necessary, breaking two of them. "I don't know what you think you're playing at, pretending to be Tans. We've negotiated a truce, we're working together, neither of us is currently attempting to destroy the other, we can even act—" I cut myself off because the word for it doesn't exist. "Not *friendly*, but maybe a level above cordial. But I'm not going to forget it's you here."

He sucks in his cheeks before shaking his head. "I know we're not friends, Grace, no matter my overtures." I make a disbelieving sound that he ignores. "Teasing isn't exclusive to Tansr. I'd hoped you'd begun to trust me, perhaps even like me, after all we've done together."

I rear back to better glare at him. "*Trust* you? I'm not sure what world you've been living in lately, but the only reason we've 'done anything' together is because you've wrapped yourself in promises to keep you from working against me."

He tosses his hands in the air. "*Of course*, I only saved you from drowning because of the promise I'd not yet made." His increased use of sarcasm makes me want to growl.

"Please, you can't expect me to believe it was wholly altruistic."

His expression turns to glass, something brittle and ready to crack. "If I can put aside that you'd willingly let my entire race die, you can surely forgive me for having multiple motives in leaving Exile."

My hands fist at my hips, landing on the two scars his past actions gave me. "That's not fair."

But he doesn't let me continue, though I don't know what else I could say. "Someday, maybe you'll realize I'm not the villain in our little crusade." He stands and looks down his chin at me. "I'll take the first watch. I'm sure you don't want to leave me alone with Mittio, in case I corrupt her." And he flicks an ember at the sticks to light them before slipping into the trees.

The tension doesn't last the night. Apparently, ignoring uncomfortable situations isn't restricted only to humans.

On the fourth day, Mittio gets restless. She still doesn't speak, but Leyden's ability to connect with her via her mind does much to keep her from crying in distress at being stuck with strangers. She won't calm down for me, but when I place her back in Leyden's arms, he whispers something to her and she settles.

"You can stop gawking," he says.

"I'm not gawking." I quickly stare at the forest ahead.

"Lies, lies, lies." Leyden's singsong tone makes Mittio giggle. She snuggles closer to him as if she agrees. Leyden raises his brows smugly in my direction.

"I'm surprised you're so...patient and accommodating with her."

He offers me an unimpressed frown. "I'm eight hundred and thirteen years old, do you imagine I've never been around children?"

I shrug. "Just because you've been around kids doesn't mean you're good with them." Father's second wife, who taught pre-k, immediately came to mind. "I assumed it wasn't in you."

"What were you imagining?" He sounds more curious about my opinion of him than I'd expected.

"I assumed most of your time was spent manipulating people. And dabbling in general villainy, so making connections with—"

He interrupts me to murmur into Mittio's ear, eyes full of mirth. "Did you hear that? Nearly a millennium in age and I've got no time for interests, only 'general villainy,' like a comic book character. Which, I'll have you know, I have read."

"When have *you* read comic books?"

"Through the window. I've never visited Earth, though that was more for conservation of magic," he admits. The windows meaning the one I saw in his memories where he spied on me and others like me. "But before and right after the wall, it was apparently quite the rage. The Greeks held much interest," he says, leaning in toward Mittio as if lecturing to her. "The savagery of gladiators and the grandeur of the Olympic games. It is a pity neither of us can experience it. "

I kick away a rock that attempted to trip me. "And here I thought all things human were beneath the Eósy."

"They might've been," he says, sniffing imperiously, but the corner of his lip twitches. "Who can say that your societies *weren't* inspired by us?"

I gesture widely to the surrounding forest. "Because we'd probably be in some kind of vehicle, a bicycle at the very least. And using a cell phone to contact social services to find Mittio's parents."

He scoffs. "That is circumstantial evidence at best. We continued visiting your realm until the magic shortage hindered us, centuries before such technology developed, though a few may have attempted to cross within the last century. There's no other explanation for your borrowing of our words."

"Like?"

"Menhir for one," he says, smirking as if he's won the argument we're not having. But when I blink at him, his expression falls. "Bittállí's original family name? The standing stone monolith, signifying that Bittállí's overinflated self-worth was not a unique trait but one shared by her blood. You must have studied the word in its Breton form."

I wrap my arms around my stomach. "I... remember you mentioning her family name was 'Menhir' earlier."

"Do you not know that it means something in English? That one of Bittállí's ancestors—" He stops as false pity seeps into his black eyes. "Oh, *Grace*. And here I thought all beings were above the Eósy. But for your human schooling to let you *down* so. Or is this not a deficiency of your people but one only found within you?"

I refrain from rolling my eyes and kicking him, but only because of Mittio's presence. "Keep teasing me and I'll go find another sàchenda and let you deal with her alone."

Mittio lifts her head from Leyden's shoulder. She remains silent, but I'm sure I see annoyance in those little brown eyes.

"I know, she has such an attitude," he says, mock whispering to her, his eyes ringing blue as he uses his magic again.

I plant my feet and fist my hands on my hips. "Is she actually saying something in her mind about me?"

Leyden lifts the shoulder Mittio isn't attached to, a one-armed shrug. "Who can say?"

You can, you jerk. But I only stew in my silence for a minute. Something skitters across my foot and I need the distraction. "Did you ever want kids?" It might explain why he's bonded so well with Mittio, because his personality otherwise can't be it.

He pauses for a moment, as if he's never needed to know the answer to that question. "Maybe? I can't recall. Ambition and a drive for power anchored into my heart soon after I hit majority at twenty."

The age when you find your soulmate. Maybe his loneliness helped his descent into irrationality and villainy sooner. "No soulmate, then?"

His dark eyes fix on my face. "Soulmate?"

But I don't answer, and he isn't expecting one as just behind the trees in front of us stands the wall I solidified. A heavy inhale comes from Leyden as I push ahead of him.

Prior to today, I'd only seen it from a distance, an opaque pearlescent block. Even at this distance, it seems larger than it should, shooting into the sky as high as the eye can see. The way it rises, white and shimmering like abalone, it's as if the world ends and there is no more life beyond it. Specks of darkness litter the space in front of the wall, but I'm too far to determine whether it's part of the grasslands or an extension of it.

I march towards it as if spellbound, like a bug transfixed by a light.

"Grace, don't!" Leyden calls from behind me.

Too late do I realize why he attempted to warn me. As soon as I step out of the trees, the dark specks grow and form into bodies.

Dozens of dead animals found their final resting place beside the wall: deer, four-headed ducks, dart-snakes, birds. A small dragon lays curled tightly in a ball, like a slumbering cat, but the flaking of its scales and utter stillness of its body confirms its death. Even some of the enterprising vulture-like birds and wolf-sized foxes, who began tearing strips of flesh off the corpses, hunker dead over their prey. That they were not part of the original dead is only evident by the hunks of meat still caught in their teeth and the corresponding rotted wound on their prey.

My knees wobble as bile rises in my throat. Leyden catches up to me and blocks my view of the dead. He's angled Mittio to keep her from seeing too.

I swallow a heave. "What happened?"

Leyden's lips form a thin line. "I can only guess."

"Please," I breathe, hands trembling as they cover my mouth. Or else the wild theory churning in my gut will take hold.

"The animals are magic, like we are. I don't know whether their connection to the land echoes ours but..." His face shutters. "If they were, they were the weaker of their species and died waiting for the rifts to let them through."

My eyes fall shut as if I can pretend that if I'm not there, those corpses don't exist, or that my theory and Leyden's are more similar than I'd like. But this was a consequence of mine, of Leyden's. Anger bubbles and I hit the shoulder not holding Mittio. Mittio grumbles while Leyden's eyes widen.

"You did this," I tell him, poking him in the chest and forcing him to walk backward.

"More accurately, *we* did this," he says.

I keep advancing, my vision turning red. "I wouldn't have done anything if you hadn't attempted a civil war." I punch him again, but he snatches my hand before it connects.

"You had many choices that day, as did I. I could have killed you when you first appeared at the Gates, or ripped through your mind until it was mush the moment Bittállí died, or used my remaining strength to send you to Earth. Then, the walls would have been down and none of this would have happened." His grip tightens until the bones of my wrist grind together. "You could have killed me instead of throwing yourself at the Gates or attempted to negotiate a ceasefire with Bittállí. Then, everything would have remained the same, and none of this would have happened. Each choice brought us here." He drops my hand and I hold it protectively against my chest as my lips curl back, ready to continue my verbal and physical attack. "Be upset with me all you wish, but don't let it risk Mittio," he says, the reminder breaking through the haze of my anger. It's only luck that Mittio seemed uninterested in our byplay and was staring back into the trees.

He continues, "From her memory, her family is somewhere close. We'll make camp inside the tree line, and I'll see if I can glean better directions from her mind."

I nod, refusing to meet his eye. He and Mittio walk deeper into the forest, leaving me alone. As it always does, my misplaced anger turns to embarrassment and resignation.

When I can no longer hear Leyden's footsteps, I walk out deeper into the accidental graveyard. I try to look at each beast, attempting to memorize their forms. Leyden was probably right that these animals were the weaker of their species, as some are more diminutive than their living brothers and hold a gauntness that death didn't create. They might also be the less intelligent, if they waited at an unbreakable barrier until death. A pang jolts my stomach; that's uncharitable. I shouldn't blame them for their plight when the ultimate responsibility belongs elsewhere.

I arrive directly beside the wall, placing my hands on it, searching for a seam or evidence that there is a world behind it. It feels frozen, like when your tongue gets stuck to a dry ice cube. As I pull my hand away, little bits of skin stay behind. If magic is hidden inside the barrier, I can't find it.

I tuck my frostbitten fingers underneath my arms and head back into the forest, looking for Leyden and Mittio's makeshift camp.

CHAPTER 18

"I'm not trying to place all the blame on you," I tell him later that evening. He's built a campfire and Mittio sits in his lap across from me. "I fully recognize my part in it. If I didn't, I wouldn't be here."

"To open the rifts and Gates," he says flatly.

"Yes. The magic will come back for the Sàrkany." I swallow an uncomfortable lump in my throat. "And then the animals will be back too."

He stares into the fire, the embers dancing across his face. "What I don't understand is how you can't acknowledge your plan's selfishness." He raises his eyebrows at my silence. "You've taken two experiences with my kind and decided the entire race should be punished."

"More than two," I say weakly. "There were some creepy ones at the Gate with you, and Carn."

"A few dozen then," he amends, shaking his head. "A few dozen out of thousands. And only a half dozen other wretched examples exist in the two thousand years with the wall erected. Do the rest of them not deserve a chance on the other side of the wall?"

"That's not fair," I point out. "If I've only met the worst of you, why wouldn't I think you're all terrible?"

He gestures to Mittio. "Is she terrible?"

As if she knows she's the subject of our conversation, Mittio wriggles in Leyden's grip until he has no choice but to release her. I reach for her, to keep her from running off, but she evades my grip, hoping nimbly around my pack and rushing into the trees. Conversation aborted, we both take off after her. The moonlight barely illuminates the small openings between the leaves above us, but we track her by the sound of disturbed underbrush as she moves.

She runs, but not at the cheetah speed from before, until she leaps into the arms of a figure who appears between the trees. Leyden and I skid to a stop, I crash into his side, and he grabs my shoulder to keep me upright.

"Praise the Fates! Thank you for finding her," the figure says, walking closer until it turns into a woman. She looks like an older version of Mittio except her skin is more sienna than gray. Mittio clings to her body much like she did to Leyden and starts playing with a leather necklace around the woman's throat. Another person joins her, a man.

I wave them off, simultaneously knocking Leyden's arm from my shoulder. "It was nothing," I say. Leyden looks like he wants to interject, knowing him to say something about how much work he did compared to me, but I elbow him in the stomach before he can.

"Are you—" the man trails off as his green eyes widen. His hands curl into fists and he jerks forward as if to attack Leyden.

Without thinking, I push in front of him to meet the man head on and stop the assault. But he doesn't stop, Leyden wasn't his aim, and he decks me across the mouth. White blooms over my vision but I can still see Leyden jolt forward and stop the man from hitting me again.

After I spit blood on the ground and my eyes clear, Leyden is holding the man back as he shouts invectives.

"She stopped our chance," he screams. "She's killed Mittio. Gracel destroyed everything!"

The woman holding Mittio tightens her grip and looks close to crying. Shock stings me as much as the pain in my lip.

"What is going *on*?" I sound stronger than I feel, wanting nothing more than to cower under his vicious insults, some of them the same words that swirl around in my mind: that I did this; that I've doomed everyone.

"I told you that you were a harbinger, inciting the masses," Leyden says, grunting as the man continues struggling, almost bashing Leyden in the nose. The man continues trying to escape Leyden's clutches until he slumps unconsciously to the ground. Mittio's probable mother whimpers and turns Mittio away but doesn't retreat.

I step closer to the man's unmoving form. "Did you knock him out? Leyden!"

Leyden throws his hands in the air. "Make up your mind, Grace. Do you want me to manipulate the minds of those who would do you harm or not?"

"I'd prefer not to be in harm," I mutter. "Why did he attack me? You're the criminal here."

The woman recovers enough to bare her teeth at me. Through tears, she says, "Because *you're* the criminal. You've doomed us; he tried to save us."

Leyden tears a strip off his tunic and hands it to me, gesturing towards my mouth. "Apparently, they're supporters of mine. And did *not* appreciate your closure of the Gates. I believe an apology is in order. I seem to recall you labeling *me* the villain in our little duo?"

"Shut up, Leyden," I say, squeezing my fists until my nails bite into my palms, the cloth he'd given me falling to the ground.

He smirks as the woman's mouth opens in outrage. But before a second stranger can attack me, he turns to her. "Revive your husband, but neither of you may attack my companion again."

She nods silently before throwing me the meanest glare I've ever seen.

We join the couple at a small campfire just outside the forest, right where the warded water ends, and the wall begins. They live alone, having left their small village on the outside of one of the larger towns, to get closer to the wall after Leyden's gambit failed.

They tell us, or technically they tell Leyden as they continue to scowl in my direction and ignore me, that they'd hoped the proximity to the wall and the rifts in the Gate might leak magic that they couldn't otherwise find in Dànna.

"Mittio's still so young," her mother, Retka, explains. "She got her speed from Ashun's side of the family but doesn't know how to control it. Half the time when she takes a step, she'll end up almost a day's trek away. The overuse of magic tires her." She kisses the top of Mittio's head where she sleeps in her mother's arms. "She can't live like this, not with the walls. Not until she's old enough to control the magic's use."

"She'll die with the walls up," the father, Ashun, says, heaving his biting words at my feet. It takes more strength than I knew I had not to duck my head. I can't escape the guilt of my actions even on *this* side of the wall.

Hope fills Retka's expression as she gazes at Leyden. "Will you try again? Will you bring the walls down?"

Leyden pointedly doesn't look at me. "Perhaps someday."

Retka and Ashun trade glances before Ashun presses his hand against his chest. "We want to help. I couldn't join the attack last fall, not with Mittio only just learning to walk and running me all over Dànna. Retka couldn't manage that alone, but we spread word to all we knew. With things as they are now, we'll do anything."

"Right now, our goal is to open a rift," Leyden says solemnly.

Retka places her hand over her husband's on his chest. "We understand."

But I don't. There's something in the subtext of this conversation that I'm missing. I hug myself tightly. I still prefer *text* to subtext.

"Let me discuss this further with my companion," Leyden says.

Retka and Ashun bow their heads towards Leyden, like one would a noble, and then enter a small tent behind the campfire, disappearing behind the flaps.

I don't know what to say, so I stay quiet, letting Leyden speak first as he understood what was unsaid around the fire.

But instead of offering an explanation, he looks at me and scoffs. "Your lip is still bleeding. While it matches your nearly blackened eyes, I'll say it again: you shouldn't offer yourself up in every battle that comes."

I lick the cut and taste bitter copper on my tongue. "I'm a bit of a walking bruise nowadays." I don't answer the implied question.

"Thank you for attempting to protect me," he says quietly. "I would have warned you he had no interest in harming me; I simply didn't expect your reaction."

I press the neckline of my shirt up my mouth. I can't explain the thought process that led me to do it, given only that morning I'd been hitting him myself. "Reluctant allies," I say with a shrug, cringing when it rubs the rough fabric against the cut.

Leyden rips another clean strip from the bottom of his tunic and presses it against my lips. "Don't drop this one. You'll get an infection, and that boy of yours would no doubt vivisect me if I bring you back marred."

I clear my throat pointedly and gesture to my hip and arms.

"*More* marred," he says, rolling his eyes dramatically. "And though Retka can heal, I imagine she'd spit on you before using her magic on you."

I doubt he's wrong, given the furious looks they both shot my way. I replace his hand with my own and hold the makeshift handkerchief up to the cut. "Do you think they'll help us with the rifts, or has my existence screwed that up?"

He stares down at his hands. "I think they'll do whatever it takes to keep Mittio safe."

"The rifts won't do that, unless you've left something out of your explanation of the walls."

"No, the only thing for her is more space and the dormant magic in Dalner."

Discomfort burbles in my stomach. "They want to cross over once they're open? They can't do that. I can't agree to that."

Kórol and Tans would kill me. Even *Fílga* would kill me, if only for letting allies of Leyden, the pinnacle of "Dark Eósy" in his mind, across. And then Rothàna would have Tans revive me somehow and make me a training toy for the clumsiest recruits.

"*They* will not be crossing." He watches me expectantly, waiting for me to understand what's unsaid.

My hands almost claw at my throat in alarm. "They want us to take Mittio across?"

His eyes are as hard as steel. "Have you seen them, Grace? There's a reason we found Mittio before they did. Ashun barely has enough magic to catch her. Retka's putting everything she has into keeping her healthy. They won't survive offering their magic to the rift, but Mittio won't survive if they don't."

I stand in shock, as if I can run away from what he's just told me. "That's—we can't do that. There must be another option. We find someone else and maybe send them elsewhere. To Carn, at the very least. She might understand and help keep Mittio safe."

He stares at me with a pitying expression. "Can you honestly tell me Carn is a viable option for Mittio?"

I slump back to the ground, my knees buckling. "No," I whisper.

He reaches out and squeezes my shoulder. I don't resist this time. "It is their choice, Grace. Do not take that from them. They would do this for their daughter."

"But where will she go? Who would take her? She's a toddler."

He splays his hands. "They're hoping for someone kind, someone who might love her as they do."

"The Sàrkany think the Eósy are monsters," I say, shaking my head in disbelief.

"And six months ago, they thought some of us were deities. A middle ground isn't unthinkable. Nor is it unreasonable to hope that someone will not punish her for something she can't change."

A thousand words threaten to spill out of my mouth, but what bursts free is not what I expect. "Okay. She crosses over with us."

Leyden's smile is faint, pained but still somehow pleased. "We're agreed."

CHAPTER 19

I wake the next morning curled around the remains of the campfire. Leyden plagued my dreams, as he has since the Wilds. But instead of bothering me, he'd spent the dream hours reading his stolen books and staring up at the sky.

Soft voices whisper behind me and pull me from my own tumultuous thoughts.

"I only wish we could do more," Ashun is saying.

"You're doing all you can." That's Leyden's deep voice, gentler than I've heard from him in a long while.

"But if there were more of us. We're not the only family affected by it."

"We left more than a handful of friends with the same ailment as Mittio when we moved here," says Retka. "If we all combined, perhaps then the wall—"

"No," Leyden says firmly. "I've learned from our last attack. We were a thousand strong, and it made a half dozen cracks. These individual pushes do nothing more than create little rifts. There must be another way. Sacrificing our entire race to bring it down isn't viable."

I cast my eyes to the ground at the frustration in his tone.

"Does anyone know? Any of those that created it?" Ashun asks.

"Bittállí killed most of them," Retka says, as if reminding them.

"What about your brother?" Ashun suggests. "He was there. Surely, he can see reason and realize the old laws are wrong."

Leyden sighs. I can almost imagine the glower on his face. "He was young when it happened. But even if he remembered enough, he'd not help. He was blinded by Bittállí without needing manipulation to push him. We had little time for talking when he exiled me, but I've no doubt he'll follow Bittállí's policies to 'honor' her," he finishes bitterly. "And even if we knew, we've an army waiting for us on the other side."

"What of her?" Ashun must mean me, and I pinch my eyes more firmly closed. "Would she stand against us or with us?"

"She made it worse, Ash, there's no point even discussing it," Retka says.

"It wasn't her fault," says Leyden. "They worked with the information they had, just as we did. The wall's barrier blocks more than magic."

Conversation stops and I use the silence to pretend to wake. Leyden greets me quietly while Retka and Ashun return to their tent. They reappear with Mittio strapped to Retka's back in a makeshift sling.

There is no sound as we trudge to the wall, seeking the remains of a Gate, one of the smaller ones to the north of Bittállí's former temple, and the closest to where I left Tans, meaning the most likely place for magic to return to him and his family. The animal graveyard appears as we close in on the wall, but Retka and Ashun act as though it is normal. If they've been traveling along the wall for months, perhaps it is.

Leyden quickly confirms the plan. It's simple, as simple as I should have assumed, given my vague memory of Leyden's actions at the wall last winter. Retka and Ashun will feed Leyden their magic, much like the land does. It sounds like something that could readily be weaponized, but Leyden assures me it could only be done with consent and intentional action by both sides. I don't ask whether a manipulated mind counts as 'consenting.' He must notice as he hesitantly reminds me that there are only two Eósy living who know how to do it and apply it to the wall, which doesn't ease my worries.

Soon, it's time. Ashun takes Mittio from Retka's back and kisses her on the forehead before placing her in Retka's arms. Then, he stands solemnly beside Leyden at the wall. Retka hesitates for a long moment, whispering in Mittio's ears, before holding her out to me. Her eyes are red rimmed, and her grip lingers as I pull Mittio to me. Retka takes a deep breath and rubs Mittio's back, who sits propped on my hip wriggling to get back to her mother.

"I promise to make sure she's safe," I tell her earnestly.

Her sadness transforms to anger quickly. "Promises from you mean nothing," she says wetly as she squeezes the pendant around her neck. Touching it may be the only thing keeping her hands busy enough not to hit me. That, and Mittio.

"I know I don't have magic, and that my promises aren't binding like yours are. But that's all I have. You must trust me—I will get her someplace safe and make sure she's loved."

Retka stares at Mittio and kisses her on the forehead. "See that you do." Then she joins them at the wall.

Mittio and I watch in silence as the three stand in a row, staring at the wall. The bodies littering the ground add to the macabre energy in the air. By this evening, two more corpses will join the graveyard. I shudder, turning us away from the sight.

After a time, she gets restless and I let her play in a wide circle around me, tying the rope I used to secure Sunflower around her waist. She attempts to zip away, but her super speed can't move me more than a few inches in either direction. She tires herself out just when I think she'll pull my uninjured arm from its socket, slumping in my lap for a nap.

During that quiet moment, I wonder if there is a better option. No matter what, we must get Mittio into Dalner immediately, meaning another rift will not open for some time. Perhaps not even then, if each rift demands the sacrifice of another. Bartering with their lives for my goals was much easier when they were the unknown ‘other,’ and not people with lives and loved ones. A bitter part of me wonders if Leyden planned all of this to force my understanding. It isn’t as though he’s had complicated and secretive schemes in the past.

My eyes fall shut as I put my hand on Mittio’s slight back, feeling it rise and fall with her breath. I have only the vaguest idea of who can take care of her when we arrive. She deserves to live, yes, but does she not also deserve the love and safety of her parents? Could they not travel to the Wilds and find solace and health there? Must they die to open the rift for me? There wouldn’t be an influx of Eósy unless others can travel like Leyden can. I could explain it to Tans and Kórol; they’d understand. We can find another way to open a rift; no one is dying in Dalner from lack of magic yet. The worst outcomes so far are learning to live as vegans, and Kórol’s dwindling sense of reason, but that might have arisen regardless. Tans will heal eventually, and maybe he and Rothàna can keep peace in the provinces, explain the supply problem and avoid a war. And I’ll—I’ll manage the soulmate situation, something only important to me.

I gently place Mittio on the ground and rush to their side. They are doing nothing but standing beside Leyden. I can’t see his face, but what I remember at the Gates in December, he’ll be muttering under his breath. Retka and Ashun are swaying, holding on to each other to remain upright.

“Stop,” I shout, slipping in front of them. Leyden looks tired too, and shivers as I break his concentration on the wall. “There must be another way. They can go into the Wilds, there’s magic there, and an entire open area for Mittio to run.”

“You would invite us there?” Retka’s voice is hoarse and she clings to Ashun.

“Yes.” I exhale the word, dragging my guilt with it.

They exchange tired glances before Ashun shakes his head. “This rift—you wish to save the lives of your people, yes?”

I nod. Leyden looks pained at the question.

"We want Mittio to live," he says. "We want her to grow up and experience joy. She deserves a life free of pain. But she is not the only one."

"We will be the spark that lights the wall on fire," Retka says, her eyes blazing. "Someday, when the wall is gone, she will know what her parents did, and how they helped."

But she'd rather have you. "What if nothing changes? What if you open this rift, and Mittio lives on the other side of the wall, but everything else remains the same?"

Retka leaves Ashun's embrace to stumble closer and peer down at me. "We will be dead, and it will matter not. If *you* are what snuffs out our spark, you are the one who must live with the guilt and consequences." She turns back to Leyden. "Let us continue."

The three begin again and I gather up Mittio in my arms. The rift hasn't even opened, and the guilt threatens to choke me. I pinch my eyes shut. The conversation I overheard that morning plays behind my closed lids. Leyden has all but confirmed he can't get the walls down alone.

The sun sets while we wait. Mittio and I play again, and I feed her a dinner of Sáven's green cheese and dried meat we made on our five day journey to her parents. As the last of the sun's rays disappear, Retka makes a distressed sound and I finally return my gaze to the wall. I can't see the sliver they're magically chiseling in the wall from my vantage point but wonder whether it will be enough, or if more must die for me to give magic back to the now enemies of these people.

Leyden stands alone, one hand leaning against it, as Retka and Ashun are curled together on the grass beside him. I gently shuffle Mittio to the ground and start towards him.

"Don't," Leyden says, stretching out one hand. Blisters decorate the palm, like what the water did. I halt midstep. "It's done. I simply need a moment."

"I can help," I say, moving towards him.

His head shakes in a stutter. "No, they are mine to attend to."

But I'm in this as much as he is, I'm why they died. "But—"

"Please, Grace. Let me have this." He turns his head to bare his right cheekbone and one blazing blue eye with wetness gathering in the corner.

I leave him be.

We plan to remain on that side of the wall only long enough to complete Eósy funerary rites for Retka and Ashun and then test whether it worked at sunrise. Then, Mittio must cross the wall into Dalner before she weakens without the constant healing Retka gave her.

The Eósy tradition is to return their bodies and spirits to the land, meaning they're burned. Leyden dragged them into a small grove in the forest, not where we slept the night before, but far away from the wall and the animal corpses left there. He placed them side by side, holding each other as if in sleep.

At first, I keep Mittio from seeing her parents' bodies; it feels almost cruel otherwise, not when she won't understand that they won't be waking up, or why they turn to ash. But it seems crueler to hide it from her completely.

I was older than her when Mom died, but grief knows no age. There was a moment, when I was getting ready for the funeral, picking out a dark dress I knew I'd throw away to avoid seeing it again, that I considered not going. I'd said my goodbyes to Mom months earlier, because we didn't know when her body would give out. But each time, it felt unreal, like we were playing a game and soon the plot would change and she'd be better. Even when she stopped being able to respond and spent most of her day asleep, I thought she'd wake up and everything would work out. We'd get our promised happily ever after. And then one day, she lost all function. The hospital accidentally let it slip that Father cut off life support, not knowing he hadn't told me. I'll never forgive him for that, and even thinking of it now makes anger churn in my gut.

So, when I sat in my room the morning of the funeral, I thought about staying right there. Then I could pretend it didn't happen, or just avoid the finality of her story ending. But Father forced me to go. We had a closed casket—the disease took so much from her—but I stared at that box and watched them lower her body into the earth. The one good thing Father ever did for me was demanding I attend, making me finally shut the book I'd written for Mom and me.

Mittio may not remember this moment, but she deserves her closure. She deserves to say goodbye, and for someone to tell her she was there.

Leyden stands at my side and holds out Retka's pendant. Together, we fasten it around Mittio's neck. "Are you ready?" he asks.

"Is there anything we can cover them with? The tent, maybe?"

Leyden studies me and I'm sure he remembers the fights I had with Father about Mom's death, and how it still hurts but could have been much worse. He runs his fingers through Mittio's long locks as she sits on my less-damaged hip.

"I can make something." He sucks in a heavy breath. "It is a magic I rarely use, something from my mother. I'm weak today and I've not been skilled at it even when I'm at my best, but I will try."

And then he sings. It's a haunting melody, and though his voice is thin and awkward, there's power and emotion in it that overcomes any conventional deficiency. As his voice rises in pitch, gleaming threads appear in the sky before us. With each note, they weave together until a brilliant golden length of fabric floats above us. Leyden's voice cuts off and the fabric sinks into his arms. It must be how he's been able to outfit himself given he left Exile with only the clothes on his back.

He flushes as I reach out to touch his creation. The stitching is a little wobbly and uneven, nothing anyone would buy at the store or market, but it feels how I expect magic would, like static electricity mixed with the bloom of potential.

After he drapes the fabric over Retka and Ashun, Mittio and I turn around. Leyden lights the makeshift pyre and we watch as flames slowly engulf it. Unlike the fire he created around the sàchenda, somehow this one seems gentle, more soothing like inside a warm hearth, blanketing their bodies and remaining low to the ground. It's an otherworldly scene, the bright colored flames not high enough to catch the trees and appearing more like an enclosure of energy over their bodies. Mittio looks fascinated by the flickering embers and colors.

I hold her tighter. "Do you say anything at funerals?"

"There are no eulogies, not like your people. We have something like a prayer, a rhyme of power. I've not heard it since my own parents' deaths."

"Would you?"

He closes his eyes and recites, "When death did knock, and life did end, we aid your walk, to fate we send. Though hope did leave, our love remains, and we will grieve, but not with pain. To earth returned, while stars will keep, your life deserved, your soul to sleep."

Silently, we watch Retka and Ashun's final send off until the flames snuff out.

Morning comes quickly. Mittio screamed most of the night for her parents, no longer interested in remaining with strangers and perhaps innately realizing we're removing her from her home. It took all we had to calm her down enough to sleep.

As the sun rises, an exhausted Leyden and I stand at the place where there is a one to two inch opening into Dalner that spans from the earth as far upward as the eye can see. My stomach falls when I realize how small it is, and what it took to create even that. It can't even be qualified as a Gate. *Is it even big enough to let magic through?*

On the other side of the opening, it looks just like a normal landscape, but that we can see *anything* at all might signify our success, and that Retka and Ashun's deaths weren't in vain. Leyden holds a sleeping Mittio and we wait anxiously for something to appear. The decay at our feet tells a story that multiple beasts have attempted to breach the wall over the months. I mentally cross my fingers that something will try again today.

And then, one of the skittering noises from the forest resonates behind us, moving from the trees closer towards our feet. A mouse hops between us, nose twitching, before it zips through the opening, popping out of the tiny opening like something from a cartoon. A dart-snake follows quickly behind, chasing it. Leyden's eyes widen almost comically, and I let out a whoop of excitement. Mittio snuffles against Leyden's shoulders and I repeat the exclamation at a whisper. He nearly beams before schooling his expression into something more staid.

"It's too small a space for us to walk through. I will cleave an opening on the other side, then you step through. Once you touch down in Dalner, you need to explicitly invite us both. Then we'll join you."

I nod in understanding just as Leyden shifts Mittio to his hip and begins scratching a rip into the air. The reality on the other side must be close to the wall as I can still see the dart-snake chasing the mouse in the distance.

I step through, but the trip was short enough it only feels like I stood up too fast, and not like my stomach wants to launch its way out of my throat. Leyden and Mittio stand on the other side of the tear expectantly. But I hesitate.

"Hand me, Mittio. I'm inviting her first."

He shuffles her into my arms, and she whines in her sleep. His eyes shift grimly. "And now, Grace?"

And that's the question. *What now?* Inviting Leyden through a second time makes everything more intentional. Our partnership becomes real; I'm committing myself to him. I know myself, and I know my limitations. It won't take much for me to agree with his goals, not when all I've experienced so far has already taken me halfway there.

I clutch Mittio closer. "Are you still on my side?"

"Always," he says sincerely. I glare at him and he amends, "Since I went into Exile."

If I want Tans to understand why I've brought Leyden, and why my motivations for the wall changed, I need to show that I've thought through the outcomes, and nothing will injure our people. "And you won't hurt the others, or my friends?"

Now he hesitates, his lips thinning. "What if they attack me first?"

I clench my teeth. "Okay, will you promise you won't hurt them unless you need to act in self-defense?"

"What if they attack you, or Mittio, or another one of our allies?"

"That won't happen." But I remember the terror that clawed over Kórol's face, and the frustration in the eyes of Tans' family.

"I must be precise in any promises, or the consequences could be harmful," Leyden says, pulling me from my thoughts.

Mittio grumbles. The gray tint remains on her skin, and I don't know if pulling out the magic is instinctual or she needs Leyden. I pinch my eyes closed. "Can you offer me any assurances?"

"Besides my promise to further your goals? That's a rather large one, you know."

I suck in a groan. "Just come through."

Leyden hoists himself through the opening and lets out a shiver as he plunges to his knees. "Thank you."

I smile weakly. "That's what allies do." Tans will understand, he *must*.

We remain by the wall for a moment longer. Leyden's eyes fall shut as he presses his palms into the earth.

"Shall we head to Tans now?" My tone is a mix of eagerness and dread. I can't even guess what he'll have to say about this plan of mine.

He smooths his fingers over the grass. "Not yet. The wall has put something of a dampener on the land. I cannot pull as much while this close, I believe. I need a bit more time to gather the magic to cleave into Samsen."

I'm less disappointed than I should be. "Should we get a little farther from the wall and set up camp?"

He stands, groaning lightly. "I've a better idea. Would you like to see Bittállí's temple?"

CHAPTER 20

I had no interest in seeing Bittállí's temple, but Leyden was undeterred. All too soon, considering he was supposedly weak near the wall, he cleaved us to the entrance of the Solstice Sanctum.

When I imagined her temple, I imagined something with Grecian architecture erected in marble, with lots of columns carved with a repeating pattern and a high portico, combined with statues inside and painted frescoes on the wall, all depicting her, given her need for attention. Instead, we're greeted by a one-story circular building made of thin white stone stacked on top of each other like piled slate. The roof of the temple is covered in grass, and the only exterior design is a crudely carved dragon on the stone just above the threshold that is repeated on the kerb stones at the base of the stacked slate. Knowing a bit more about Bittállí, and how she felt spurned by one of Kórol's ancestors, I wonder if she got any smug satisfaction about co-opting their symbol for her gain.

Surrounding the building are a landscape of ancient markers, the only evidence that there's something important here as the temple's shape blends into the natural contours of the land. Given all the rolling hills and valleys, someone might never notice that inside this hill holds an architectural surprise.

Though it's early morning, the construction of the temple keeps most of the morning light from following us inside. A stone passage widens into a central chamber with an arched roof made of overlapping rock slabs. More crude carvings and symbols cover the walls. Leyden lights one finger like a match while I place Mittio on the ground of the circular chamber. When she sprints around the circle repeatedly, I block the passage entrance and study the rest of the temple's features.

At the back wall of the chamber is a long stone slab table, where jars of something golden are stacked in a pyramid. Leyden picks one up with his unlit hand and turns it upside down, the liquid viscous.

"Honey?" I ask.

Leyden turns. "Yes, dearest?"

The joke is so reminiscent of Tans, I don't know whether to laugh or burst into tears. Leyden doesn't notice, as he gathers a few jars and settles on the ground next to me. Mittio, either having worn herself out or sensing a sweet treat, clambers into Leyden's lap, grabbing for the honey.

"What do you think of Bittálli's grand sanctuary?" he asks as he hands Mittio an open jar. I may not know much about kids, but I know he'll be cleaning her off later instead of me.

I sit cross legged beside him. Besides the honey jars and the unique architecture, it's otherwise unremarkable. "I expected something bigger with statues of her, maybe some fineries piled up in the corners. And a vat of the blood of her enemies in the center."

He huffs a laugh. "You must remember she was pretending to be a benevolent deity, the embodiment of purity and love. Those beings need worship, not material things."

As if worship isn't material. "She still made them leave her honey," I point out.

"That was more for inconvenience. We don't have bees like you do, more a bee-wasp hybrid. Harvesting their honey is asking to be stung." He shifts Mittio off his lap when she attempts to drink from the jar. "If we return during one of the Solstice's, you'll see its more striking feature and the intricate use of astronomical alignment. It is actually quite extraordinary, although it would have been awful to—*Eat* the delicacy, Mittio, do not wear it."

I smother a grin as Mittio tries to climb up Leyden with sticky fingers and a dripping chin. "You're in charge of finding water for clean-up."

Leyden's eyes twitch. I wonder if he's thinking of the Carn's warded water. "Lovely. If we're lucky, it will rain and we can avoid taking a dip. With her speed and your clumsiness, I would rather not tempt fate near a body of water."

I sit up in excitement. If a single rift means the Eósys with weather magic can send rain, I'm nearer to my goal of fixing things than I thought. "The rain is back?"

A puzzled expression crosses his face. "What do you mean 'the rain is back?' The rain has never left."

"From the walls," I explain, but his expression remains blank. "Weather comes from the Eósy, they make storms and send them into Dalner. With the walls up, there's been no rain."

"That is absurd," Leyden says dismissively. I don't know why, but the immediate censure feels like a slap to the face. "The Eósy do not control the weather. Yes, some have weather magic, but the storms themselves come from the magic in the land."

"But then...how do you explain the lack of rain for the past six months?"

He shrugs. "A dry year? With the magic dormant, Dalner probably had few storms regardless, but even then, they'd most likely appear during a wet season. Perhaps there's limited rain around Ilsen, but it would shock me that the entire country has had no rain in six months."

I suppose it makes sense. Dalner's wet season might be the late fall, the only times I've seen rain.

Leyden eyes me critically. "What are they teaching you in Dalner?"

I cross my arms around my waist defensively. "When *your* history books are lost or edited because of a despot, I'll make sure to be just as snide to you about *your* lack of knowledge."

His expression softens. "I meant no offense. The claim that the Eósy control the weather is propaganda from Bittállí's supporters on this side of the wall, no doubt, perhaps combined with a splash of truth given her most devoted supporter has weather magic. If you'd like, I can look at your syllabus and tell you if there are any other glaring problems."

Mittio drops her jar and looks ready to sprint again. As she makes the first circle, her speed splashes the honey clinging to her skin and clothes onto us like a sticky rain.

"Maybe." I wipe the honey splatters from my cheeks. "But right now, I wish you did control the rain. I'll be dealing with dried honey for days."

We clean ourselves and Mittio in a nearby stream, much like the little puddles I saw throughout the hills when I first arrived in Dalner. Neither of us almost drowned, making the endeavor a success.

That evening finds me lounging outside the temple watching Leyden show Mittio how to uncover the magic underneath us. It is fully nonverbal as the two sit on the grass and Leyden presses Mittio's little fingers into the earth.

"You've got it," he says tenderly as her skin transforms back to the sienna color of her mother. She smiles and starts vibrating.

Before she can sprint off, I heave myself to their side and slip Sunflower's rope around her waist. She pouts up at me.

"I'm sorry, Mittio. But I can't have you running away. Even if there are few predators around here, it's still dangerous. It would be one thing if I could catch you, but you're too fast."

Her doe eyes blink guilelessly and then she zips away, moving so quickly that I get dragged forward an inch or two with an *umph*. Leyden takes the rope from me, smirking.

"That's cheating," he says, gesturing to Mittio's makeshift waist leash. "Like those women at the mall that bothered you."

This is the second time the reminder that he's been in my head doesn't make me flinch or want to hit him. Instead, it's almost nice to have someone here who knows Earth like I do. He'd probably understand the term 'sugar daddy,' at least.

"I've learned the error of my ways. A few days as a caregiver and I take back everything I thought about those moms." I elbow him in the hip. "Besides, reading her mind is cheating too."

"It is better than letting her flounder without her parents and unable to understand how to pull in the magic, Grace."

"I didn't say reading her mind was bad." And wow, that was painful to admit aloud, but I've committed myself to this path. I take a deep breath and look Leyden in the eye. "What's the plan?"

"I suppose we let her run until she tires out, then feed her honey, though I'm told sugar isn't good for—"

I eek out a laugh. "No, the plan for us, and Mittio, and—and the wall. What our next step is."

Leyden stares out at the distance, his neon blue eyes fading back to black. "What a question. For five hundred years, I've had a single goal. Remove Bittállí and remove the wall. I achieved part of it, but now…" He glances at me. "There are hundreds of Mittios across the wall."

"I know." Hundreds of innocents. "And they need magic."

He wets his lips. "Yes."

"And the Sàrkany need magic."

"Yes," he breathes.

I can't quite take the leap he wants. Not yet. "But the wall went up for a reason. There were Dark and Light Eósy for a reason."

"Propaganda, Grace," he says, the muscles in his jaw tensing. "There are good and bad humans, good and bad Sàrkany." He closes his eyes. "The wall went up because of power and fear. Bittállí's father intended her marriage to secure his control over the Raddare land. The Raddare wife was killed because of his plan, and in his grief, the Lord of Raddare sought to wall off magic, fearing the mental manipulation that led to her death. He was shortsighted and too hasty, never realizing he'd doomed us all."

"And Bittállí?"

"A woman who built a wall of ice around her soul and thought of nothing but revenge against the Raddares who broke her spirit *and* her heart."

"I get that, Leyden. And you certainly haven't been subtle in pushing me towards the goal you want." I huff as I cross my arms around my waist. "So much for indirect interference."

"That only matters when we're walled off from—"

"But it's a big ask. You go from mentally abusing me and my friends to expecting us to willingly let you run amok in Dalner. There must be a middle ground. We can't just remove the wall and expect everything to work out, not when you all have godlike abilities and we don't."

"You need the wall down too, Grace."

I press my palms against my eyes until spots dance behind the closed lids. "I only need the rifts. I need it back the way it was."

"Grace-"

"And then I see Mittio. If I could invite each Eósy like her, I would." I watch our toddler guest continue running back and forth, giggling to herself.

"That wouldn't work," he says. "It must be all or nothing."

"I know. But for every innocent that needs the wall down like Mittio, there will be another that will rejoice at getting to subjugate the Sàrkany. You're immortal, and full of powers that I can't even comprehend. What's to say we don't tear down the wall and someone does exactly what you and Bittállí did to our minds?"

He growls in aggravation. "What's to say a bandit doesn't attack you? What's to say a serial killer doesn't come across you? Those risks exist with or without magic."

"I could avoid a bandit by staying in my home. I can't avoid a mind reader."

His black eyes are bright with intensity as he speaks. "There's nothing more I can say, Grace. We need it down; your people would benefit from it down."

"We need a middle ground."

"There isn't one," he says mulishly.

We both watch Mittio, who now sits in the grass, playing with who knows what. There must be a compromise; the world isn't that binary. Even Leyden must understand that he can't simply retread that same ground. Except—

"Once I release you from your promise, tell you that my goals are met or we open enough rifts to help the Sàrkany, and we go our separate ways—will you attempt to bring down the walls again?"

His mouth opens but no words come.

I sit in front of him, blocking his view of anything from me, and stare into those beacon-like eyes. "Leyden. Will you try again?"

"Yes," he hisses. He shoves me aside and stands, moving closer to Mittio. "You're right, my initial reasons for deposing Bittállí weren't wholly altruistic. She had her revenge plans, and I had mine. I wanted her gone, and I wanted the walls down to get *my* magic back and no longer feel as though simply living hurt, damn the rest of my race." He turns back to me. "Half of those at the wall with me were the same. They *hated* me. Hated what I did in Bittállí's service, hated what I didn't. With her death, I made them remember they were in pain, and creatures in pain will do the impossible to avoid it. But the other half—they were like Retka and Ashun. They followed me because there was someone else in their lives that needed help, and they were willing to sacrifice their souls for the hope of it." He gives me a rueful smile as something shifts behind his eyes. "I'm not that good, and my motives weren't initially benevolent, but even I know it's the right thing to do. So, yes. I'll keep trying without you."

The conversation ends without resolution, as Mittio, bored with playing, returns to us demanding a meal. We end the evening inside Bittállí's temple eating the remains of what I packed for my solo trip to the Wilds and Bittállí's honey.

"We can't put this off any longer," he says quietly when Mittio naps in his lap. "Are you on my side?"

My eyes fall shut at the question I posed to him, one he could answer immediately but I can't. "There's a difference between being on your side and actively agreeing to hold the pickaxe you'll use to attack the wall."

He runs his long fingers through Mittio's hair. "Wouldn't it be better if you were involved? Then you could monitor me."

At the expense of causing Tans to go bald. "What if I acted as a mediator?" He looks skeptical, but I don't let him respond. "I'll go with you to the Council, and you can explain about the magic and the information they're missing and come up with the middle ground."

"That would go well. Would I give my speech from the gallows, or would they allow me the pretense of freedom first?"

I wince. "Dalner doesn't have gallows."

"Well, then let's head there now."

I drag my pack to me and rummage through it, looking for excess paper. He peers over my shoulder where I attempt to keep my purloined books hidden.

"Did you bring *books* with you?" He scoffs. "I suppose I should commend your continued dedication to prove that 'likes books' is a personality trait, but perhaps something more practical would have been better? I wouldn't have minded a few more dinner options aside from that green goo."

The tension dissipates and I grab hold of the conversational lifeline, one that isn't fully focused on Leyden's immediate death and whether Kórol would consider me a traitor to the Kingdom. I show him the children's history book to sate his curiosity. "A new acquisition. And at least I packed something. I haven't noticed you foraging for our meals."

He narrows his eyes. "Don't think I wouldn't."

"Maybe another dart-snake will make it through the rift." I bare my teeth in a facsimile of a smile. "I can teach you how to leach out the poison before we eat it."

His skin turns as green as Sáven's creation, but still, he tilts his chin. "Sounds delightful." He gestures to the parchment and Mittio in his lap. "Though I'm quite preoccupied now."

I don't remind him that sunset is several hours away, instead handing him the paper and lifting Mittio into my lap. "Write out everything you've told me about the wall's construction and the magic and how it killed the original Sàrkany."

"Why?"

"We don't know enough. It's like you said, the wall kept out more than magic. The Sàrkany has been working off flawed information. Once we know the full picture of the wall and what happened, we can brainstorm how to bring it down. And, in the meantime, we'll approach the Council with the information and come up with a compromise."

He rolls his eyes. "I told you, there's no middle ground. I might as well promise to let them kill me."

A thunderous thought rumbles through my brain, and I nearly kick *myself* at what we've forgotten. "That's the answer!"

"Yes, my death would solve some of your problems," he says, sounding hurt.

"No, a promise. Sometimes I forget we're in a fantasy world with completely impractical things, like a species whose weakness is an inability to lie." *And the horrifying prospect of magical soulmates.* But I smother a wince at the reminder. "You could all make a promise, like a treaty."

"A one-sided promise."

"To protect the weaker side from powerful immortals."

"Fair point," he says in a clipped tone.

"And the Sàrkany could promise something too, if it helped your people agree," I say, liking the idea even more. It gives me a reason to get approval from Kórol and Tans, so they don't assume I'm betraying them when the walls disappear. "It would just be based on trust rather than magic."

He frowns. "It would have to be an incredibly precise promise."

I gesture to the paper. "Lucky you, you've got some time to plan for it." And me to plan how I explain it to Tans and Kórol without joining Leyden in Ilsen's version of a prison.

Leyden grunts and stares down at the paper while I flip the history book open and look over the stories I've yet to hear. The original owner annotated the margins, but unlike the last time I read notes from an unknown author in Dalner, these jottings ask questions of the subject instead of complaining. I run my fingers over the delicate signature on the first page, pronouncing that this book belongs to F. Caern. The penmanship is strong, almost pretty and easier to read than the book itself; something about them seems familiar. Perhaps that's why I don't need to murmur the words aloud like I did with other books since Leyden took away my ability to understand the language.

Leyden taps the pen nip against his bottom lip, keeping his eyes down. "How do you intend on bringing the walls down? Now that you know what must be done to complete it."

"I—I don't know yet. Like you said, mass sacrifice isn't feasible."

"How benevolent of you," he says under his breath.

I ignore him as I replace the book in my pack. "But that's why you're writing everything we know. If we can discover how they went up, we can discover how they come down. Nothing is *that* permanent."

Leyden huffs. "Pender might know, but he will be as difficult to convince as any in Ilsen. Worse, even."

Now it's my turn to frown. "Your brother?" After he nods, I ask, "You think he'd be against it?"

His expression looks disturbed, as if half his face wants to display one expression and the rest another. "He'd rather cause trouble for the world than do anything *I* suggest."

"I get the emotional component with Bittálli, but he must want to keep his people alive. Himself, if nothing else. Spite can't be worth that much."

He doesn't answer, instead pinning me with his gaze and roaming it over my face. "Why did you leap into the Gate with me?"

"For my family," I say immediately, though my eyes narrow at his evasiveness.

"You wanted to prove something to them. Just as I wanted to prove something too."

Then I understand. "He's part of your not-initially-benevolent motive and revenge plan?"

He cocks his head. "And might be as likely to kill me as your King, given what I've done. If he deigns to do so himself, instead of demanding one of bloodlines allegiant to him do so in his stead."

Mittio shuffles in my lap. She'll want to run off her excess energy one more time before dinner and sleep. "We'll take it slow. Baby steps. First Kórol, then your brother."

He grunts as he turns back to the parchment. "If those steps are anything like hers, I'm dead already." He lifts his head and smirks. "Shall we say one chapter at a time instead?"

"Now, whose personality can be boiled down to 'likes books'?"

He laughs but doesn't deny it.

We don't take shifts that night. Instead, Leyden drapes himself over the passageway hoping to keep Mittio in place. It's her attempts in racing that wakes us in the morning, as she hops on Leyden's form with a giggle, spilling the handful of charcoal smudged pages resting on his stomach. He gently snags her leg and corrals her back in the chamber.

"Figured out world peace yet?" I ask as I gather up the pages. The letters are slanted and squeezed together. I squint to read some of his notes.

The Lord Caern disappeared shortly after his son, though likely he died in the War and wasn't recovered. Caern heir thought to have died too because—

Leyden snatches the pages back from me, shuffling them into some semblance of order. "The history is simply too dense. My time would be better spent reviewing what the Sàrkany know and filling in the gaps, rather attempting to write every single thing down. It is two thousand years of history," he whines.

Shaking my head, I dig through my bag for more paper and my notes from my studies. "This is what they know," I say, handing over the bundle. "I made notes on everything Fíl—the historian has on the wall, the Separation, and the immediate aftermath."

Leyden skims through my sparser notes. "This is everything? Surely, you're teasing me and you failed to summarize it all. This is...almost nothing."

I shrug. "There are no books left. Most of the records were destroyed in the fire around the time of Raddare the Eleventh." Fíl helped me read the only relevant pieces when I started my research on the wall.

"Then where did this, albeit incredibly limited, history come from? I can't imagine a single Eósy with this knowledge remains living on that side of the wall, given they promised to limit their magic use. They'd all have died centuries ago."

I shrug again. "Oral tradition."

"Some of this is oddly specific though," he says skeptically. "Something only the heirs would have been privy to. I can't imagine one of the Raddare royal family caring enough to maintain the knowledge. They were more considered... what's the word from your world?" He casts his gaze to the sky. "Himbo, I believe."

A laugh stutters from me. "They are not."

"It isn't an insult. Kind, charming, empty-headed. Beautiful, but not all that smart, making outrageous strategy decisions, trusting Bittállí. Derul, Alac, even your Kórol."

My smile fades. "Don't talk about Kórol."

"You cannot tell me he's made sound decisions lately," he chides. "You feared for war before coming out here."

"Because you—" I release a long breath. "He's not a himbo."

His brows furrow but he doesn't respond, instead catching Mittio on one of her spins around the temple. "Perhaps my opinion of him is wrong," he says finally. "I can correct it right before he inevitably kills me. Speaking of, are we on to Ilsen and my probable death?"

"Not yet," I say, gathering our things to avoid looking him in the eye. "First, Samsen, like we originally planned. Tans and his family can be our practice for the Council."

"They can kill me in Samsen just as well as Ilsen, you know," he mutters loud enough for me to hear.

"They wouldn't kill you, just maim you."

He huffs. "Gracel the inciter, the provoker, instigating a *negotiated* revolution. Though that doesn't have as strong a ring to it."

I roll my eyes without comment as Mittio starts vibrating in place, eager to dash off her morning energy. "Maybe we can walk there," I suggest, wrapping her makeshift leash around her waist and letting her start down the pathway out of the temple.

Leyden's brows raise. "Can your hip manage the walk? You appeared pained the last few days in Dànna."

Surprise lines my features as I stare him. But he doesn't act like he's completely upended my world view by showing common courtesy. "I'll be fine," I finally say.

"Very well. Far be it from me to deny your whims, especially when they keep all my limbs in place for longer."

I elbow him as I leave the chamber, and his weak laugh follows me outside.

CHAPTER 21

"Of course, the Caern heir died. He'd die in the Wilds, if he'd deign to stay there," Leyden says, grimacing.

We're almost to Samsen and Leyden and I are attempting to pass the time. Both of us seem to want a distraction, but for wildly different reasons. The meadow stretches out before us, the rolling hills and shallow valleys bathed in the soft hues of the setting sun. A gentle breeze rustles the grass, carrying the scent of petrichor. I can't help but compare it to the last time I wandered through the landscape, unaware of how my life would change for the better.

I give Leyden a sideways glance, the being responsible for all that's happened to me, the good and bad. "It's possible the heir could be around. Maybe he found somewhere else to live. With the Raddares, perhaps."

I remember Carn's memories and the flashes of a boy-turned-man that visited the tower, and the abandoned room full of cherished items. The room reminded me of the decor in Ilsen. The child would have loved the warmth of the grand halls and the rustic elegance of the library.

"Then he is most certainly dead. Any of the ruling family would have slaughtered him to avoid another uprising. If he'd managed to successfully hide among the common folk and under the Raddares' promises," Leyden says, his facial expression implying he believes that to be an impossibility, "then he'd die painfully from magical drain centuries ago."

"No need to be morbid," I say lightly, looking at Mittio snuggled in his arms.

"It was *your* idea to only speak in Sàrkany," he says, somewhat snide.

Through the side of my mouth, and in quiet English, I say, "Because we don't want to further traumatize her." I smile down at Mittio, only slightly forced.

"No, the Wilds were his only choice, if some other enterprising family did not kill him before the War and his claimed disappearance is a skillful coverup," Leyden continues, barely acknowledging I'd spoken. "If he was anything like the other heirs, he was an entitled little prince who never had to work a day in his life. He'd not allow a hair out of place, much less learn to survive on his own. Appearances are all that would matter, and something would have eaten him because he was distracted by his stained tunic."

"Glass houses," I say, eyeing his artfully tousled short hair. The tunic had seen better days, but that wasn't by choice.

"I remained beautiful *while* inciting a coup, thank you. No one can say I didn't put in the effort."

"And so successfully too," I say before I can swallow the retort. "I'd call you a…" I search for the word in Sàrkany, but none come to me. "A himbo," I finally say, combining the two languages again. "Except you're missing the 'nice' part of the descriptor."

He smiles smugly and whispers into Mittio's ears in Sàrkany and loud enough that even the townspeople of Samsen could hear. "Did you hear that? She thinks I'm beautiful."

"And ignorant," I mutter.

"Star-crossed lovers from two different worlds. Drawn together by fate, unable to be separated. With their love forbidden, one world must bend."

I wrap my arms around my stomach with a huff. "How about I kick you, then we'll see who is bending?"

"I deliver a tender homage to our relationship, and you threaten me? Think of the child, Grace," he says, pressing her head against his chest as she giggles.

"No, you're delivering a delusion."

"Or a prophecy," he says slyly.

I blanch. *To all the Fates that the Sàrkany pray to, please don't let this be a world of soulmates* and *prophecies.* I cough to clear the thought and lean down to look Mittio in her dark eyes. "Just remember: don't 'bend' for some man."

"Burn the patriarchy," Leyden says, smirking.

"Fight, fight the patriarchy. But I guess burning it works, too."

"Burn burn burn!" The voice that squeals that out stops Leyden and my teasing, as Mittio says her first words in the nearly two weeks we've known her.

"Little fire starter, are you?" Leyden says, laughing, his entire face brightening.

"Burn," she repeats gleefully.

"Let me not disappoint my lady," he says as he hands her to me. He scans the meadow. Shadows have lengthened as the day went on, the valleys hiding their depths. Apparently satisfied with his inspection, he wiggles his fingers like a tv magician. I slip Mittio onto my hip and plant my feet to watch whatever spectacle he intends to put on. The already quiet landscape seems to hold its breath in anticipation of the vast amounts of magic it hasn't seen in centuries.

Leyden's wiggling movements spin into finger shapes that would put any shadow puppet performer to shame. Fire arcs and rises from the tips like a flaming water dance you'd see from a choreographed fountain. Only Mittio's giggling exclamations and Leyden's soft huffs break the quiet surrounding us.

Until a figure emerges from the horizon and their stuttering breath fills the space. Leyden's fire dance extinguishes as if he plunged his fingers in water and the three of us turn towards the strange newcomer.

A man stands only two valleys away from us, his long dark hair blending into the shadows, half-hiding him. He shuffles on his feet, the setting sun illuminating a weathered face and wary eyes.

Leyden tenses. "Stand behind me," he orders quietly. "I will handle this."

My hand snags his shirtsleeve before he can do more than lean forward, bustling Mittio between us. "Handle it how?"

He turns back to look at me flatly. "I have no plans to kill him, Grace. Simply...help him forget what he's seen. I am somewhat of an infamous figure nowadays."

"No one here knows who you are," I start.

He scowls. "And yet, they are certainly aware there is no magic here. Do you truly want that known before we meet with your boy and his King? Would you rather I be executed before I can even propose your ridiculous 'partnership' plan?"

"You will *not* be executed." I press Mittio into his arms, who starts wriggling to escape. "And you're not mind-manipulating people anymore, remember?"

"I only promised to leave your mind alone, dearest," he says with a sharklike smile. "I also promised to help you and keeping you from being attacked by a probably bandit is certainly part of that promise."

"You don't know he's a bandit. He just looks like a traveler, not—" Not like the men who attacked me, after Leyden technically led me to them.

His eyes widen as he must realize the trail my thoughts went, and he coughs nervously. "Looks can be deceiving."

"Yes, you look like prince charming when you're really an irritating toad."

"She's calling me beautiful again, Mittio," Leyden tells her, though he sounds less confident now that I've reminded him of the many, many reasons I have to be annoyed with him.

I slash my hand through the air. "Stop distracting me and changing the subject."

Our whispered conversation let the man get closer. The wariness in his expression bled into something more like fear. Mindful of the risks to his mind and Leyden's life, I jump in front of Leyden, causing the stranger to flinch. I smile as pleasantly as I can and hold up my hands, again hoping it remains the universal symbol for 'we're no trouble, please don't murder us or sic the wardens on me.'

"Hello," I say, tone friendly. "Lovely evening we're having."

Leyden groans behind me. Spinning around, I shush him.

The man sucks in a sharp breath as I turn back to him. "That...that was magic." His gaze flickers between me and Leyden, his eyes stopping on Mittio.

"It was, but—"

A flicker of interest bursts over his face. "Are you bringing it back?"

A weary sigh escapes me, the complexity of our goals and how we can accomplish too difficult to give a simple answer.

"We plan to try," Leyden says, his expression resolute but his eyes flashing blue. I elbow him in the side.

"You're an Eósy," the man says, almost stuttering. "That means—"

"It means I'm not lying when I say that."

"And he won't hurt anyone," I finish. "Meaning there's no need to be...alarmed."

The man studies Leyden's face searchingly. Various expressions flicker over it before something solidifies over his face. "I need to tell—" he cuts himself off as he slowly slinks backward from us.

"Wait!" I jolt forward, trying to grasp him, but he slips into a valley and my hand misses, grasping empty air. He spins and runs, surprisingly spry.

When I turn back to Leyden, he's glaring. "Now, may I correct this, Grace?"

I sigh as no good options present themselves. "No. We couldn't keep you hidden forever. This is just a...complication."

Leyden bends to rest his cheek against Mittio's head, his gaze still fixed on the man's diminishing figure. "This is a mistake."

"We'll deal with it. Let's keep going."

Leyden huffs. "At your command."

The remaining walk passes quickly in silence. The sun dips below the horizon, casting long shadows behind us. With each step, my feeling of unease grows, a lingering sense that I've put us on a path that will end in ruin. Hopefully not mine, not with Tans in my corner, but likely Leyden's. Possibly Mittio's, if fear of the Eósy's turns irrational against their entire ethnic group.

Samsen finally rises in front of us, the small wooden and stucco houses lined in circular rows. The wind from earlier today has vanished, leaving the flags slumped against the roofs. The unease in my gut morphs into nostalgia, though I'm unsure which encounter with the town could truly be said to be 'better.' At least Mara could never do whatever she threatened that involved swimming.

With night nearing, candlelight quivers in the windows. A distant hum of activity reaches our ears, louder than my last two visits. As we round the main lane, the hum roars into a cacophony. A crowd had gathered, their murmurs escalating into an agitated buzz. Leyden crushes Mittio closer to him as we both see the man from before in the center of the horde. Together, we come to the same realization: we're the focus of the unrest.

"Looks like you *are* inciting something," says Leyden.

I restrain myself from slugging him and instead crane my neck for a familiar face or at least a recognizable landmark that will take us to Tans' house and away from the potentially dangerous situation. The crowd's energy sharpens as we walk towards them. Shouts and accusations flow through the air, though the jeers blend into a mob of sound and I can't make out what they're yelling. But the wild looks on the citizen's faces tell me all I need to know.

"Go that way," Leyden shouts over the din, gesturing to another street to the side of the crowd. He grabs my hand with his free one and starts dragging us through them. We only get a few steps until—

"Stop!" A voice overcomes the ruckus, sounding somewhat familiar. The crowd parts to let Breg emerge, a few of his wardens behind him scowling. When he approaches, his piercing gaze bores into Leyden, flowing to Mittio, and then down to Leyden and my conjoined hands. "Grace," he calls out, his tone measured. "Who's your friend?"

I shake off Leyden's grip as relief settles over my roiling nerves. "Breg! I'm so glad to see you. Can you get us out of here? I need to speak with Tans."

"Tans has left for Ilsen," he says gruffly, barely audible over the din. "But I will take you where you must go." With a sharp gesture, his men fan out, two holding their bows with notched arrows ready to launch and the others holding rudimentary-looking handcuffs.

This was a mistake, Leyden had said. *Without Tans, what hope do I have?* I cringe away from the wardens, closer to Leyden. "We've done nothing wrong," I say, lifting my chin. At least, not recently.

Leyden huffs behind me as he offers Mittio's tiny wrists up to a guard. "He's met you once, dearest. Why would he give you the benefit of the doubt?"

Breg's eyebrows raise at the endearment. "We'll sort this out, but we must do this the right way."

One warden pulls Mittio from Leyden because the handcuffs won't fit. She screeches and reaching back for him, her body vibrating. In another second, she might break free.

"This is the right way?" I snap, taking her from the warden.

Breg rubs the back of his neck. "You hold the child, and you may both remain uncuffed. But your friend must be restrained."

"Fine." My answer comes through clenched teeth as I grip Mittio tighter. Breg places a hand on my shoulder and directs us through the crowd, the two armed wardens standing shoulder to shoulder with Leyden.

"Look at that. She didn't even disagree that we're friends," he tells them as we edge through the crowd.

When we break free on the other side of the mob, the shouts and murmurs congeal into a single repeated word: "Gracel, Gracel, Gracel."

Leyden bursts out a laugh that makes the two wardens clench their bows with white knuckle hands.

"Shut up, Leyden," I say, shaking my head.

I enter Tans' home the same way I did several weeks earlier: without a welcome. But I doubt the outcome will be a childish joke this time. I crane my neck looking for Mara or Tans' parents, but the room appears empty. The benches are more organized and a paper sign has been tacked to the wall behind the podium, "TRIAL" written in large letters. I cling to Mittio, and she makes an unhappy sound.

Breg leads us towards a door in the back of the room, not one I'd noticed the last time. The stairwell leading up to the residential floors is empty, telling me they're taking us somewhere else. Stomping sounds rattle the ceiling above us and Breg hisses through his teeth. He holds up a hand and stops us in the middle of the chamber. But instead of anyone appearing from the stairwell, a burst of red barrels into me from the side. I spin sideways to protect Mittio from the unknown threat. The blur turns into Sáven, who squeezes the two of us tight.

"Glad you're alright," he murmurs into my ear. He releases me, his gaze tripping over my face, likely noticing the faded bruises on my cheeks from Carn's assault and the thin scratch from Ashun's hit. He offers a wincing smile before focusing on Mittio. "Got yourself some new friends?" he asks, ruffling Mittio's hair. Curiously, she smiles at him and reaches for his hair. "Wild, right? Never was good at braiding." He runs a finger down her cheek. "Maybe I'll cut it short like yours."

"You'll lose the desirable farm boy look if you do," Leyden says from behind us. A forgotten cover of one of the 70s novels I found in the bargain bin right before falling into Dalner flashes through my head. It was called The Farmers' Desire. I blanch. If Sáven were shirtless, he could act as a body double for Desire's, the main character, lover. Leyden's smirk meets my eyes when we turn towards him, as if he knows what I'm thinking. He might not be reading my mind anymore, but he had several years of memories to flip through. And apparently embarrass me with.

Sáven flicks his gaze over Leyden, sharp and like the predator he once was. Leyden turns his gaze from me and puffs out his chest, a smug expression on his face. Even with the honey and dirt-stained tunic and dust coating his arms and neck, his skin is still luminous with an otherworldly spark. And, irritatingly, the handcuffs haven't dulled his charm, or overcome his looks. The magic of Dalner really does suit him.

"And you are?" Sáv asks.

My shoulders slump at what will be the first of many uncomfortable conversations today. "Sáven, this is Leyden. He's...the Voice."

Sáven's brows raise. "The Voice. You mean, the—"

"Her long-time guide and partner," Leyden says, flashing shining teeth.

"Not partners," I correct. "Just—"

"We most certainly are partners," Leyden says. He sounds affronted, but there's a gleam in his eye that rings false. "We even have a child together."

"No, we don't. Stop spinning words." I turn to Sáv. "It was an accident. I needed his help. And he helped." My voice turns desperate. "We're doing what I told Tans I'd do. I think we can make it work."

Sáv's eyes fall shut, and he heaves a breath.

My heart stutters at losing my best ally here, now that Tans is gone. "Sáven?"

"Imagining punching him in the mouth." He opens his eyes and smiles at me. "Needed a second to beat back the urge."

Leyden laughs, making the wardens flinch again. "From what I know of you," he says, raising his brows with intent, reminding us exactly how he knows Sáven. "You'd not hit an unarmed man."

"You're not unarmed," I say thoughtlessly. The warden closest to Leyden squeaks.

The thumps above us move closer to the stairwell. Sáven winces and offers us both an apologetic frown. "You're right. I wouldn't, but no promises on anyone else here."

The stomps get louder as two booted feet come into view, followed by a long skirt. Breg moves closer to Leyden and crosses his arms, as if protecting him from an attack. Leyden peers around him, eyes gleaming but still black. At least everyone's minds are free from his influence and meddling so far.

The skirt turns into the lithe form of Mara. She huffs when she sees Breg and his guarding of Leyden before planting herself by the opposite wall. She glares at Leyden, then me, and finally giving a small grin to Mittio. Mittio waves back. Zorin follows Mara out of the stairwell. He waves before rearranging his face to a comically severe expression and standing beside Mara.

Mara's dark eyes narrow at me. "Hello, Grace. You've been busy. Is bràuntaklys shorter when the partner is Eósy?"

Sáven chokes beside me, his hand faltering on my back. I stretch my neck to stare at him, raising my brows in question. His face reddens to match his hair, and he shakes his head.

"It means pregnant," Leyden helpfully translates in English.

The wardens all shiver at the foreign words. One raises his bow to point at Leyden.

I tear towards Leyden, handing Mittio to Sáv. She goes willingly and traps a sizeable chunk of his hair in her tiny fist. I can just hear Zorin whimper behind me as I try to get between Leyden and the possibly trigger-happy warden. "Don't. It wasn't magic, or anything bad. He was speaking in my language."

"That doesn't make it better," Breg says.

"Protecting your newest beloved, Grace?" Mara asks, fists clenched at her side.

"No, protecting you," I snap back.

"There're more of us than him," says the warden who isn't pointing a weapon in my face.

"She didn't deny I'm her beloved," Leyden adds helpfully.

"I noticed," says Mara, sniffing.

"It's not the time, Leyden," I growl. I flex my fingers and inhale deeply, attempting to calm myself and appear more competent than I feel. "We opened a part of the wall." A miniscule part, but a part, nonetheless. "There's some magic here now."

"We know," Sáv says.

Mara straightens and turns to Zorin, whispering something. Zorin steps away from her and shakes his head. "Apologies, Miss

Mara. With my Lord Commander gone, and Lady Grace as his proxy, I answer to her before you."

Hope blooms through me, and not only because I may have yet another ally in Tans' stead. "Was the magic enough to mean something here?"

"I don't see why that matters," Mara says.

"There was a...spark," says Breg, frowning at her. "We all felt it."

"Tans healed enough to ride. And burned one of his sheets," Sáven says.

"Sáv went beasty for a minute and Mara scorched the wall," adds Zorin, like he's sharing a secret.

I'm not sure why, but I turn to Leyden to share a pleased smile. He nods at me, his lips turned up in the corners. Satisfied, I direct my attention back to the tense room. "Is it still working?"

"When my wardens are near the wall, magic still seems to work. But after the spark, no one in town has recreated their gifts," Breg says.

"You did it," Sáven says. It isn't a question, but I still nod. He gestures to Leyden. "And you brought *him* back with you?"

"We need him. He knows what to do to tear down the wall, I mean the rifts." I stumble over the slip, but no one seems to catch it. "We're...accidental allies."

"Turned partners," says Leyden.

"Platonic partners," I add firmly. "For this endeavor only."

Leyden shrugs. "We'll see."

Sáven nods thoughtfully. "I see it now."

"And the little miss?" Mara eases her tone to something warmer while looking at Mittio.

"Her parents helped in creating the opening. They were lost to us," Leyden says. His expression appears impassive, but after having no choice but to stare at his face for several weeks straight, I see the cracks in it. He blinks and the sadness vanishes as if it was never there. "Now, might you uncuff me? I could do it myself, but I fear you'd attempt to imprison me in something stronger and I am in no mood to break out of another prison."

"Pris—" Zorin says faintly, clutching his weapon close.

"We can't uncuff you," Breg says, though not unapologetically. "You breached the peace. Among...other things." *Like attempting to take over the world*, I think. "You'll both need to wait overnight—"

Sáv's voice drowns out my shocked exclamation. "Breg, you can't mean it."

Zorin marches forward. "Sir, does she not have immunity?"

Breg shrugs. "That is up to the citizens."

"What did I do?" I ask, frowning.

Mara raises a brow. "Besides bringing a fugitive into the country?" *So much for Mara 'thanking' Leyden for taking down the Great Matron.*

"And brought back magic." Petulance colors my tone as I cross my arms around my waist.

"That the outcome may be worthy doesn't mean the actions to obtain it are worthwhile," says Leyden slyly. "Isn't that right, Grace?"

Without thinking, I elbow him in the stomach. He grunts faintly as the warden, still aiming an arrow at us, falters. After a breath, he drops his bow to the side.

"We have a citizens' review set for tomorrow. They will decide whether to charge you," Breg explains. "If they find enough evidence merits a trial, it will be set before our judge that afternoon."

"That's me," Mara says with a sinister smile.

"Mara," both Sáven and Breg say, with equal disappointment.

She sniffs and lifts her chin. "Father may find himself unavailable tomorrow."

"I'll see that he won't be," says Breg. "Unless you and I need to speak further first."

Mara pouts before the smile slides back onto her full lips. "We could always discuss a plea deal over a pleasant swim. What do you say, Gracie?"

I swallow a gulp. I'm not sure what would be worse.

CHAPTER 22

E ven after explaining my plan to the group, Breg and Mara still want to arrest us. Breg, at least, looked apologetic about it and appeared interested in the proposal, whereas Mara seemed convinced I'm cheating on Tans. That I've teamed up with a criminal doesn't seem to bother her.

Breg and the wardens take us through the mystery door, which opens into a stairwell down to the cellar-turned-jail. Multiple dimly lit corridors were dug out of the earth and covered in stone. After a short walk away from the stairwell, we're taken to a hallway with five small cells. Breg lets his wardens direct Leyden into the first cell. The one who attempted to shoot him earlier holds keys that clink loudly in the silence.

Leyden lets them place him in the cell, uncuff him, and lock the door before he smiles wide. "You realize I could escape? Or better, convince you to let me go?"

"We'd never do that," the warden says, shakily.

"Not willingly, no."

I heave a heavy sigh. "Leyden."

The smile turns more teasing. "Of course, dearest. One chapter at a time."

Sáv and Zorin followed me down there, the former still holding Mittio.

"Got a bed for you upstairs, you know," Sáv reminds me.

"I know." There was a loud argument upstairs about it after we explained our reason for coming to Samsen, about how fair it would be and whether I 'deserved' it. In the end, I agreed because

I *did* team up with and bring a fugitive into the country. One who got people killed, including people known and loved by people in this city. I deserve whatever censure they have for me. "Will you be alright with Mittio?"

We'd decided if she was willing to stay upstairs and sleep in a proper bed, she should. I'd already warned them all of her speed. Sáv shifts her onto my other hip. "We will be. Mara's good with kids too." He laughs at the expression that must be on my face. "I know, but it's true. She and Breg wanted one for a while. Mara babysits for practice."

"If you're sure."

He nods, and the second warden directs me inside the cell next to Leyden. After closing the heavy iron door behind him, the group leaves. A metallic clang of heavy chains echo through the chamber with each step they take, the sounds getting fainter and farther away.

The air in the cells is stifling, with no windows and the weight of a trial settling on me light a lead weight. The straw strewn across the cell floors emits a faint, stale odor, intermingling with the scent of cold stone A single flickering torch barely illuminates the narrow corridor, casting long, eerie shadows that dance across the uneven stone floor. Muffled thumps vibrate above us until they, too, vanish. Now, we're completely alone.

Leyden starfishes on the hard stone, his hands and feet touching each wall of the cell, with his head right beside the bars separating us. A whiff of decay spirals towards me from the dust he kicks up "The increase in magic is lovely, but you'd think they would provide some amenities. My last cell at least had a bench."

I wrap my arms around my stomach and scrunch my body until a small ball. The chill from the stone seeps into the thin fabric of my pants. "We can give them a review tomorrow after they decide whether to execute us."

He rolls onto his side, kicking up more dust, and rests his head on his bent arm, peering over at me. "They won't execute us."

"Not me at least. Smuggling a fugitive over the wall doesn't carry the death penalty." I'd know, Fíl read me the more serious crimes and punishments for my stint as Tans' proxy on the Council. I could spend some time in this cell, though, long enough that my goal in fixing magic would be worthless.

"No, they won't execute us because I'll take us directly to Ilsen."

I lean my chin on my knees. "I'd forgotten about that."

He sits up quickly, disturbing more dirt. "Truly? I thought this was part of your plan. Play nice, present me as a courteous gentleman rather than the slightly crazed villain the stories tell, and gain support in the event your King disagrees. Let us leave now. Grab Mittio, or not. I'm sure that lovely brunette upstairs would care for her. And we'll be in Ilsen before the moon rises."

The reaction to my plan upstairs makes me want to wait longer, if the Sàrkany and Eósy can handle it. If I can't get Mara on board, who at least trusts Tans' opinion of me, what hope do I have of convincing the other eleven Council members? Like Pirre. Or worse, Rothàna. I just need more time. "Why are you rushing to meet Kórol now? This morning it was all you could do to avoid it."

He tosses his hair. "I'd prefer to never meet him. Particularly not in Ilsen. That will probably feel as dreadful as if we'd remained in Dànna. But I've agreed to aid you and aid you I shall." His nose wrinkles. "Although waiting through a farce of a trial seems counter to that plan."

"Think of it like a dry run."

His black eyes lock on my face and he frowns at whatever he sees there. "You know all those criticisms about you needing to choose your battles and not fight every foe that presents itself? This is not the way to go about it."

Faint noise above us turns into loud thuds around the hallway, which ends further comment on my shortcomings. The flickering lamp light illuminates Mara, who drags a chair behind her. Silently, she places it in front of my cell before sitting and fussing with her skirts. When they've been sufficiently settled in a configuration known only to her, she raises her piercing eyes to stare at me.

"Hello, Gracie. We're due for a conversation."

Even though Mara called for the conversation, she spends the first five minutes just watching me. Leyden appears bored with the lacking interaction and starts attempting to goad her into reacting.

"And we're related! Can you believe it? After all that, and Grace's boy and I are distant cousins." He leans forward and purrs out, "Quite distant, sweetness. There would be no concern should you join me in this cell."

That breaks Mara's silence. While I roll my eyes at Leyden's antics, she sharpens her gaze. "Would that make you jealous, Gracie?"

"No," I say. It's true. Mara is attractive and Leyden can agree without it affecting me in the slightest, as Tans holds my heart. But my irritation presses forward with the snide, "Though I'm not sure it says much for soulmates if you'd move on to Leyden that quickly."

"Soulmates," Leyden says, cackling.

Mara stands, knocking her chair to the floor. "I knew it! This is about the conversation before you left."

The fight drains out of me before it could even begin. "Of course it is, Mara. I told you; I told *him* why I was going. Meeting Leyden really was a coincidence."

"A necessary one," he adds under his breath.

I can't help but roll my eyes. "Yes, a necessary one. He is one of the few people who know how to reopen the, the rifts."

She makes an irritated noise. "And he told you that?"

"Yes." Both Leyden and I speak in unison.

"And...you believe him?"

Leyden's overly dramatic outrage drowns out my affirmative answer.

She picks up her chair while shaking her head. "Honestly, Gracie. I hoped you weren't as naïve as Tans made you out to be. You're becoming such a disappointment."

Before I can react to the slight, Leyden stands, drawing himself up like a serpent ready to strike. "I am the first person to detail Grace's flaws, but I've earned that right. You have not, Mara, daughter of Elo."

"Leyden," I start, but he holds out a hand to stop me, his rage palpable.

His eyes flare blue and long pale fingers wrap around the bars closest to Mara. "What would you have me learn of you, Mara? What would you have me tell your little miss Gracie?"

Mara's eyes widen in fear, her hands clawing her throat. When he read my mind, it was never painful. For scant seconds I wonder if Leyden can choose for mind-reading to be painful, or if she's simply too afraid of what he might discover.

I shake off my inappropriate curiosity and bang my hand on an iron bar separating our cells. "Leyden!"

Leyden's eyes bleed back into their normal black as he offers a clenched smile. "I am simply attempting to further your goals, dearest."

"Mentally attacking people who irritate you isn't furthering anything," I say, glaring back at him. Even though a tiny part of me relishes what he attempted. How odd to consider Leyden in my corner in the same way I'd consider the remains of the Pack. Before arriving in Dalner, no one had ever stood up for me.

Leyden indolently raises one shoulder. "Agree to disagree." And then he winks at me, like he knows what I'm thinking, no matter that he physically can't.

Mara watches us with wide eyes before she steels her frame and resettles in her chair, fluffing her skirts just as she did earlier. "You will not do that again or you will regret it." She pins Leyden in place with narrowed eyes. "While no Eósy magic binds my tongue to the truth, you can take my threat for what it is: a promise."

"And then you interest me again," says Leyden.

Dryly, she responds, "How fortunate for me." She angles slightly away from Leyden, enough that it wouldn't be noticeable except for the bareness of the cells emphasizing even the slightest changes in the atmosphere. "Now, is he truly forced to tell the truth? Or was that another farce created by that false idol? The Great Matron, pah!"

"And again. In another life, we might have been friends," Leyden says, resting his chin on his fist, looking more innocent than he should.

I snap my fingers to refocus their attention. "Yes, he's forced to tell the truth."

"I demand a demonstration," she says.

Of course, she does. "He could die," I offer, though after his display of magic, I doubt it will dissuade her.

I'm immediately proven right as she laughs, full and throaty. "Gracie, saying such does not diminish my desire."

Leyden lights his fingers on fire and blows her a kiss.

"You must realize you'll have to prove it," she says, ignoring him. "Your 'partnership' agreement with all the-" She pauses and eyes him with irritation. "All those monsters will never work unless you prove their part of the agreement is ironclad. You cannot expect them to take it on something as vekganengà as faith."

"Asinine," Leyden translates into English automatically for me, and then he retreats to Sàrkany, telling Mara, "They did so before."

Mara sniffs. "And look what happened to them for their trouble."

A rock drops into my gut. While I knew my treaty plan was somewhat harebrained, I'd convinced myself over the past day that it would work. There was nothing else, at least that I could think of, to keep both the Sàrkany and Eósy safe. The Sàrkany need the magic of the wall, if not down, then at least reopened at the rifts. And the Eósy would never agree to tear down the wall, or reopen the rifts, if they didn't get the magic they needed from the other side. Particularly if it involved sacrificing a willing number of them.

Although I stood during most of the interaction between Leyden and Mara, the realization cut my balance at the knees, and I slumped back to the prison floor. *What would Tans say when I presented it to him? Another one of my half-baked plans? That it might work, but at the expense of my health and safety again?* Or will this just be another failure, like the Sìnnách, like the wall, like my solitary search ending in the dragons?

"I expected as much," Leyden says, sounding resigned. "Pity for you, sweetness, that we can test it without my death."

I wipe away a tear that snuck through, keeping my head down in hopes Mara and Leyden won't notice. "How?"

"Was that display worry for me or regret that it won't kill me?" Leyden asks in English. It was too much to hope he'd leave the emotional demonstration alone.

"Neither," I respond.

"I see. Fear of failure again."

"Don't—"

Mara snaps her fingers at us. "Enough of that. You'll inspire no trust if you continue to speak nonsense at each other."

I swallow the anxiety while Leyden sits up and rearranges his limbs as if in prayer, resting on bent knees. "Very well, sweetness. Ask me a question you know has an objective truth, that I cannot wiggle out of. I'll attempt to lie, which will cause me pain until I ultimately pass out."

"And it won't kill you?" I ask.

"Not unless I keep lying. A sustained lie is something constant, that will stop my heart. But a single, discrete question? No."

"Again, I say pity," says Mara. "Very well. Is it night?"

Leyden rolls his eyes. "How should I know? There are no windows, you irritant. While it may have been evening when we were dragged down here, I cannot determine how long you have bothered us. It could very well be sunrise."

"That would be the 'wiggling' he mentioned?" Mara directs to me.

I watch Leyden for a minute before replying, in case this was the test, and we couldn't tell if he was in pain yet. When he remained infuriatingly serene, I answer. "It's based on what he knows too. If he was color blind and was asked if the sky was brown, the truth depends on what he knew of the sky at that minute."

"I don't know if that is more reassuring or less," Mara admits. "Let us try again. Is her name Grace?"

"No," I say before Leyden can answer. "More specific. While here in Dalner, do I refer to myself as Grace?"

Leyden's lips pull into a smile. "That one will work. The answer is n-"

And here's where the plan might succeed, if we can come up with a promise the Eósy can't squirm free of. It looks like Leyden has swallowed his tongue, as each time he attempts to form the letters to say "no," he chokes on the air, coughing and gasping. It continues for what feels like long moments, but that could be because watching another being suffer is so uncomfortable that it slows time. Even if that being is Leyden.

After a sixth time trying to answer, his skin mottles gray, like it was in the memories after I'd defeated him at the wall. before he crumples. Mara watches impassively as I rush to the bars separating us. I can't reach him, but I can see the dip at his throat, which trembles, and the small bits of dust he disturbs with each huff of breath against the floor.

"Is that enough of a demonstration?" I snap at her. Fear shows itself as anger, and I was apparently afraid for Leyden. Which just made me angrier, that I'd moved him from reluctant allies to someone I wanted to stay alive. And while I still lie to myself, I can't convince myself the only reason for my fear is because I'd lose my chance to correct the consequences at the wall.

"It provides some trust," says Mara, her gaze glued to Leyden. "I do wonder if he forced himself to lose consciousness to prove it, rather than it being a true effect of a lie."

That has me stand and march towards her, finger pointed in accusation. "Seriously? Someone would willingly hurt themselves just to further a...a what, a game?"

She shrugs without responding.

"We didn't tell you what happened to Mittio's parents, did we?" I don't wait for an answer. "They died. They orphaned their daughter and sacrificed their very lives to make a fingernail sized hole in that wall. Because she needs the magic buried in Dalner that can't be found in Dànna. They literally let themselves die to do it. And more and more of them will have to do that, over and over and over, if we want any more of the wall down, if we want to keep the Sàrkany alive. Unless we find another way, which isn't looking likely." I point to Leyden's still form. "So, even with everything he's done, and Bittállí has done, and any of the rest of the complete and utter *demons* on the other side of the wall, if they partner with us, they're doing so walking through the blood of their kinsmen who willingly laid down their souls for us. You don't know the promises Leyden made to me. But I'll tell you right now, he's one of those willing too."

"It isn't totally altruistic, Gracie. If they're receiving benefits too." She stands and grips the back of her chair with clawed hands. "And they've killed our people, no matter if they plan on killing each other too. You'll be fighting with more than simply distrust when you present your plan. You'll be fighting against the grief each of us have experienced when he brought his brutes through the wall, and the heartbreak that grows with every death and injury after."

The fight leaks out of me. "I know. I can barely reconcile it myself. But it's like that saying, 'the enemy of my enemy is my friend.' Right now, we have a joint enemy of death. And we're aligned in attempting to stop it. It won't make up for what they've done, or my hand in it and what I did at the wall. It's no excuse, but it is an explanation and a reason we're moving forward together now."

She smiles, the first real one since I arrived today. "Adequate, Gracie. Tans said you had conviction and fire. You'll need it when you see him and Kórol again. But for the Council, you must work on your statecraft. Watch Sirgen tomorrow, you'll see what I mean." She picks up the chair and gathers herself to leave. "Now, are you romantically involved with your companion here?"

"No."

She shakes her head. "I'm asking him."

I turn to see Leyden still on the ground but with black eyes intent on us. "No, we are not. Not in the slightest," he croaks out.

"You could have trusted my answer," I tell her, crossing my arms about my waist.

"Why deal in trust when I can verify?" She starts down the corridor but doubles back. "I will not tell Breg what happened tonight. I assume I can *trust* you'll also keep this evening to yourselves?"

Leyden makes an affirmative sound as I nod. And then she ambles down the corridor and away from our solitary cell block.

I shuffle back to sit cross legged against the stone wall of my cell. "How long were you listening?"

"Long enough."

My eyes drift closed. "Good night, Leyden."

"Good night, dearest."

CHAPTER 23

$\mathbf{M}$orning comes slowly. Even though I spent several months sleeping outside, including the last month, I've never slept as poorly as I did on that hard prison ground. When I did, the dreams showed Leyden in his cell, meditating and pacing.

The underground prison feels more desolate in the morning, the cool stone damp. At some point, Leyden tossed a magicked blanket through the bars and I wrapped myself up in it to hide from the chill. I have a vague memory of him croaking out a song and creating the cloth. As he wakes, my fingers run over the sparking fabric and I swallow down my curiosity about why he spent his magic on me.

"Were I to rank my nights, I would place this near the middle," he says, sounding overly cheery. He leaps upward and makes a spectacle of brushing the dust from his tunic and pants, but all he does is rub it in. "Now, can we finally leave, or do you truly intend for us to go forward with this show trial?"

I hesitate. Mara thinks I need to watch this 'Sirgen,' and I'm still not convinced Kórol won't, justifiably, murder Leyden the second we arrive. "We're trying to prove the Eósy aren't all that bad. Escaping would just play into their already formed opinions of you."

He offers me a flat look. Whatever frustration he was hiding under the false cheer has reappeared. "And how will it look if we waste their time going forward with this farce only to vanish when they intend to sentence us?"

My mind races for a better solution, but none come, not when the grips of exhaustion still hold tight to my brain. "Maybe they'll agree with us."

Above us, an ominous thumping reverberates through the ceiling. The rhythmic echoes suggest the arrival of the citizenry, heavy footsteps and indistinct voices growing louder.

"Grace, that excuse is—" He stops himself and focuses his attention on the ceiling. The sound intensifies, the vibrations reaching down the walls and onto the stone, a reminder of what might meet us upstairs. With his gaze on the ceiling, the corners of his lips turn upward. "Perhaps you're right." He reseats himself as though completely unworried as the smile grows. "I foresee things working out well today."

His eyes remain black, not a speck of blue in sight.

The thumping reaches a crescendo as Breg and a warden appear down our corridor. Without doing more than silently nodding a greeting, the two release us from our cells. Leyden is handcuffed again and escorted in front by the warden while Breg lightly clasps my forearm and directs us to follow.

No matter Leyden now seems more at ease than I've ever seen him, and that's saying something, I still try to question Breg. "Should we be worried?" My voice is barely audible over the murmurs and sounds of the crowd above us.

Breg doesn't answer.

When we breach the stairs and appear in the main chamber, we're pushed backward because of the overwhelming mass of people. Candles sit atop sconces lining the walls, casting a warm, but unnecessary glow. Someone has thrown open the windows and the light feels blinding. The benches, packed to capacity, creak under the weight of eager onlookers. Those that couldn't find a seat squeezed into the remaining open areas, some even pressed over the windowsills, leaving no space for us to even maneuver to the front.

But Breg's height and authority allow us to push through the crowd, forcing Leyden and I in step as the warden takes the rear. At our appearance, the din transformed into something more charged, quiet murmurs and the rustling of clothing spread among the assembled spectators. The hushed conversations don't allow me to catch any of the words. I exchange an anxious glance with Leyden, but his eyes don't reflect the shared dread of what awaits us. Instead, he smirks and nods his head at those attendees who meet his eyes. Men and women alike blush at his attention.

At the front of the room, the wooden podium is covered with bound parchment. Standing on the raised platform shared with the podium is Mara, Elo, and Prieten. Beside them waits Zorin and another warden, who has his hands on the shoulder of another man in chains. He looks weary, in a simple tunic in better condition than mine. Sáv and Mittio are nowhere in sight.

Breg delivers us next to the other cuffed man, who inclines his head at Leyden and me. Leyden tips his chin and stands straighter.

Zorin lingers behind me and when the wardens' attentions are elsewhere, leans down to whisper in my ear. "He was brought in from another part of the province. He violated the travel ban." The whisper is almost a shout and I cringe as the few eyes that *weren't* on us refocus on our forms. Mara moves to stand beside me and elbows my side.

Prieten bangs his hand on the podium, while Breg and the wardens bark out demands for silence. The room quiets, punctuated only by soft coughs and shuffling in their chairs.

"Thank you all for coming," Prieten says in his gruff voice. "I see many of the same faces who appeared at our petition day, and I know the difficulties you all experienced after the battle at the wall, which only grew after the travel ban was put in place. However, in times of uncertainty and challenge, it falls upon us, my family as your Council representative and you as the citizenry, to uphold the laws that safeguard our Kingdom. Today, we bring forth three individuals for trial, each accused of violating the King's mandates."

He gestures and a warden pushes the cuffed man beside us forward. Prieten stares at him in silence for a minute, before speaking again, louder this time. "The first, Marpon, a person who, in defiance of the travel ban, sought to cross the now-forbidden boundaries. We cannot ignore such crimes, as they threaten the delicate balance we strive to maintain for the greater good of our society."

A few voices appear to heckle, but it's unclear if they're jeering at Prieten or the accused, Marpon. The wardens can't tell either and appear ready to intercede, but Breg's stiff headshake stops them. Marpon is pushed back to our side.

"The second accused, a figure whose actions are far more... insidious, stands accused of the unthinkable—being one of the very creatures that subjugated our society for centuries. Although he was not the Great Matron—"

Here the jeers are clear. Whether or not the crowd will lay her crimes at Leyden's feet, they are furious at the reminder.

I shuffle closer to Leyden, letting the audience's noise cover my voice. "We may need to get you out of here."

He doesn't respond, keeping a placid smile directed outward.

The wardens finally get control of the crowd and Prieten continues. "Although he was not the Great Matron, he is an Eósy. He has breached the walls and intends to use magic." Prieten gestures again, but none of the wardens will touch him to push him forward. Instead, Leyden lifts his cuffed hands and waves.

"Finally, we bring forth our third accused." Prieten urges me forward.

My brow furrows as I realize Leyden's crimes are less than I expected. They didn't mention the wall or his being the mastermind at the battle there at all. *Maybe this* will *work out.* I step in front of Leyden and offer a wincing smile to the room.

Prieten watches me for a long minute, something like sadness swirling in his eyes. "You may recognize her as Lord Commander Tansr's proxy on the Council. Others may remember her as our savior at the wall." He cuts himself off as the room explodes a second time.

Someone starts up the chant from yesterday, shouting "Gracel, Gracel, Gracel," until the entire room has joined in.

Prieten bangs his hands on the podium. "I must finish. Grace brought the second accused through the wall. She used his magic to breach it. While the magic is a boon, it offers the chance for more Eósy to come through."

Surprise ripples through the room. Dozens of questions meet my ears. "They did that?" "They can break it open?" "I thought they had to be invited?"

"Though the nature of these charges may be unbelievable to many, I assure you, my fellow citizens, that we and your Council bear the responsibility of following the demands the Raddare line has laid out," Prieten continues. "We must ensure fairness and execute the laws that govern our land, no matter whether you agree with the law. As we navigate the challenges before us, let us remember that justice, however strict, is the foundation of the realm we hold dear."

The crowd doesn't appear sure how to respond to that last appeal. And it's unclear whether Prieten is saying he agrees we should be prosecuted or not. But undeterred by their lacking reactions, Prieten gestures towards the back of the room. "I turn over this tribunal to Sirgen."

Anticipation zings through my body at their introduction. Something shuffles through the audience, too short even while standing to be seen over the heads of people seated on the benches. I rise to my tiptoes to catch sight of the person but Mara yanks me down by my wrist.

Finally, they emerge. A navy cloak embroidered with images of plants cascades down their body, their features hidden in the shadows of their hood. They take off a hat and reveal a short woman with two scars bisecting her cheeks. Standing at, what I'd guess is, only four feet tall, she carries herself with a confidence I can hope to emulate one day. She dons a floor-length dress made of deep greens and browns that matches her earth-toned hair trailing down to her thick waist. Lines of experience etch the corners of her hazel eyes, even though she looks the same age as Mara. Instead of ascending the small platform and standing at the podium with Prieten, she plants herself directly in front of the man being tried.

"I would present from here," she says in a smoky voice.

Prieten looks like he's going to protest, but he ends up nodding. Given her statute, she probably couldn't see over the podium, anyway.

She turns to the audience, letting her body frame Marpon's. His body grows out of hers like a double-headed statue. And then she speaks.

"Marpon may be charged with violating the King's travel ban, put in place after the battle of the wall and a difficult growing season. Marpon's reasons for the travel matter not. He could have been visiting family who live outside Gramad, searching for opportunity in Gremeg, or planning to steal from the coffers of Làna. What matters is that he traveled.

"In recent times, we've seen changes that have tested the very fabric of our society. The King, in his...wisdom, has imposed restrictions to ensure our safety. And while we acknowledge the importance of safety, we also value the fundamental freedoms that have defined our existence."

Prieten and Elo share a weighted glance as murmurs sound through the audience. Sirgen ignores them all, her voice rolling through the crowd in its own form of magic.

"Prohibiting travel between provinces, imposing boundaries that keep families separated, and restricting work outside our towns have altered the landscape of our lives. Our ability to connect, to reunite with loved ones, and to seek sustenance from the lands we once roamed freely has been taken from us. They have separated us during a time when we should be coming together as a people to overcome the shifts in our way of life."

I whisper to Leyden. "Is she suggesting what I think she is?"

He shifts closer and speaks from the corner of his mouth. "Do you now see why I believe things will be well?"

"Does she know about the mosquito theory?"

"Quiet," the warden beside him hisses. Leyden inclines his head, but it's unclear if he's answering me.

"Our unity, our shared dreams, and our determination to forge a better future are the bedrocks upon which the Kingdom was built," Sirgen continues. Even with the warden scowling at him, Leyden echoes her words in English, translating the difficult phrases I've not yet learned. "And it's these principles that we must draw upon as we navigate these trying times. I stand here today to remind you that the spirit of our ancestors, who traversed these lands freely, flows within us.

"The sense of adventure that led them to explore new horizons and build connections across provinces is not lost—it is merely suppressed. In this era of change, we must craft our own destiny, and become stewards of the legacy we hold dear." She stalks forward, pinning the entire audience in place. "The King's intentions may be noble, guided by a desire to shield us from the unknown. But in safeguarding our safety, we must not surrender our freedoms. We are a people capable of self-governance, of finding solutions that balance security and liberty."

The murmurs rise like a tide, building through the room.

"Let us not be confined by the borders drawn on maps but united by the shared yearning for a return to the vibrant tapestry of our interconnected lives. Let us not forget the essence of who we are. For as surely as the sun rises, so too shall the spirit of our people triumph over the shadows that seek to confine us. Let today be the first step in overcoming the shackles that bind us. Let Marpon free."

The sound of the audience snuffs out like a candle, dying with Sirgen's ending call. She turns to Prieten, who is staring at her as if she's suddenly nude. Elo touches his side and his open mouth clacks closed. He steps back up to the podium and clears his throat.

"Those in favor of charging Marpon, with the trial to occur this afternoon."

The room stays silent. Mara's breath quickens beside me.

He nods, as though he expected that. "And those in favor of releasing Marpon without charges."

The room explodes with sound, claps and jeers, a deafening array. Some stand and stomp their feet and it feels like the chamber could collapse around us. Breg and the wardens yell again, the contrasting voices overwhelming the room.

"Does she know?" I repeat, using the disorder to hide my inquiry.

"If she doesn't already, I plan on making sure she does," Leyden answers, his lips slowly stretching into a wolfish grin, full of teeth. At least one citizen faints at its appearance. Prieten raises his arms and finally, finally, everyone settles down. "Marpon will be freed. Now, our second witness, Alban."

As the wardens uncuff Marpon and he disappears into the crowd, another man stands from near the back and presses forward. It's the man we met yesterday. When he gets close enough, he waves. Leyden waves back.

He steps up to the podium and rubs the back of his neck. "I've never done this before. It's nice to stand on, uh, on this side of the stage for once." A few titters run through the room. "I'm not as well-spoken as Sirgen. That's why she does this more than, uh, me and you. But I'm game to try, seeing as I found the two. These people are accused of similar things. Gracel, I mean Lady Grace, is accused of aiding a fugitive. And the man, uh, Eósy, next to her is that fugitive. As far as we know, they've done nothing wrong."

Mara elbows me again, hard. "You're welcome," she hisses through pursed lips.

"For Grace, intent should matter," Alban says, slamming his fist on the podium. "What's her motivation for bringing the Eósy with her? For opening the wall? It's for us. She's trying to bring back what we lost. We all felt their first bit of, uh, success. Imagine if it all came back. My best fruit tree gave up fruit for the first time since the battle!"

He points at Leyden with a dirt smudged finger. "And him. Yes, he's Eósy. Yes, we were tricked for ages. Yes, they tried to kill us at the wall. Yes we, uh, I'll stop with the 'yeses' for a minute. But just because he's one of them doesn't mean he's bad. Not if he's trying to help us. Now, I get it. The King thinks we're better off without all that magic. Easy for him to say, when he can just wait for winter and get himself some ice."

Another titter echoes through the room. The wardens shift uneasily.

Alban winces as he looks over at Prieten and Elo. "Sorry about that. Wouldn't like to be, uh, up here for treason next week. Back to the accused. All I'm asking you is to see past the rules for a moment and look at what these two are trying to do. They're not villains, they're dreamers. Dreaming of a time when we had something special, something that made our world a bit more... uh, magical. Let 'em try to make things better. Let 'em go and let 'em try." He bows quickly and shuffles away from the podium. A smattering of applause follows his speech.

It wasn't as compelling as Sirgen's, but at least Alban didn't speak against us like I'd feared.

Prieten sighs and raises his hands when Leyden interrupts.

He steps forward, a predatory smile spreading across his face. "Might I address this honorable tribunal?"

"No." Prieten and I speak in unison.

"If you're scheduled for trial, you can chatter all you want," says Mara.

"I don't chatter," he responds, sounding affronted. Several members of the audience laugh like he said something charming and clever.

Prieten ignores them all. "Those in favor of charging Grace and the Eósy known as Leyden, with the trial to occur this afternoon."

Only a handful of voices shout in favor. I release a heavy breath.

"And those in favor of releasing them without charges."

The rest of the room springs to their feet, their shouts filling the air.

After Breg and the wardens clear the room, we're left alone with Tans' family and Zorin. Soon enough, Breg stomps back downstairs, followed by Sáv and Mittio.

Mittio wriggles the minute she sees Leyden and squeaks to be let go. Sáv releases her and she zooms over to Leyden, hitting his knees and knocking him backward. Somehow, he still looks smug while laying half on the ground. Mara leans over and whispers, but it could be to Leyden or Mittio. Sáv shakes his head before coming to me and wrapping me in a hug.

"Sorry I couldn't be here. You okay?" he whispers.

I shrug into his neck. "Do you think Tans will hate me after this?"

He doesn't get to answer as Mittio's high-pitched squeal snags our attention. She's hopped off Leyden's lap and attempts to race around the room. Breg snatches her and spins her in the air, like a tiny jet plane.

"Careful now, little miss," he tells her. She giggles and squeals and he keeps spinning her. Mara moves to join her parents but has stars in her eyes watching Breg and Mittio.

"Someone should speak with Sirgen," Elo is saying when Mara's attention turns to her. "I fear that speech may open her up to greater turmoil."

"I will." Mara says. She looks over at Leyden and winks, but Elo can't see it. "Her wife's death has led her to be less...careful."

"That can't be an excuse for her radicalization," Elo says, pursing her lips.

Mara exchanges a weighted glance with Breg who appears unconcerned.

"We will overcome this," says Prieten. "For now, life will go on as it has."

Mara kisses Breg hard on the mouth and blows tiny kisses to Mittio. Breg flies Mittio through the air to 'catch' the kisses and Mittio giggles even harder.

When Mara leaves and closes the door behind her, Prieten turns to me, still squished up next to Sáv. His gaze hardens. "Grace, I look forward to seeing you again under better circumstances next time."

Shame heats my cheeks. "Thank you. I'm...I'm sorry for bringing this to your door." Leyden stands beside me and I stifle a wince. "And I'm sorry for my choice of companion—"

"I beg your pardon," Leyden says, holding his hand to his chest in mock offense.

"But this must be done," I finish.

Prieten frowns. "I cannot say I understand what you intend to do, or the path you've chosen to complete it, but I know why."

Elo wraps her arm around Prieten's waist. "Unlike my husband, I do not support your plan, Grace. I believe it is short-sighted and will only lead to more turmoil. But—" She sighs and tears form in her eyes. "I have worried for my youngest since he mentioned you and what may happen when he hits his twentieth year. I know it is not your primary motivation, but I thank you for attempting to give him options."

Leyden looks intrigued while I swallow the immediate irritation rising through me. I'd hoped the soulmate revelation, and her opinion about 'magicless me' would stay out of this conversation. I'm trying to save her entire species. You'd think the why wouldn't matter.

Prieten places a gentle hand on my shoulder and rakes his eyes over my bare arms, the pale scars on display. "You've made this place your home, and my people your people. I know the expense you've paid. If what you've said is true, he is our only choice."

"It is." My voice is resolute.

Sáv squeezes my side. "Grace's got a 'hero' thing going for her."

Prieten nods. "Often, heroes emerge not from the purity of their choices but from the wisdom to understand what the greater good demands. Good luck." And he and Elo return to their home upstairs before I can think more about what he's pronounced.

"Assume you'll be on your way soon," Sáv says, looking down at me. "No time to waste, from what you've told us."

I nod. We can't put it off anymore. Though I doubt it will go as well as today did. If only Kórol knew how some of his people felt about his pronouncements, he'd agree with my plan in an instant.

"What about Mittio?" Zorin asks.

Breg now has Mittio sitting on his shoulders, riding her around like he's a horse. He pauses mid gallop to say, "Mara and I have discussed it. We'd be honored to care for Mittio. If she'll have us."

"Mittio is Eósy," Leyden reminds him. "My impression of your wife is that she doesn't enjoy my kind."

Breg furrows his thick brows. "Perhaps she simply didn't enjoy you."

"Alas, our love was not to be." He learns forward with a sly grin. "Though she got me on my knees."

"Should've gagged him too," Sáv mutters.

Breg ignores Leyden, instead focusing on Mittio and pulling her from his shoulder and into his arms. "Mittio, from what I know of your mom and dad, they loved you more than life itself. Since they aren't around anymore, we'd like to take care of you. You could live with us. Me and Mara." He touches her little cheek. "Remember her? She took you swimming this morning."

The word pops out before I can stop myself. "Swimming?"

Sáv laughs next to me, a short, startled sound that breaks the remaining tension in the room. Mittio doesn't speak, at least that I can hear, but after whispering to her, Breg breaks out into a wide smile.

Leyden lets out a put-upon sigh. "Let me tell you everything you must know about her magic and raising a nearly immortal Eósy."

"And about her parents," Breg says. "We want to know everything about them to keep them present in her life as best we can."

"Well, Breg, let's talk," Leyden says, his voice a rumble of dark amusement. He puts one hand on Breg's back, as far up as he can reach, as the three of them ascend the stairs. "You know, your wife piqued my interest last night. Even with love lost between us, there were certainly sparks. Have you ever considered a third?"

Zorin stares after them with wide eyes. "A third what? Would Mittio not be their first child?"

"I'll tell you when you're older," Sáv says, laughing again. But then his smile dims. He sits on one of the empty benches and stares down at his hands. "Can't lie to you, Grace. Tans may not understand, but he'd forgive you anything."

I slide next to him on the bench. "That's better than I can hope for, I guess."

"He wants to protect you," Sáv explains. "Can't do that if you keep running off into danger. Especially with the creature that put you in the most danger in the first place."

I stare at the raised platform and empty podium, thinking about what Sirgen said and how she moved the crowd. "Sometimes you have to walk in shadows to banish the looming darkness."

Sáv's brows raise. "That come from one of your books, or did you think that up yourself?"

"That was me," I said, tilting my chin up before biting my lip with pride. "Do...do you think the others will buy it?"

"Buy it?"

"I mean, will it convince them?"

"Some of the Council will understand the path you've chosen," Zorin says tentatively. "The necessity of the uneasy alliance forged with one wearing the mask of a villain."

Impossibly, it looks as though Sáv's eyes raise even higher. "Got a head for policy there?"

Zorin blushes, pleased. "I did a lot of escort duties at Council meetings for the Lady. Before that, my post was the library."

Sáv smiles fondly at the reminder of Fíl, which Zorin notices. Longing dances over his features and I leap back into the conversation to avoid more drama.

"It isn't just a mask, Zorin. Leyden did those things. To me, to the Sàrkany, to Kórol." My gaze focuses on the stairwell where Leyden is no doubt verbally terrorizing Breg. I almost miss the phony advisor act he had; at least he sounded competent then, not like an angsty teenager. We've already got one of those. "He's got an explanation for it, but it doesn't excuse it."

"I cannot speak against my King," says Zorin, slinking towards us. His neck swivels as he checks every corner and ducks under the benches to confirm we're alone. Both Sáv and I bite back a smile when he finishes. Finally, he leans in close and gestures for us to do the same. In a whisper, he says, "But since the battle at the wall, he rules by fear. My King deserves a life not dictated by fear. We all do. If contracting with the Eósy can extinguish that fear and return the magic they gave us, then I would expect his mask won't matter."

"The Eósy didn't—" But I pause. That misunderstanding doesn't matter right now. "Will *Kórol* forgive me, do you think?"

Sáv winces. "You've been around him a lot more than me."

"He'll likely attempt to execute you," says Zorin. When he realizes it was him who spoke, his eyes widen, and he slaps his hand over his mouth.

"Tans'll never let him," Sáv is quick to add.

"They've been on opposite sides of an...issue before," I say. "It was absolutely awful."

"What issue?" Sáv blinks as understanding passed over his face. "Ah, yes. I'll say the same thing I said way back when. Even with the...damage, their friendship's iron-strong."

My lips thin. "A 'woman's never come between them' before, I recall you said. And do you remember what happened next?"

"No," Zorin answers. But Sáv looks visibly torn, likely revisiting the turmoil and trauma that befell us all before Kórol and Tans worked together to go after Bittállí.

I slump into Sáv's side. "They work better as a team."

"A trio. Wasn't just them in that room with that she-demon," he reminds me, hugging me again.

Leyden strolls back downstairs. "Shall we be off? I, for one, would love to discover whether my winning streak continues. Perhaps there's a stamp we can collect."

"Stamp?" Sáv mouths to me.

"You know," Leyden explains brightly. "Buy three, get one free or the like. Although in this case, it's 'avoid three executions, get the fourth free.'"

I huff. "That's my joke."

"No, yours was about kidnappings. Mine is entirely different."

"Great reminder." I break free from Sáv to smack Leyden in the shoulder.

Zorin raises his hand. "What is the fourth 'one' that would be free?"

Leyden answers lightning quick. "Some other guilt-free crime, of course."

I press my fingers against my eyes and take a breath. "Okay, if you're done playing the rake, we can go."

"I'm merely livening up a rather challenging time," he says.

"By making it more challenging?"

Sáv and Zorin watch us like spectators at a tennis game. Before Leyden can make another retort, the door opens and Mara strides in.

"Why are you still here?"

CHAPTER 24

A fter saying our goodbyes, we sneak back into the cellar to leave without an audience.

Sáv asked me to tell Fílga hello and promised that he'd return to Ilsen the moment the travel ban was lifted. He didn't feel comfortable chancing his innocence in another province. And Leyden wasn't offering to take him straight there. Zorin was, as expected, thrilled they were staying alone longer. I can only hope the tension doesn't boil over.

Leyden directs us to the cell closest to the stairwell, rather than our musty 'home' from last night. He takes a deep breath. "Still believe this is the best course of action?"

No. I hug my waist. "Can you think of a better way to get the walls down without a civil war?"

He doesn't respond, instead breathing deeply and lifting his finger to rip through space. It's as nauseating as the first few times, reality flapping open in the phantom wind. On the far side of the opening is Raddare's Pass, and in the distance, the Gates just outside Ilsen. There are a few guards standing to either side of the entrance. At this distance I can't see the marks on their uniforms to know which unit they're assigned to, whether they're the men and women I'd befriended.

"Why aren't we going straight to the castle?"

He frowns at whatever he sees in the distance. "Wards. The castle proper is warded from this cleaving magic."

"That's why Bittállí flew in through the window," I realize.

"She ripped through the wards once," he says, almost idly. "It almost killed her, but she was…highly motivated. I'm told Derul increased the wards when they did whatever they did to put up the walls, thinking she couldn't get back in."

"And then she got invited back and slipped through the windows to avoid the problem altogether," I say, rubbing my eyes. Nothing is ever easy.

Leyden bows low with one arm gesturing towards the opening. "After you, dearest."

The opening is two feet off the ground, and I heave myself through it. This time, my skin catches against the side of the opening and something zips through me. Like the icy shock I'd felt at the wall, but slimier. I stumble to my knees as I make it through and heave. The trip wasn't as bad as the first one, but the oozing sensation running down my arms and into my stomach creates a nausea worse than I'd felt in a while. I curl on my side and shudder.

Leyden hops through behind me, zipping up the hole. He smirks down at me. "You touched the sides."

It wasn't a question, so I don't answer. He holds out a hand. Without considering denying him, I let him help me up.

Leyden dropped us halfway through Raddare's Pass, near the south side of the mountain range pass leading into the town at the base. I'm reminded of the first time I saw Ilsen, its silhouette a jagged monstrosity of black spindling spires, towers reaching for the sky like fearsome sentinels standing guard. If a child thought up a haunted castle, Ilsen would be the design.

At the end of the Pass is a formidable stone barrier wall crossing perpendicularly to the castle and town beneath it. Adorning the rugged stone is creeping ivy and patches of emerald moss, a bright contrast to the tar black of the rocks. Beyond the protective area lies the town, with labyrinthine streets winding around timber-framed houses. I've sprinted through the town several times: when I arrived here the first time, when we've left for adventures elsewhere. Only once have I visited, when I'd created a commotion much like what we'd just seen in Samsen. At the time, I thought my appearance spurred a negative reaction. But hearing Sirgen and the other recent rumblings here makes me wonder.

The guards at the far end of Raddare's Pass haven't noticed us yet. If we're lucky, we can pass through without alerting them to our violation of the travel ban. And maybe I can see the town, without the dramatics this time.

And maybe putting off entering the castle a little longer would be nice, too.

There's a small patch of something that smells like garlic growing in the ground between boulders. Sáven's mother used it for spice, and I'd seen a healer or two carrying it around. I veer off to the left to pick a few sprigs. Leyden follows.

"Alixan," he says, touching the head of one of the small ruby red flowers clutched in my palm. "Intending to entice the Council with a good meal?"

I gesture to the small contingent of guards several yards away. "Looking for an alibi. Jokes aside, I don't want to go through another trial." At least not for something as preposterous as the travel ban when my actual crimes are closer to treason.

He hums thoughtfully. "Clever. Though if the populace is anything like Samsen, we might be freed yet again."

"We got lucky. There's no 'citizen indictment' here. The serious crimes go straight to the Council. The less serious have something like an elected judge." I remember the delicate sneer covering Elo's mouth. "I don't know if the judge would be as lenient."

We take a few steps closer to the gates when the guards notice us and stand at attention. I brace myself for a confrontation.

"Had we gone to trial, with Mara as our judge, we still would have fared well," he says as he hooks his arm through mine.

I grit my teeth but don't push him off. The guards would likely catch the strife and come running faster. "She seemed...slightly in favor," I admit. Enough that she was willing to adopt Mittio and appeared to respect Sirgen, who was a half-step from talking *actual* treason.

"She's no fan of mine, but she doesn't dislike my kind on principle," he says as we approach the guards. "The truth of it is that Breg is feeling the effects of the walls up more than he'll admit to the others."

My brows raise and I urge him to continue.

"His magic is based in his strength. Without it, he says it's like an everlasting cold but without the symptoms. Mara had been planning on moving them into the Wilds, suspecting there might be something there, even before Mittio. There was some talk of a butterfly that gave them hope." He looks at me expectantly.

I don't react. "How did you find all this out?"

A dark smile curls over his lips. "I'm very charming."

"Halt," a high-pitched voice calls out to us. A guard with a sword on their back has jogged towards us while Leyden distracted me with gossip. The second guard stands at the entrance with a drawn bow. The speaker looks familiar, her blonde hair braided and bound to her head.

With nothing to lose, I take a guess. "Shivio?"

The woman's entire body seeks to blink. "Lady...Lady Grace?"

The second guard, an unfamiliar man looking no older than Zorin, leaves his post at the entrance and runs in our direction. Leyden subtly shifts in front of me.

"Lovely afternoon we're having," Leyden says smoothly. I restrain the urge to poke him for using the same greeting I did yesterday with Alban, which Leyden teased me about.

But neither guard pays him any attention, focused entirely on me.

"Lady Grace, you'll need to come with me," Shivio finally says, holding out her arm.

I swallow back the nervous anticipation burbling in my gut. "Would you believe us if I said we were gathering spices?"

"For two months?" says the other guard, wrinkling his nose.

"It was a long walk," I offer lamely. I hadn't assumed my absence would be a secret, but I didn't expect even strangers in the guard to know. "I'm sorry. I don't think we've met."

That turns the guard's expression to one of excitement. "Rungin, Lady. I recently moved into Commander Eida's unit after Enlistee Zorin abandoned his post."

"He didn't abandon—" I cut myself off. I can work that out with Tans when I see him. "Will you take my companion and I to Tansr?"

"That was our intent," Shivio says, still holding out her arm.

"Good, that's good," I say, letting out a breath. A nervous laugh follows. "I was afraid you were arresting us."

"Did...did you do something that would require us to?" Rungin says, his hands tightening on his bow.

"Rungin," Shivio hisses. "Apologies, Lady. Rungin is quite new to this position and needs to finish his trainee test on interacting with nobility."

"I'm not nobility," I say, but neither are listening, instead directing me back towards the gate.

"When we cross through—" Shivio starts.

Leyden clears his throat loud behind us. Rungin jumps while Shivio gives an almost imperceptible flinch. "I hope I haven't been forgotten."

"Not possible," I say under my breath. To the guards, I say, "My companion also needs to meet with Tansr and then the King. As soon as we can."

"My King is preoccupied with the Council and the trials, Lady," Shivio explains. "It is unlikely you can get an audience with him unless you *were* arrested."

"What about as a Council member? If I'm still the proxy for Gramad, I could attend with my companion as my guest and speak during the open forum." An uncomfortable thought rolls over me. "I *am* still the proxy for Gramad, right?"

Rungin is quick to reassure me. "Yes, Lady. But with several Council members returning to their provinces before the travel ban could be enforced, leaving only three of the twelve remaining, the King will not halt the trials for anything, for fear of the others leaving."

"Rungin," Shivio hisses again. "We don't question the King."

"Begging your pardon, Lady," Rungin says, falling into a deep bow. "Please don't tell him."

"I won't," I say. The relief I'd felt at the confirmation that I'm still on the Council was a momentary reprieve. I exchange a glance with Leyden whose brows are furrowed in thought. "How many trials have there been?"

Now it's Shivio's turn to share a heavy glance with Rungin. "We'll explain on the way."

Leyden tramples the alixan as it falls from my fingers.

One hundred trials, as of this morning. One hundred trials for grievances considered 'serious enough' for the King and Council to hear it, rather than the town's judge. Shivio and Rungin paint a picture of an almost authoritarian regime with Kórol adding new violations and removing more freedoms daily. Given it was already a democratic monarchy, the fall to an autocracy doesn't take as long as it would in my former country, but it's still horrifying. Even Leyden looks shocked at what's happening, and

Bittállí's reign didn't seem like one with a lot of standards for the government.

There are new curfews and prohibited occupations, all under the excuse of "keeping the people safe." With no travel in or out, the citizens are isolated from the rest of Dalner. Rungin tells me that, as far as they know, all of Dalner is under this substitute for martial law.

Shivio took us around the city, following the stone wall until we could slip a side of the castle not used by many. I miss my opportunity to see the city once again, but time is clearly of the essence.

"We'll do what we can," I promise the two when they deliver us inside.

"We know," Shivio says. Rungin nods in agreement.

Leyden, who'd remained silent after we entered the gate, stops them from leaving. "Why did you not take us through the city?"

"We wanted to keep the peace," Rungin explains.

"There would have been too many arrests," Shivio adds.

Leyden nods, as if in understanding, but I don't get it. "What peace would we disrupt? Would we be attacked by the populace?"

Shivio tilts up her chin. "There would have been a revolution in your favor." And then they leave us with that bombshell.

I try not to give Shivio's words much thought. People can support me without it meaning they'd overthrow Kórol.

Although a coup attempt was one fear that sent me running towards Samsen.

I direct us away from the throne room. We can tackle Kórol with Tans at our side, and instead slip us up a side parapet towards the map room. Shivio said it's likely we'll find Tans there.

As I guide him through the circuitous hallways past the kitchen and winding staircases, I can't shake the unease clinging to me like a shadow. This was the only option; I was sure of it. Leyden will try to bring the walls down with or without me, not all the Eósy are monsters and don't deserve to waste away anyway, the Sàrkany need to be protected from those who can manipulate minds and take away their free will. And, at a minimum, I owe them a warning before we do this. But bringing Leyden here... This sprawling fortress is my home, the first place I can call home since Mom died. I steal a glance at Leyden as we circle closer to our destination.

I can't decipher the wistful expression playing over Leyden's features. His eyes, wide with curiosity, dart from one tapestry to the next, entranced by the centuries old stories woven into the stone walls. Stories of his long-dead sister, if I remembered the family trees he and Fílga lectured about. Both offered tidbits of the Eósy history like a slow dripping faucet. But I'd been patient and filled a tiny cup of knowledge, hopefully enough to convince the Council of the wisdom in my plan. My unease threatens to boil over, in tears or nausea, I can't be sure. Once or twice, Leyden perks up and stares down a side hallway or at the floor, like he's discovered something interesting. Fates only know what. I continue fretting as we walk, unsure whether his presence here might unravel the delicate balance that keeps me rooted here. I'm already the girl that got rid of magic. What will I be now?

With a heavy tread, I take us down the last hallway, until the door to the map room stands in front of us. My fingers reach for the handle but pause in midair.

"Will you promise to wait in this spot until I call for you?"

Leyden looks like he'll refuse, but with a pout, agrees. The smallest tingle of relief chases through me, that I might prepare Tans for Leyden's presence.

The door opens with a loud creak, and I close it behind me. Tans sits slumped in a chair at the far end of the table, leaning on his elbows with his hands covering his eyes. Tiny flags dot the map before him, dozens surrounding Ilsen and the wall but leaving the rest of Dalner bare.

"I've instructed all my men to leave me be when present here," he says, his voice muffled.

My voice shakes when I respond, "I'm not one of your men."

His head snaps up, and he's halfway across the room before I can blink. When we're within reaching distance, we crash into each other. His arms wrap around me, tight enough to sting. My own fingers find refuge in the familiar contours of his back, as I drop my head into the crook of his neck. His long hair tickles my cheek as he rests his head against mine. His scent clings to me, the intoxicating blend of smoke and cinnamon. With each breath, I feel the stressors of the past weeks, the pain in my body and head, release.

"Butterfly, how I missed you," he murmurs into my hair. Without releasing me, he leans back far enough to stare into my face. "Are you well?"

"Well enough." I blink away a few relieved tears. "I figured out how to bring back the magic."

"I know. You'll imagine my surprise when my back no longer ached," he says, a teasing smile on his face. His own eyes look relatively wet too.

"That was just the start." At this I drag us apart, leaving only our hands connected. "That's why I'm here. Before we take the next steps, I wanted to...run it by everyone."

He smirks, but it's shaky. "My butterfly is seeking confirmation of her plans *instead* of simply going forward and advising us afterward?" His gaze roams my face, likely seeing the exhausted bruises under my eyes, the gauntness of my cheeks. "Is this truly my Butterfly?"

I think so. I gulp. *I hope so; I hope you'll still think so after I bring in Leyden.* "Absolutely."

"We must—" he cuts himself off with a weighted inhale and forces forward a facsimile of his usual smile. "Let me prepare you a bath and bring you something to eat. Without Sáv's experiments, the offerings are blander but likely more edible."

I squeeze his fingers tight. "No. I need to meet with Kórol. I...brought someone to help. Someone who can help fix it. With me."

Before he can react, I shout towards the door. "Leyden?"

Tans' brow furrows. "Leyden, who in Fates' name is—"

Leyden struts in the room, chin tilted towards the ceiling. The lit candles wink against his blond hair, which looks almost white in the light. He stands before us and crosses his arms, flitting his eyes from Tans' form to mine and finally landing on our still connected hands.

I burst out an explanation before Tans can say or do anything more, the words erupting from me. If I'm fast enough, maybe I can forestall the actual volcano of reaction coming. "He's an Eósy, one of the few who knows how to bring down the wall. And he's connected with their leadership, so he could be a good messenger or proxy if the Sàrkany and Eósy could contract together. Like a treaty, you see, and—"

Tans tries to grab his braids, but our conjoined hands stop him. He drops my hands as though they scald him and tries again, as my heart plummets in my chest. "Is this..."

"I am indeed who you think I am," Leyden says, giggling and looking like he's received an early birthday present. "Little Grace found a very specific Eósy."

Tans appears to stop breathing. And I understand why. With the candlelight above him and the posture he's positioned himself into, he looks just like he did standing at the Gate. The only difference is his skin doesn't sparkle with gold paint but is pale and smooth as alabaster. Coupled with the innocent-but-menacing nickname, he's more than confirmed exactly who he is.

"I told you to stop calling me that," I say under my breath, restraining a shiver. But the damage has already been done.

"Little Gr—" Tans stares between us, eyes and mouth widening to comical degrees.

The room itself seems to hold its breath. And then it exhales as he pounces, charging past me and into Leyden. Leyden manages to sidestep him, but Tans isn't deterred.

He attempts to rain an onslaught of furious punches at Leyden, who effortlessly ducks each blow. They lunge and parry around the large table. The frustration on Tans' face grows into an almost maniacal rictus, with each failed hit stoking the flames of his rage. This is as unhinged as I've ever seen him.

"Tans, stop!" I shout, rushing forward and trying to intercede. But no matter the turbulent dance between the two, there appears to be an unspoken agreement that I'm not involved, as they skillfully evade my attempts to intercede. Each time I seize Leyden's tunic or Tans' arms, they spin away, circling the table and leaving my fingers grasping the air. I bang my hands on the table, knocking the flags from their positions. "We need him!"

That pauses the one-sided brawl. Tans spins to fix his fiery gaze on me, his hands still fisted in midair. "The only place he's needed is the bottom of a deep grave!" His breath is harsh, his skin glistening with exertion.

Leyden stands behind Tans, barely winded. There's no remorse on his face at his part in creating this melodramatic interaction. Instead, he looks amused.

I return my attention to Tans, who hasn't calmed from the involuntary break in sparring. With each breath, his anger appears to increase. If magic still existed here, the entire room would be on fire. I cover his fists with my hands. "Every arrow, remember?"

He quakes lightly, as if he's forcibly holding himself back. "He isn't a weapon in our favor, he's a kreschehátseltak!"

The miniscule hope I'd held on to, that I could convince Tans and then together persuade Kórol, snuffs out like a dying candle. Never had Tans used a Sàrkany word I didn't know. Never, even in our most intense disagreements, has he not remembered who I was and respected my limitations.

"Terrorist," Leyden says from behind him in English. Where there was no remorse before, there now is the bloom of something, something pained. As though he realizes what this meant for me.

Tans flinches at the sound of Leyden's voice and drops his fists, the fight in his expression extinguishing. "He is no ally, Grace. Not after what he did to you, to Kórol. To our people."

"I've forgiven him for what he did to me." The words spill out before I realize what I'll say.

Leyden looks more shocked than I feel. "Truly?"

I shrug. Apparently. I'll never forget what he's done, to me and especially to Kórol, but we must move forward.

Tans shudders and he stalks towards Leyden. Instead of attempting to hit him again, he clutches Leyden's wrists and pushes him forward.

"He's not resisting, Tans. And he didn't assault you earlier when you tried," I say desperately. "Doesn't that mean something?"

"A snake that sheds its skin remains a snake," Tans says, his face falling. "Remain here, Grace. We can discuss this further later."

Leyden inclines his head as he lets Tans drag him from the room.

CHAPTER 25

Tans only had a few seconds on me, but by the time I breach the doorway and burst into the hall, he and Leyden are gone. I run down the stairs and surrounding hallways but can't find them. When I make it to the bottom floor, I search for areas I haven't explored before.

After I turn a third corner, I smack into the first person I've seen in the halls today. A muscular chest strikes against my cheek and a half dozen books fall to the ground. I drop to my knees to help gather them when a long blond braid dangles in my eyeline. I snap my neck up to see Fílga in front of me.

"Fílga!" I barrel into him, knocking him back onto his knees and me partly on the ground in a half-embrace.

"Grace! I had not heard you were back." He helps me back to stand, leaving the books on the floor. "Your greeting was more effusive than I'd expect from you. I take it you missed us?" His teeth flash in a crooked smile. "I can only imagine the welcome you would bestow upon Tansr."

At the reminder, I burst into tears, all the pain and worry and guilt leaking down my face. Fíl flutters his hands about my sides, as if he's not sure how to react. Finally, he pats me on the back, the only form of reassurance he's capable of.

"Should I locate Tansr?"

That makes me sniffle louder and he quickly resumes patting my back and appearing more and more alarmed. Fílga looking completely out of his element helps calm me down, rather than continue to upset yet another one of my friends.

"I'm sorry." I wipe my nose against my sleeve. "It's just been a rough few months."

"Likely a difficult year," he says, frowning. "The anniversary of your appearance isn't far off. I imagine nearly repeating the trek has brought forth many competing emotions."

"It's not that." I hadn't even thought of that. "I did something."

He gathers the books in his arms, back into unemotional scholar mode now that my tears have stopped. "I'd heard. Tansr reported there was a burst of magic near the former Eastern Gate and believed it was from your actions."

"It was. I'm planning on bringing the whole thing down."

The books fall from his hands, his expression frozen in horror. "You cannot."

My shoulders slump; I must be doomed to repeat this argument over and over until I lose all my friends. "I have to, Fíl."

"You would let the Dark Eósy into Dalner." He grabs my shoulders with clawed hands, shaking me once, hard.

"We learned there wasn't Dark and Light, remember? Just Eósy."

He releases me to pick up the books, snarling at them instead of me. "You're correct, Grace. There is no division in them as I'd believed. They are all Dark. The worst of them sacrificed their families, their lives, for something as base as power, to support men who would ruthlessly murder their allies based on a slim chance they could increase their already vast power." He presses the books against his chest and pins me with a sharp gaze. "The best of them agreed to turn over those who were defeated at the wall as near slaves. I'd forgiven that, given the circumstances, but knowing what we know now, knowing who has controlled the so-called "Light" faction for centuries, they deserve to remain walled up." His tone remains calm as he delivers the condemnation. The only evidence he's barely keeping together is his slightly discordant breath and the gritting of his teeth.

"It isn't for the Eósy," I tell him gently. He'd never discussed the wall going up, not in any specifics. The hidden agony on his face looks like he's taken the actions of their ancestors personally. I wonder if it's a historian thing, when you immerse yourself too deeply in history. "Not really."

The lines on his forehead deepen. "What benefit would it be then?"

"To the Sàrkany. With the walls up, there's no magic anywhere but in the land."

"I cannot see why that matters." He offers me a flat look. "Now, while I am pleased to see you, I must—"

"Because the Sàrkany are the progeny of the Eósy and they still need magic to survive," I snap. Fíl stares down at me like he's never seen me before. I gather my composure and continue, hoping for a little less irritation in my tone. "They can't get it from the land. You're the one that taught me people died when the wall went up. It wasn't because they lost 'knowledge,' but because they lost the magic. They promised the Raddare King they wouldn't use magic and died. The children that lived evolved into not needing as much magic, but it's still there. You're all still using it. But with the rifts closed, you can't get it anymore."

He clicks his teeth in thought. When he speaks, it's as if he's talking to himself and not to me. "I'd never considered...I'd simply assumed the skills in their blood were lost over time because it was no longer *needed*." He remembers I'm there as he focuses his stare on me. "No one can withdraw from the land? Where did you learn this?"

Now I can't meet his gaze. "I brought someone with me. An Eósy."

"Another—an Eósy?" His posture stiffens. "Thank you, Grace. I must leave. I'm to deliver these books... I cannot delay any longer."

"No, please." I grip his sleeve. "Where would Tans take a prisoner?"

He sounds distracted now. "To the dungeons on the westernmost part of the castle." He glides away, moving as fast as if someone was chasing him.

"Wait! What do you mean 'another' Eósy?"

He turns the corner, letting my words hit the air at his back. With a grumbling huff, I follow his vague directions, going as west as I can before finding myself in an area of the castle I'd never visited. A single staircase appears out of a dead end, the only steps that take us into the bowels of the castle.

I tiptoe down the stairs, the air turning bitter with each step. The stairs end at what looks like another dead end, but flickering shadows confirm there's a hidden hallway. It looks like an illusion: if you stand in front of the wall, it appears solid; if you walk up to it, the opening exposes itself. I start down the left side.

Quickly, I find what I'm looking for. Torchlight flickers against the cool stone walls, unveiling intricately wrought iron bars that confined the cells. A thread of gold curves through the stones, bright veins in the black marble. The scent of rust and corrosion lingers from the iron bars, chains, and hinges. The unmistakable tang of metal, tinged with the subtle undertones of age, permeates the air, leaving a metallic aftertaste on my tongue. Each cell was sparsely furnished with straw-stuffed mattresses, scuffed wooden benches, and ornate locks. Dust on the locks and cobwebs in the ceiling corners reveal a history of disuse. I've never even seen a spider here, or Sekai's hybrid monster version of one.

I follow the cells until I hear voices.

"Once he's fed, leave. We cannot predict how his mental manipulation will work." That's Tans' voice, sounding authoritative and tired.

"Even without magic?" a stranger asks, their voice shaking.

"There is no way to know. One of his kind hasn't been here for centuries."

"Have no fear." That's Leyden now. He sounds distressed. "The dampeners still work well."

Tans ignores him. "Let no one else enter."

Footsteps echo, getting louder and coming in my direction. I duck into the shadows as Tans stalks past me. I wait a few minutes, but the stranger with Leyden, likely a guard, remains. Sighing, I retrace my steps back upstairs. Tans and the guards clearly think the Eósy can't access his mental magic here since none of the Sàrkany can. Apparently, everyone thinks so. *If it gets too bad, Leyden can cleave his way out.* After confirming that I'm not *completely* abandoning the ally I forced here, I head back to my room to plan anew.

When Tans and I had recovered from the battle at the wall in December and reconnected emotionally, we'd started sharing his quarters. They were bigger, for one, and had the best bathroom. It made sense. But with Ilsen large enough to support hundreds of dignitaries and families of Council members, a lot of rooms remained empty. Kórol's minister, Sethen, seemed too preoccupied dealing with Kórol's declining emotional state to reassign my room.

I drift towards the far spindle-like spire that holds my former room, skipping over Tans' floor. A single candle is lit at the end of what was once 'my' hallway and I snag it. With clammy hands, I open the door.

The sun sets off in the distance, barely visible from the six-inch wide windows. The view from the floor displays the stables, residential block, and training grounds, meandering upward to the sea in the far southern distance. It's an image for a postcard. Father used to talk about wanting a 'postcard' family, which would never include me. But I still have a chance for happiness here, if I can manage it. I light the sconces around the room and rest the candle on my tiny table by the door.

The white canopy bed is still made from the last time I used it. I lay on the bed, letting my legs fall over the side and pressing my fingers hard against my closed eyelids. Echoes of Leyden's meddling bounce from wall to wall, our last few conversations before I took the stand at the Gate.

If you know what I am...

I am almost always here...

You did us a favor. Me most of all...

Tans and Kórol stood with me at the Gate. Fílga and Sáven supported me. The Kingdom went to battle based on my drawn ramblings. They trusted me, and that trust got us in this position. In working with him now, am I choosing alliance over allegiance?

"I'm told you have yet to eat since arriving." Tans stands at the door, his face in half shadow, holding a plate.

I pull myself to sit cross legged on the bed. "I've been preoccupied."

With a fortifying breath, he enters my room and joins me on the bed, placing the plate between us. A few vegetables accompany a soft cheese, white instead of Sáv's green variety, and the petals of the alixan flower spice the meal. He picks up a piece of a dergen and shuffles closer. Gingerly, like he's afraid he'll be refused, he wraps an arm around me. I lean into his shoulder as he trails his arm down my side until it can hook around my hip. His fingers rest on one of my scars.

"I will not ask about how in Fates' name you can forgive him for what he's done. You have always been a more gracious person than I," he starts.

"That's not true and you know it." I turn to better tuck my head into his neck.

"What happened to you was personal and if you have seen fit to forgive him, my feelings on the subject are entirely irrelevant," he continues without pausing. "But I cannot forgive for what he has done."

I lift my head and take a piece of cheese to buy time. "I'm not asking you to. I'm asking you to trust me and trust that I know what I'm doing."

He grabs my hand and runs his fingers over my forearm. "Your skin has been marked anew." He traces the fresh scars, a spill of white against my tan skin.

"Because of my choices."

He flicks his amber eyes up at me, torment bleeding from them. "There must be another way."

"There isn't." I say it desperately. "You need the magic. *Kórol* needs the magic. We're the best option right now." I snatch his hands before they can root in his hair and squeeze them tight. "If there's any other option, tell me and I'll do it."

He pulls me even closer, his eyes wide and anguished, locked on my face. "It isn't your problem to solve." Now it's my turn to pull from him. "I'm not arguing about this again. Your asinine attitude will just hurt more people. The citizens in Samsen cert—"

"Asinine?" he says, the ghost of his usual grin on his face. "Is that a new word?"

"Tans..."

He stands and stalks towards the table, his hands gripping the edge. "Must we discuss this? You've only just returned."

I let myself fall backward and throw my arm over my face. "Fine. It's a tomorrow problem. We'll meet with Kórol and the Council and figure it out from there. But no matter how awful it seems, Leyden must be a part of the solution." With what we know, there's no other choice.

Tans doesn't respond, but his silence is as loud as a bullet. I slip onto my elbows and peer up at him. He isn't looking at me, but at the candle I purloined from the hall.

"Tans?"

"I'll discuss it tomorrow. With Kórol." His eyes meet mine for a minute and attempt a playful smirk. It doesn't work. "Perhaps we can restart your training test regimen."

I take the olive branch for what it is and toss a piece of cheese at him. He ducks.

"One of them focuses on aim, you know," he says slyly, as he snags another piece of dergen and kneels on the bed. He shuffles towards me until he's straddling me. "Yours could use some work."

And like the tropes I used to read, I let Tans and I bury our disagreement and argument under a mountain of physical chemistry to deal with the problem for another day.

CHAPTER 26

Tans and I talk about our weeks apart until we run out of words. He doesn't mention Kórol and the fast descent into (what sounds *a lot like*) authoritarianism, and I don't talk about Leyden or tearing down the wall. Meaning the conversation ends quickly.

When we're beneath the sheets, he leans close, wrapping his arms around me. I press my face into the soft skin of his chest.

"I've been thinking about the conversation we had before you...left," he whispers, trailing his fingers down my spine.

I shimmy out of his grip, but he snags me back. "Is that not something we can leave until tomorrow too?"

The moonlight from the slim window illuminates his face, his mahogany eyes dark. He nods. "Tomorrow, we'll handle everything tomorrow."

He kisses me again. It's hesitant, like we're not the same people we were when I left for the Wilds, like we aren't the same people from only an hour ago, simply a brush of his mouth over mine. Then, deeper, slower, longer as he pulls me atop him. His eyelashes flutter against my cheek, his taste is in my mouth. There's a rush of blood in my ears and a thrum of desire in my belly. And then it's only need and need and need until we finally sleep.

I wake the next morning in my old room, the sky outside still dark. Shuffling over, I reach my arms out for Tans but only grip empty sheets. Something, some fear or nerves, pushes me from the bed instead of falling back asleep. Tans said 'we' will handle it this morning. And after living with a creature that spins words for fun, I know that 'handling' it from Tans could be devastating. And Tans never said I was part of the 'we'. He certainly wasn't part of my plan with Leyden.

All my clothes are in Tans' room, and I dropped the travel pack in the map room, leaving me no option but to force myself back into the dirt and travel stained outfit from yesterday. Sparing only a second to bemoan my lost opportunity to get completely clean for the first time in months, I race through the hall and down the winding stairs of my spire. A night's sleep in a bed, no matter how restless, helped my hips and legs recover and I don't hobble when I make my way down the stairs. *Good*. Reminding Tans and Kórol of my injuries won't endear them to Leyden any.

Moving purely on instinct, I pivot towards the throne room. If they aren't there, I'll try my next idea. Luck is with me as I hear soft voices from the hall. I heave open the heavy door and slip inside.

Leyden is kneeling before Kórol, Faburth standing over him with a sword resting on the back of his neck. The sun's slow ascent barely illuminates the red stained glass, leaving grisly looking rays bisecting the floor around. Kórol sits on his throne on the dais, face pale and mouth nearly frothing. As I lurk closer, his pale skin looks sickly gray. Beside him, wearing identical masks of dread, are Sethen and Tans. The only thing keeping me from freaking out and breaking into a run is that Faburth's sword isn't raised.

Tans sees me first, his expression freezing, leaving only horror in its place. Beside him, Sethen shakes his head with minute movements to ward me off. But I can't.

"Kórol, wait!" My voice reverberates around the room. Everyone except Kórol flinches at the harsh sound.

But Kórol's gaze never strays from Leyden's. "You have not been called before me, making your presence unneeded. Unless my Lord Commander minimized your part in this demon's appearance into my realm?" He looks at me then. The deadness in his gaze when he was spelled by Bittállí looked less terrifying than the lifelessness he reveals now. "I've been advised you do not belong beside him. Is my Lord Commander wrong?"

Tans pleads silently behind him, attempting to shoo me away. But I don't get a chance to answer Kórol as Leyden starts shaking from his place on the floor, his whole body convulsing. Faburth's sword quivers against his neck and opens a thin line of red into his skin. Purposeful or not, Leyden pulls attention to him, letting me shuffle closer. I creep between the benches towards the dais and Leyden kneeling before it.

Kórol's lips pull back into a sneer as he turns to Sethen. "Tell me our prisoner is not expiring before I have the joy of executing him myself." If someone could freeze from a look, Kórol could do it, his eyes hard as diamond and just as cold.

"Simply laughing," Leyden says, lifting his head and revealing a jagged smile. "That Grace would let something as base as an 'invitation' keep her from going where she likes. Whether she belongs here, she would find her way to meddle."

Kórol stands then, reaching for his waist and finding his knife holsters empty. I'd be almost touched that Kórol is enraged on my behalf if I actually believed it was in my favor. Leyden could insult Kórol's greatest enemy and Kórol would find fault with it.

Rightfully so, I remind myself. *Given what Leyden's done to him.* The guilt at bringing this pain back to Kórol festers inside me, nearly bringing up bile.

"Kórol, please," I start gently, my hands out in front of me like a poor shield. "Do you remember when I leapt into the Gate?"

He blinks; the entire room seems to take a breath.

"We thought it had to be done, remember? There was no way to stop…" I swallow a gulp. Perhaps bringing Leyden's crimes to the forefront of Kórol's memory isn't the best tactic. "We needed to close the gate. There were more of them than us and they were better prepared. And do you remember what you did? You held Tans back, because you thought I had to do it. Even if you didn't understand it, if Tans didn't understand it. And I did it for you. For you and Tans and everyone here."

Kórol sits back down, some color leaching back into his face.

"But I was wrong." I gather my thoughts with a deep inhale. "I knew my blood and the interaction with my *phone* and the Gate affected magic. I thought it would close the Gate and keep more of them from coming. I didn't know it would remove the Sàrkany's only access to magic," I say miserably, confessing my guilt aloud. "But I know how to fix it now. And I'm asking you to let me, even if you don't understand it now."

"Grace, stop this," Tans says, concentrating on Kórol as if afraid he'll explode. "The Eósy did this. This isn't your fault, or your responsibility." He pinches his eyes shut tight. When he opens them, the muted mahogany swirling within looks mournful. "This isn't like your books. You aren't the main character, responsible for all the good and bad that happens."

He could have stabbed me and it would have hurt less. Phantom twinges of my own scarred stab wounds speak the truth of it. "You think I don't know that? You think I'm pushing this narrative forward because I, what, like nearly killing myself? That I like constantly fighting and feeling like this is all my fault?" I throw my hands up in the air. "I would love for there to be a better explanation. Or a better answer. I don't want to be the hero of this story! But none of you will go into Dànna and none of you will try something else." I take a deep breath and try to force away the anger. "I need to fix it. It's my duty. I need to return magic to keep your…our people alive. I need you to trust me that, no matter what he did to us, we need his help now."

"If it will speed things along," Leyden says. My eyes fall shut as tension reappears in the room. "While I can't feel regret for my actions, I can certainly apologize for whatever repercussions they may have inflicted upon you. I compelled no one beyond what their own strength could handle; that was Bittállí's game. To me, you were simply tools, useful tools with specific roles. My actions were a matter of necessity rather than personal sentiment."

Sethen's hands cover his face. Even Faburth looks to be wincing with concern.

"Shut up, Leyden," I hiss.

"He should understand that," Leyden says, raising an elegant eyebrow, at odds with his dirt smudged and slightly bloody face. "He may not have been king long, but I recall him speaking to you about duty. Choices must always be made to further one's duty."

Kórol bursts upward, reaching for the small knife Tans' stores in a thigh holster. It's only luck that kept Tans from bringing his bow and arrows today. Tans wrestles it away from him.

"Kórol, we must follow the procedures," Tans says, keeping his hands on Kórol's chest. "You cannot kill him."

I'd point out Tans' hypocritical behavior from last night if all my attention wasn't pinpointed on Kórol's enraged face.

"Now you wish to behave appropriately?" Kórol roars. "You play the buffoon and tease when it serves you. But when your King truly needs you, you deny your commitment?"

Tans' expression crumbles. "Everything I have ever done is to support you."

"Then do as I say," Kórol says through hissed teeth. "If you are too much of a weakling to do so, then give me your daggers."

Tans forces Kórol backward. "I will do much for you, my brother in arms, but there must be limits or we are no worse than the creature kneeling before us."

"You are a disgrace!" Kórol spits in Tans' face, who doesn't even flinch, before turning his attention to Faburth. "Your Lord

Commander is derelict in his duties, you must fulfill them. Execute the prisoner!"

I reach out for Leyden uselessly, knowing my hands are no match for the speed of Faburth's blade. His own lessons tell of the futility of succeeding. And Leyden's hands are cuffed behind his back so he can't escape that way, but perhaps he could manipula—My mind shudders at what I'm considering, at what desperation would push me to do to those I love.

Faburth raises his sword but hesitates, his callused and wrinkled hands clenching around the hilt. "We haven't yet had his trial. The law requires—"

"I am the law!" Kórol howls.

"They don't understand it," Leyden says, almost conversationally. He looks calm for someone with a sword above his head. "The gradual unraveling of your sanity. The void that lingers where the magic should be. It's a brutal rot, like something gnawing at the core of your existence. Your mind, your very being, succumbs to a chaos that others can't fathom. At least not until they, too, feel the absence of magic. Your commander looks a little gray himself. Perhaps your bloodline had it affect you first, a strength that couldn't be bred out. Perhaps you were simply more powerful. Whatever it is, you are not yourself."

Leyden's words hang in the air. Tans and Sethen look struck with the realization that there might be another reason for Kórol's behavior. I'd left Tans in Samsen before I could explain what Leyden had told me during those irritating dreams.

Kórol snarls again, slashing his thick forearms through the air. "Commander Faburth, do your duty!"

"Tranlig!" I shout. Kórol freezes, Faburth drops the sword. "I call for tranlig." A phrase that doesn't exist in English, it's a right given to citizens to be heard before the Council, saved only for the most serious of situations. Instead of being prosecuted, the accused takes the lead instead of facing prosecution in a conventional trial. If any circumstance called for it, it's now.

Kórol pants like a bull ready to charge. "How dare—"

"We acknowledge the request from the proxy for the Council member from Gramad," Tans says. "Minister Sethen will confirm and prepare the room for your presentation."

Faburth quickly stands and grabs Leyden's cuffs, likely to return him to the prison. When they're near the door, Kórol shudders, placing a mask of civility over his face and calling out.

"Commander, Miss Grace will await Tranlig with the prisoner. Escort her to the dungeons."

Faburth offers me a compassionate smile, but it's pinched in the corners. I follow behind him.

"Kórol," says Tans, his voice piercing.

"I, too, have limits, Lord Commander."

I attempt small talk on the trek to the bottom floor, to avoid thinking about the situation I've put us into. "I've been practicing my hand-to-hand combat," I tell Faburth.

Faburth, whose attention remains fixed on Leyden in front of him, as if worried Leyden will make a run for it, hums. "Did you run as I suggested?"

"No," Leyden says brightly. "She attacked a woman with fire for hands. It went as well as you'd expect."

Faburth holds in a laugh. "I should have expected nothing less."

The mood lightens, but only for a minute, when we step down the stairs into the dank prison and can't avoid what we're doing and why we're there. The pervasive odor of decaying wood and rust wafts through the cramped space.

When we get to the false wall, Faburth directs us right. Leyden stumbles once and slumps his shoulders when he regains his footing.

I dart my gaze around at the barren cells. Mildew and disuse cling to the very air we breathe, evidence of the slow degradation of the prison. "Shivio and Rungin told me a little about what's been going on since I left. Is it as bad as they said?"

Faburth stops, yanking Leyden to a halt. "There's a reason these cells have remained empty."

"Because of the executions," Leyden says, though his voice croaks.

I hiss air through my teeth. "Yes, thank you, Leyden. I got that."

Leyden looks ready to respond but Faburth nudges him forward until we arrive at a hallway with a dozen cells all in a line. He opens the first door and directs him inside before turning to me.

Leyden throws himself onto the straw mattress and speaks into the rough fabric. "We can share."

"No," I'm quick to reply.

Faburth appears relieved and opens the cell to Leyden's right. "I will return for you the moment the Minister allows me," he says, leaning forward and touching my cheek. "Take heed, Lady. We will overcome this."

I wait until I can no longer hear Faburth's footsteps before focusing on Leyden. "That could have been worse," I admit.

"That I live shows the truth of that statement," Leyden says, his voice muffled.

"Thank you for not using your magic and destroying the plan before it could begin."

Leyden groans, rolling over onto his back on the mattress, dust mites wafting up into the air. "They believe me neutered here, that there is no magic for anyone, and I see no reason to correct that misunderstanding. However, while I would love to accept your praise, it wasn't willing restraint on my part. There's something in the dampeners here reducing my ability to use my magic as I'd wish."

I'm across the cell and at the bars separating us before I realize I'd moved. "What? What do you mean?"

He gestures carelessly to the stone wall and floor. "See the veining? It's likely in that. I tested it last night and did not enjoy the outcome." He holds up two fingers that I hadn't noticed were burned. "The effects had almost worn off upstairs. Alas, the longer I remain down here, the longer it will take to regain my full strength."

"Fantastic," I say, putting the bars at my back and sinking to the floor.

"Thank you for sparing me the loss of my head upstairs," he says. "Although should I assume the risk remains for this 'tranlig,' whatever that is?"

I press the backs of my hands to my cheeks to cool the tense flush that's appeared. I'd called for it to avoid Leyden using his magic to avoid murder upstairs, and to get in front of the Council rather than Kórol. And if they didn't approve our plan, we'd rip away with my guilt at a more manageable level. But now...it's a last resort, since there's no question that we're both guilty. Tranlig isn't about evidence, but which side puts forth the most compelling and persuasive speech. "Maybe. It's like a business presentation, instead of a trial. We try to move the Council to support our position, while a representative of the crown does the opposite. I'm hoping the person speaking against us is a friend."

"Given we *have* committed treason, it will need to be an impressive presentation."

"Helpful," I say, somewhat snide, no matter I was thinking the same thing.

"It sounds easier than the trials in Dànna," he says, lounging on his mattress. "We must complete a trial by ordeal, enduring elemental bindings."

I pinch my eyes closed. With my luck, we'll go through that next. "Worst case scenario, we could try to delay long enough for your magic to reappear."

"I suppose we could—" He jolts to sit up and his head cocks like a flustered bird.

I leap to stand. "What is it?"

"I secured your bag." Fíl's emerges from around the corner, holding my dusty travel bag aloft. He falters when he sees Leyden before appearing to brace himself and glide past him without acknowledgement. "I apologize for opening it, but you could not receive it before someone searched it. I volunteered to confirm there was no vektágsal."

"Contraband," says Leyden. His stare hasn't left Fíl's form since he appeared.

"Tansr hoped you could use your notes within to prepare for whatever presentation you make this afternoon," Fíl says, frowning. "I apologize that Tansr could not appear himself."

"It's fine," I say, lying as I grab the bag and force it through the bars. "Thank you for bringing it."

"Of course, Lady Grace." He spares a glance at Leyden before refocusing on me and offering a warm smile. "Good luck."

"Until later, friend," Leyden says, wriggling his fingers in goodbye.

Fíl jumps, his braid whipping behind him as he stalks from the room.

I reseat myself on the floor. "What was that about?"

Leyden ignores me, now standing at the barrier, fingers clutching the metal and staring at the space where Fílga disappeared to. His cheeks press against the bars. "Who was that?"

"Fílga." I dig through my bag, Leyden forgotten. "He took some of my books!"

Leyden sits beside me on the other side of the bars. His cheeks have two red lines slicing through them from the metal. "Fílga the...historian?"

"Yes." I check out the notes, but they're all in order. Leyden's writings too, with his written knowledge of the wall and how it went up. But I'm missing something. "Why would they take those books?"

"Which ones?"

"The ones I took from the Caern stronghold." I scowl down at the open space in my travel bag.

Leyden isn't as annoyed by the theft as I am. "Perhaps there was something illicit within them."

"They were children's books!" And they might not have been mine, but I'd earned them fair and square.

He shrugs. "Is the historian also the one teaching you?"

I cast him a dirty look. "Yes, why?"

"Might I look at your syllabus?"

"Why?"

"I'd offered previously, if you'll recall. I find myself...curious." There's a sheen of sweat on his forehead and a trembling in his frame that takes the fight from me. If Leyden wants to look at my syllabus, I suppose he has that right, given what I'm requiring of him. I scoop out the worn syllabus and pass it through the bars.

While Leyden peruses the stack, I try to put my thoughts into order. I don't know which Council members are still in Ilsen, whether they're ones interested in facts and law or prefer passionate pleas. My head falls into my hands. Maybe wasting time until Leyden can break us out *is* the best option.

Leyden hums as he turns to the last page, then straightens the parchment as best he can, handing it back through the bars. "It seems all in order, covering everything I'd consider appropriate to teach you were I in charge of your education," he says, his sickly pallor fading. "I'd expect as much, with what I now know of your teacher and what knowledge he could impart to you, given your claim of lost knowledge and destroyed books."

My brows raise. "Information is lacking. I didn't make that up." But Fíl keeps leaving things out, information he avoided telling me and topics he's removed. "Whether it's *appropriate* shouldn't be the standard. No one should police knowledge."

He cocks his head. "I've no idea what you're talking about."

"How about one topic that may not be 'appropriate' for me to learn but shouldn't be kept from me. Soulmates."

There's no reaction from him except a baffled blink. "*Soulmates?*"

I shove the notes back in my pack. "Yes, soulmates. Love of my life, aren't we so lucky our magic chose each other. The fated matches all you magical people get."

When I return my gaze to him, I expect a look a pity or laughter, as he saw firsthand the struggles in my relationship with Tans and my complete lack of magical anything. But his baffled expression slackens to nothing, like a frozen computer that loses power. I'm about to poke him through the bars, fearing the stones caused permanent damage when he ducks his head. A small snuffling sound comes from him that builds into a light giggle, high-pitched and giving me flashbacks to his days pretending to be my childlike guide. It shifts into a full belly laugh.

He grabs his stomach as my own fills with a mix of apprehension and annoyance. I reach through the bars to slap him on the shoulder, but it only makes him laugh harder.

"If you don't stop laughing and tell me what's funny, next time I'm aiming somewhere more sensitive. Magic sickness or not."

He cuts himself off with a cough and wipes actual tears from his eyes. "I'm unsure I can even explain it. It wasn't altogether funny, but the seriousness in your face and the senselessness of your words started a laugh that I couldn't contain." He giggles hoarsely. "It has been centuries since I've allowed myself that."

"I'm so glad I could provide you some joy at my expense," I say dryly.

"Don't pout, dearest. It was a good jest." He opens his eyes again. 'Soulmates! And you sounded so sincere, I'd almost believed you were serious."

I cross my arms around my chest until comprehension blooms on his still pink face.

"You are serious." His brows raise in alarm.

I throw my hands in the air. "Why would I make that up?"

"I may have been in your head for years, Grace, but even I can't understand all that occurs within. Why would you think it's true?"

"Because they said it was," I say petulantly.

"Did Fílga?" He asks with a seriousness I can't interpret. When I shake my head, he gentles his tone. "What exactly did they tell you?"

I speak to the ground to avoid seeing the pity that must match his voice, explaining what Tans and Sáven said, and how Mara and Breg described it. Even Elo understood its significance.

"Is that not simply...love?" The hesitancy drags my attention back to him. He's not looking at me, but his long, pale hands. "The soup analogy is good, but it isn't enough that the ingredients may match. You feel a connection to another and your feelings simmer, but you must give it care. If you leave it be, it can boil over. If you don't add flavor, it can turn bland or taste poorly. Not that there is some fated match for you, but that there's someone whose essence might work with yours, and who can create magic together. Here, the magic is a shared recipe for love."

It sounds like something out of one of the old books I'd read, ones he likely read along with me when he was creeping into my life. But the significance of his speech... I want him to be right. I want choices for everyone, including me. Assuming my relationship with Tans can withstand what I'm putting us through. But all I can say is, "I didn't know you could cook."

He wets his lips and exhales. When he finally raises his head, the vulnerability is gone. "Yes, well, I haven't in centuries. And like my cooking abilities, soulmates likewise do not exist." His eye twitches. "Though it most certainly was a bit of propaganda from Bittállí. Before the wall, it wasn't unheard of to call your beloved your 'heart's match.' Bittállí convinced Derul's son that he loved her, and she was thus *his* heart's match. I assume as the story was passed down, it evolved into the idea of the translation you mentioned earlier, that magic brings you together."

"And it all culminating at age twenty?"

"The traditional age for betrothal. At least you can take solace in the fact that your teacher did not teach you any lies." He returns to his mattress. "Now, I intend to nap until it is time for this 'tranlig.' Unless you have any objections?"

I shake my head, silent and staring down at my travel pack.

Soulmates and fated heroes. Two things the Sàrkany were so sure were true. I look back up at my Eósy companion, the red burn lines fading but still present on his porcelain skin. *What else are the Sàrkany wrong about?*

CHAPTER 27

B y the time Faburth returns to escort us back to the throne room, I've pushed the soulmate discovery to the side, something to reveal to Tans when all is well, and have two long outlines. The first is full of facts and history, the second modeled after Sirgen's speech in Samsen.

Faburth handcuffs Leyden again but has us walk together rather than him leading Leyden and me trailing behind. I'm not sure if it says something about his increased trust in Leyden or a new distrust of me.

Leyden looks green when we're brought upstairs, stumbling enough that I feel compelled to keep him steady. With one hand on the notes I've been allowed to keep and the other on Leyden's narrow shoulder, I lean closer and whisper, "Do I need to worry about a 'gold paint' situation?"

He blinks at me before huffing a pained laugh. "My sanity is fine. The wards are simply...an obstacle."

An obstacle that could kill us if my presentation isn't good enough. "Maybe give me a signal when you're back to normal."

"The signal will be an opening that takes us elsewhere," he says, wincing as he stumbles again.

"To Dànna," I say firmly. We're enacting our plan. We must.

He groans, the sound only half-forced. "You're going to demand I speak with Pender, aren't you?"

Before I can respond, Faburth places a hand on each of our backs and directs us through the door. I appreciate the nudge, or I might have grabbed Leyden and ran. Better than failing this early. Tans would understand, someday. Maybe his mistaken belief in soulmates means he'd move on quickly. I smile grimly at my own joke.

Kórol, Sethen, and Tans are in the same positions they were in this morning. Now, Fílga has joined them, holding reams of paper. I heave a sigh of relief; he's likely Kórol's representative. While he wouldn't lie for me, he could certainly go easy on us and lean the tranlig in our direction.

The benches have been shoved together towards the back of the room, like they were during the trial with the dragon. A small, raised platform has been pulled from storage and three chairs are placed equidistant on top. Rothàna sits in the chair closest to Kórol, Pirre in the middle, and Zovà closest to the window. It isn't the best combination of Council members to present for, but also isn't the worst. Pirre exploits his birthright at every opportunity and justifies his derogatory behavior and disrespect towards others as a privilege granted to him alone. To persuade him will take a delicate balance in flattering his ego and appealing to his sense of entitlement, that he 'deserves' magic. Rothàna will weigh the consequences and favors strategic maneuvers rather than impulsive actions. Our appearance here, before we cross into Dànna and undertake our plan, may weigh in our favor. But Zovà is cautious by nature, more of a faceless follower without personal ambition. He'll likely let the other two decide and agree with one of them.

When we're directed down what used to be the aisle, Zovà and Pirre rearrange their expressions into ones of severity. But Rothàna's face is devoid of emotion. I can only hope I don't utterly destroy her opinion of me.

Sethen clears his throat and begins the ceremonies. "Lords and Lady of the esteemed Council. We gather here today to review Miss Grace and the stranger Leyden's treason against the crown," he announces. "The accused shall present first, with a limit of five minutes, followed by the accuser with a limit of three minutes. Then, the Council will deliberate to determine the outcome, which must be decided before the sun sets on the day tranlig was demanded."

My eyes dart to the colored windows, the day is more than half-over already.

Sethen continues, "Lady...err, Miss Grace has requested approval to enter a compact with the Eósy to jointly raze the wall. The crown seeks their execution. In the event of a tie, the King's vote shall carry."

I look down at my notes, scribbles legible only to me. When there were twelve Council members present, Kórol's tie-breaking made sense. But with only three, we must convince all three Council members to side with us or else Kórol's decision will prevail. Our fate rests on these three Council members, only one of which I know likes me enough to, *maybe*, vote in my favor to keep me from execution.

I sneak a look at Leyden. Delaying until his magic is at full strength seems like an even better idea. Leyden still looks green, but at least he's standing straight with a hint of smugness in his expression. I frown; his attitude will offend Rothàna, but Pirre's arrogance might appreciate it.

Kórol remains silent, flapping his hand at Sethen as if he's bored. In the late afternoon light, the blood red of the windows and Kórol's graying skin look even more worrying.

Sethen nods. "Present your cases," he declares and the tension in the room ratches to a stifling level.

I suck in a deep lungful of air and reread my first line once more. But before I can begin, Leyden takes over.

"People of this Kingdom," he says, pressing his hands into his chest, the cuffs clinking together. "Hear me now not as an outsider but as a kindred spirit, bound by the threads of a shared destiny. I stand before you as a shared ancestor. Your King, indeed, his entire line that arose after the wall's construction, came from my sister."

Kórol's eyes twitch, but he otherwise keeps up his impression of a statue. Rothàna raises a single brow.

"I don't think that's helpful," I hiss to Leyden's back.

He tousles his hair and ignores me. "I tell you that to remind you of our once connection. And the threads of unity that once wove a tapestry of a thriving Kingdom are not easily forgotten."

I look down at my notes. The tapestry line is something I co-opted from Sirgen. But Leyden's version sounds more compelling. *Maybe this will work.*

"Step outside these walls and see the faces of your neighbors, your family, your friends. Do you not see the hunger in their eyes, the longing for something more? We are not beings meant to be confined by borders or bereft of the magic that gives us life."

Pirre looks to be tuning out. He's dressed more ostentatiously than normal, with embroidered embellishments on his tunic and a dozen beads in his long black hair. He probably hasn't spoken to his 'neighbors' in years.

Leyden continues, gesturing outward with his hands, but the handcuffs dull the effect. "We stand at a crossroads, not just in this room but in the very fabric of our existence. Magic isn't a force to be feared; it is a wellspring of potential, a gift waiting to be unwrapped. I ask you to consider, not just my fate, but the fate of us all. Together, we can weave a new narrative—one where the borders that confine us are but shadows of the past."

"Pretty words for a pretty boy," says Rothàna. "But this tells us nothing of your actual proposal and why we should let you free. I would hear more from Lady Grace, who must explain why she believes this is the right choice."

I look down at my notes again before abandoning them to the floor. "This isn't a question of magic or no magic. This is about keeping you alive."

Kórol scoffs from his throne.

I point out the window. "That wall isn't a barrier between you and those you see as enemies. It is a dam withholding the lifeblood of your people. Unless we tear down the walls, every Sàrkany will wither and die. And it isn't only the Sàrkany. Our supposed enemies are not as invincible as you assume. This is a fate you all share. *That's* why they attempted to tear down the wall."

"Is this true?" Zovà asks Leyden.

"Yes," he answers.

Pirre scoffs. "Their deaths matter not. Why would we not reopen the rifts and continue as we have?"

Here I hesitate. "Because only the Eósy can reopen them, and they likely won't do so without some benefit to them."

Pirre scoffs. "Ah. You're presenting blackmail in the form of a contract." He claps his hands. "I believe I've heard enough. The gentleman's words were persuasive, and the—"

"Not yet," Rothàna says. "You are not in charge of this proceeding, Pirre. Quiet down and listen." A dull color blooms on Pirre's face and he pouts but stays quiet.

I stutter forward. "My proposal is not to forge an alliance with the Eósy out of naivety, but out of necessity. We work together to tear down the wall. They will apply magic to the wall, sacrificing that magic until the wall bursts. I've seen it happen." I leave out the amount of Eósy lives that would be sacrificed to do it, no matter it would likely convince Kórol and Pirre just *because* of the death. "In exchange for agreeing to tear down the wall, the Eósy will enter into a treaty with the Sàrkany, to keep them from..."

"From playing with your lives again," Leyden adds helpfully.

"Why have they not attempted to tear the wall down these six months? Why go through this farce with the Sàrkany and ask permission for something they already have the power to do?" This time Fílga asks the question, surprising the other audience members.

Leyden smirks at him. "Because only two Eósy know how to do it. One who is not inclined to do so and myself. And I've promised to help Grace with her goals."

I step in front of him before Leyden's antagonism ruins our chance. "The mechanism to tear down the wall is...unpalatable to most of the Eósy. If we receive your support, our next steps are searching for an alternative magic source to bring down the wall."

Rothàna narrows her eyes at me, a glint of intrigue appearing. "And if we do not approve your plan?"

"Assuming we are not...executed?" I stare down at my hands and the scars there. I remember the conversation I had with Tans before leaving for the Wilds, with Leyden after the bath. Though it is Fíl's question, I lift my head and focus my gaze on Tans. "I'm not asking for permission. I'm asking for support. We will present the same proposal to the Eósy. It's their promise that matters, as it will bind them from harming the Sàrkany. We can bring down the wall without Sàrkany support. And we will. But I want Dalner behind us."

Tans' eyes fall shut but Rothàna nods and leans back in her chair.

Sethen steps forward again, cutting off any further presentation. "Now, the crown will present."

At the pronouncement, Kórol stands. The room gasps in unison. In no account of tranlig has the King ever spoken for himself. As a member of the 'jury,' it can't be fair. But no one comments, instead everyone watches Kórol in anticipation.

A pall of unease blankets the room while he stares at the motto etched in glass. "There comes a moment when the well-being of many requires us to make choices that may seem unpalatable. For example, replacing Council members is always an unpleasant business. Revising our justice system would likewise be disagreeable." He speaks idly, sounding overly casual for the implied threats he's just made. "Sentencing a beloved friend is certainly unpalatable." He spins to gaze directly into my face. "But we must do our duty." And then he takes a seat, leaving nothing but the hushed cadence of our breaths to fill the void left by his loaded statements.

The hush is finally broken by Sethen. "With that," he says, stuttering. "With that, please tally your votes."

Leyden slides closer to me. "Not to alarm you, but my magic has yet to reinvigorate itself." My stomach twists into a mass of anxious knots.

"I vote with the crown," says Kórol, waving a lazy hand.

"I vote with the accused," Rothàna says. "I have come to know young Grace and I would have us stand with her, rather than against her." She tilts up her chin, as if daring Kórol to go through with his threats.

Pirre stares down at his embroidery for a full minute, before smiling shakily. "I vote with our eminent King."

My heart descends into my stomach like a stone.

Although it no longer matters, Zora echoes Pirre. "I vote with the crown. I'm sorry, Lady Grace."

Faburth is beside us in an instant, grasping my shoulder tight like he's afraid I'll run.

"Perhaps the trial by ordeal would have been a better option," Leyden says, sounding unbothered. "You've always wiggled out of those rather well, recent scars or no. Certainly better than any of your speeches."

"Shut up, Leyden." But I say it this time because I'm watching what's happening before us. Fílga is whispering with Rothàna before she nods and he scurries from the room, trailing papers behind him. Tans is hissing animatedly in Kórol's ear, his hands punctuating whatever he's saying.

Kórol ignores him. His voice is barely more than a whisper but laced with acid. "As is required by our laws, those convicted of treason are to be executed."

"Kórol, this isn't you," Tans says, nearly shouting now. "He might be right about the effects of the magic—"

"Do not question your King," Kórol snarls.

Rothàna stands and narrows her eyes. "What effects of the magic?"

Kórol stalks towards the door. Before he breaches the seal, he spins back to face the room. "Whoever questions my decisions will join Grace and the demon tomorrow morning." And then he shoves the door open and vanishes from sight.

"Grace," Tans says from the dais.

"It's okay." My voice wavers, as I make my last words to him a lie. "It will all work out."

He vaults down and catches Faburth before he can cuff me and escort us from the room. Sethen and the two male Council members watch him aghast, while Rothàna twists her lips into a grim smile. Faburth looks between Tans and me and makes a show of digging through his pockets for a second pair of cuffs. Leyden drops his head to stare at the ceiling with a groan.

But Tans ignores them all. One shaking hand pulls me close while the other caresses the bottom of my chin and tilts my head up. With a desperate noise, he descends on my mouth in a passion-driven kiss. He pulls away sooner than I'd like, but given the audience and Kórol's pronouncement, I understand why.

I open my mouth to say something, anything, but he presses his finger to my lips and leans close to my ear.

"You never needed my permission, but you will always have my support. Do *whatever* you must, my darling Butterfly. And we will find each other again. That is my promise to you, and I need no magic to make it binding."

And, finally, Faburth escorts us from the room.

CHAPTER 28

F aburth pushes us back to the prison faster than I'd expected. I try to delay him, to give Leyden more time to overcome the magic block, but he was unrelenting.

When he returns me to my cell, he doesn't linger. "I will not forget my own promise," he says before racing back the way he came.

Leyden resettles on his mattress while I watch Faburth go. "What promise?" I ask aloud.

"That you'll overcome this," he answers, staring at the ceiling. "We have until morning."

I create a cocoon of my arms and hug myself tight, a poor imitation of Tans' arms around me. But I've got nothing, no grand plans on how I'll overcome this. Leyden's magic was my deus ex machina. "You sound oddly cheery for someone about to be executed in the morning."

"Because we won't."

I rub my eyes as a few tears leak through. "Has your magic returned?"

He rolls over to look at me scrunched into a ball on the ground. "No. Because that guard is right. You will overcome this."

"So, faith." I curl further into myself. "Your big idea is faith? Might as well pick out our tombstones."

"Stop it, Grace," Leyden bites out. "Stop feeling sorry for yourself and figure out a way to escape. Fates, that was the most irritating part of being in your mind. How often you bemoaned your fate, acted as though you were going to give up, and then somehow it worked out regardless. If I weren't on your side now, I would rue your abnormal success."

"Pardon me for irritating the creature that violated my mind," I snap.

He groans. "It is exhausting, Grace. We go through this performance repeatedly. Can't we simply…skip to the end? Your mind will come up with any number of implausible ideas and one will work. It always does."

"My implausible idea this time involved you creating a tear in reality and getting us out of here," I say snidely. "Look where that's gotten us."

His tone is disdainful and expression sharp. "Then think of something else."

"What if I can't?" My voice is whisper soft.

His expression doesn't soften. "Then we'll die, won't we?"

"Helpful." I inhale unsteadily at the prospect.

"As much as you may think otherwise, I *am* attempting to be. You've talked yourself out of dozens of scrapes and wriggled your way out of many seemingly unwinnable situations. Why should this be any different? You leapt on the back of a sàchenda and brought it down. You've ridden a dragon, after you *shot* it first. You bested Bittállí and her mother. For Fates' sake, you defeated me *and* convinced me to align myself with you."

"I didn't do any of that on my own," I snap. "I did it all with…" I lift my head as I replay what happened in the throne room, and what happens every time I'm in need. "With my friends."

Leyden crosses his arms and pouts. "I helped with the sàchenda," he mutters.

Unbidden, a smile blooms over my chapped lips. "I was including you in that category, though that probably means the wards are affecting me more than you at this point," I tease. "Now stop talking, I need to think."

"There's my girl," Leyden says.

"Not your girl." I can't stop the spontaneous laugh that erupts. "Seriously, Leyden, shut up."

"You have a plan?" Leyden asks later. He's turned greener during this third visit to the prison, but that's part of the idea.

"Something like that..."

No matter what Kórol pronounced, Tans and Fil won't let me die. Rothàna too, probably. The first idea is not even an idea, but a prayer, that Tans or Fílga gets the keys and releases me. The more likely scenario is they send someone else to check on me. From there, the idea blooms into something simple: assuming they aren't already planning on releasing me, I'm going to leverage the information I have about the unrest and get the person, likely a disenchanted guard, on my side. The greater world seems invested in returning the magic, and as far as they're aware, I'm the best way to do that.

The more troublesome part is dealing with Leyden, as none of my allies care about him. As soon as I'm released from my cell, Leyden will fake an illness. None of the guards that Tans would send for me are callous enough to ignore a sick prisoner, not unless the lacking magic has already hit their personality. Assuming it hasn't, and it's a necessary assumption, when the guard attempts to attend to Leyden, Leyden will either run out. Or the guard will be sympathetic enough to my goals that they'll want Leyden free to return to the wall and release him at my urging.

My third idea is too callous to think, much less say aloud, but Tans did give me permission to "do what I must."

Leyden wrinkles his nose when I finish explaining the more agreeable plans. "We're relying on a sympathetic ally or a guard rebellion? That's your idea?"

"You weren't offering a better one. And this one is just as likely to succeed as the others."

"Why not break through the stone and discover a long-forgotten, underground escape route that predates the prison's wards? Or find a hidden artifact under your bench that can temporarily nullify the wards? Or a mysterious magical stranger, shrouded in shadows, reveals himself and zaps us away? Or a rare alignment of stars triggers a surge of magical energy—"

"Because those are likely." I roll my eyes. "This isn't a book, remember? There's no missing artifact or mysterious stranger that will simply appear and fix things. We need to fix it." With our allies, unwilling or no.

"I'll have you know—"

Footsteps echo down the halls. Leyden and I fall silent. I offer him a weighted glance and he rolls his eyes. But, still, he tosses himself back on his mattress and covers his stomach as if in agony. But before the person reveals themselves, he sits up and beams.

Fílga appears, rushing towards the bars and clasping them tight, a large sack dangling from one wrist. "Grace, are you well?"

"Fílga!" I shout, duplicating my reaction when I ran into him yesterday. *Was it only yesterday? How long ago was Bittálli's temple?* "Did Tans send you?"

Fíl furrows his brows. "He did not. I have not spoken to him since Kórol's pronouncement. I've been making arrangements."

A rock sinks in my gut before I shake it off. That Fílga's here means hope is not all lost and my first idea, that my friends break me free, is still viable. "Can you get us out of here? Do you have the key?"

He hesitates, releasing the bars and rubbing the back of his neck with one hand. The other holds the sack aloft. "I do not have the keys. But—"

"He's our mysterious stranger," Leyden mock-whispers. In his normal voice, he addresses Fílga. "Will you melt the bars, or can you simply bend them?"

"Stop trying to scare him off," I say, frowning. "Fíl, if you don't have a key, why are you here?"

Fíl opens and closes his mouth as the color fades from his cheeks.

"Because he's an Eósy," Leyden says, as if it is obvious. "And only those with mastery over minerals could overcome the dampeners. See how his palms remain unburned?"

I turn back to Fílga, his face steadily paling. "Stop teasing him, Leyden."

"I am not," Leyden says, affronted. "I cannot lie, remember?"

"But you *can* be wrong. You aren't all-knowing and could—"

"Grace," Leyden says, interrupting me. "Don't make me give you yet another pep talk about your skills. I've barely recovered from the first one. You can fit clues together without my babying you through them."

Fílga's mouth snaps shut, the sound of his teeth clacking together loud in the silent cell. It looks like he's holding his breath.

"But...he called them Gods," I say, my mind stumbling over the facts attempting to fit together. "He talked about the Sìnnách like she was a spiritual thing. If he was Eósy, why would he—"

"The walls hide many things, dearest," Leyden answers. "Information most of all."

My brows raise. "So much so that you'd think your own species was a heavenly being?"

"It is simply a name. Remember your question of me when Mara demanded her test?"

That asking my name was too vague because I could call myself any number of things and it would be true. But confirming what I had already referred to myself as was more concrete.

"Panic at the revelation faster," Leyden says dryly. "If your friend continues to deny his magic, he'll likely lose consciousness. And given I am the only one feeling the dampeners, it doesn't seem fair."

I squint at Fílga, as if I can see the Eósy in him. I can't, just his face paling in fear. *No,* I realize dimly. *Not paling. Graying.* Dozens of clues race through my mind until they slot neatly into the picture before me: that Fílga *is* an Eósy. He's the 'other' he accidentally mentioned earlier. I slam my hands on the bars to hopefully shock him into admitting it. "Fíl, if it's true, tell us!" A high-pitched laugh spills from my lips. "I don't think I can handle you passing out after the day I've had."

Fíl shakes his head, more of a grimace, and the bag in his hands clangs hard against the bars. But before his eyes can roll back in his head, he gasps out a sharp, "It's true." Disgust covers his face as it slowly returns to its regular pallor.

Leyden's laugh interrupts whatever reaction I might have had. "Mysterious stranger who reveals himself. I win."

"He isn't a stranger," I say, keeping my attention on Fílga, who looks ready to bolt, the disgust mixing with shame. "And he's my friend, so it should count as my plan. Eósy or not. You are my friend, right, Fíl?"

Fílga's expression pinches in the corners. "Yes, of—"

Leyden ignores the byplay. "But it wasn't truly your plan, dearest. You planned for a guard—"

"There isn't time for this," Fílga growls, squeezing the bridge of his nose again and gliding away from the bars.

"We've got plenty of time, comrade." Leyden bares his teeth. "Until morning, at least. Unless you plan on making a run for Kórol's crown? Between the two of us, we've the pedigree for it."

I growl. "Shut up, Leyden." To Fíl, I ask gently, "Not to be insensitive about what you've just revealed, but *are* you planning on using your magic to release us? You still have magic, don't you?"

His shoulders slump but still he gives one sharp nod. "I had planned to disturb the bars enough to release you and let you merely guess at how it was done, rather than reveal myself."

I try to swallow down my questions, but they burble out. "And your magic is manipulating metal?"

He brandishes the sack. "Among other things. I also brought these in hopes they would help you on your journey." He presses the sack into my hands.

I peer inside, scores of shiny coins glint back up at me. "I just—I mean—how? Were you invited and then just never left?"

"He was here before the wall," Leyden says. "Bittállí's information campaign snagged him early."

"Your companion is partly correct," Fíl admits. "I never left what is now called Dalner. I spent a significant amount of time in the area known as the Wilds. I visited Ilsen at various times over the centuries."

My eyes flicker, caught in a moment of sheer disbelief. "How did you manage that without lying?"

His nose wrinkles. "A few centuries between visits. And...I have many names."

"As fascinating as this is," Leyden says. "Can you get on with it? The dampeners may not work on you, but I may be forced to enact Grace's plan and vomit over your shoes."

"Now you want us to hurry," I say under my breath.

"That was your plan?" Fílga says, scandalized.

I cross my arms around my stomach and restrain a pout. "One of them."

"Mine involved magic," Leyden says. "Hence why your presence is a tally in my favor."

Fíl sighs, looking like he does when he's tired of Tans' antics. Without commenting further, he crouches and wraps his fingers around the bars in the corner of my cell, the part farthest from Leyden. In an instant, he bends the metal to create an opening small enough for me to wedge through.

When I wriggle free and stand, Fílga clenches my shoulders, his expression pained. "I am sorry it came to this, Grace."

Mindful of the grime on my clothes, I gingerly hug him from the side. "Me too. That you had to reveal yourself."

"It couldn't last," he admits softly. "I have been walking on hot coals since your time in the Gate. Your lessons alone, when the only support for my statements was my own firsthand knowledge, was a flint ready to light."

"It explains why you kept putting me off when I asked for more information." I grin at him slyly. "And seriously, soulmates?"

He laughs. "You see my issue?"

Leyden clears his throat dramatically. "Again, I find myself asking: have you forgotten something?"

We turn to see Leyden glowering in the center of his cell, sweat pouring off his pale skin.

"Are you sure he is necessary for your plan?" Fílga says, rubbing his beard. "If he remained, Kórol's demand for justice would be sated and you could likely escape without further trouble."

Leyden makes a displeased noise as I shake my head. "I need him."

Fílga frowns. "I doubt—"

"Still in a cell," Leyden snaps.

With another irritated sigh, Fíl bends another hole for Leyden who scurries through.

"Come on now," Leyden says, clapping his hands imperiously. "To the next part of our escape. I need to get farther away from these rocks." He glares at Fíl who doesn't react.

I snag Fíl's arm before we leave the hallway. "Wait, do you have any paper?"

After leaving a discreet note I hope gets into Tans' hands, we sneak through the prison. Faburth stands at the top of the stairs, holding a heavy set of keys and gawking. Leyden glides into a defensive position while Fílga stammers, skin turning gray as he tries to think of an excuse that wasn't a lie.

They both relax when Faburth gathers me into a hug. "I should have known you'd find your way free."

"She's wily," Leyden says, leaning against the wall. "Like a roach."

Faburth eyes Leyden suspiciously. "Are you entirely sure he must go with you?"

"Why is everyone so keen on leaving me behind?" asks Leyden, pouting.

"You know why." I elbow Leyden in the ribs before he can comment. "His presence is nonnegotiable," I tell Faburth.

"Very well. But your absence will be noted as soon," Faburth says. "The King denied you a meal, but Lord Commander convinced the cooks to prepare one. It will be delivered soon, by whichever guards the King chooses. While I know my recruits, I cannot guarantee which guards will hold back if they're engaged to capture you."

I glance at Leyden. Hopefully my first implausible idea comes through soon. "We can handle it."

Faburth clasps me on the shoulder. "No, you must leave immediately. This is a fight you must run from, so you may fight another day."

"While a fight without magic sounds thrilling," Leyden says, emphasizing 'without magic,' and dashing my hopes, "I agree with your guard ally. We must clear the castle. I cannot cleave us from here until I regain more strength."

"I will take you to the stables," Faburth says, straightening. "There is a shortcut."

I clutch his arm, squeezing tight. "What about you? Will you get in trouble for having the keys?"

He flashes bright teeth, looking decades younger. "I've already accounted for that, Lady Grace." With a hand at my back, he prompts us down the hall.

Fílga lingers as the three of us start down another corridor.

"Fíl?" I hiss, checking for other passersby. "Are you coming?"

He stares back at me, conflict swirling in his gaze. "I planned to leave the castle. But if Commander Faburth's actions conceal mine, then perhaps..."

I jog towards him and cling to his hands. "Fíl, ignoring that Leyden's powers are well known and *someone* manipulated metal that can't be explained away, why would you stay? If anyone else figures out what you are, you're dead."

"It's highly unlikely—"

"Kórol isn't behaving rationally. Hurchá, the world isn't behaving rationally. You need to get out and protect yourself."

"No need to curse at me," he says mildly.

An idea hits me. "Try to get to Samsen, to Sáven. They seem a little more liberal in their views about the Eósy right now. Take the long route through the Wilds."

Fílga purses his lips. "And do you think Sáven will...accept me for what I am?"

"Of course, he will." I pull him into a tight hug. Before releasing him, I whisper in his ear, "But you'd better tell him soulmates aren't real."

An unbridled laugh escapes from his lips and he shows his crooked smile. "Good luck, Grace."

And we run in opposite directions towards our created destiny.

CHAPTER 29

There's no subterfuge on this trek to the stables. While Faburth knew a shortcut, it still takes us into the guard's stronghold by the training grounds and soldiers' residential block. But the rhythmic clatter of dinnerware and distant laughter promises that most guards are absorbed in their evening meal.

The sun fell during our brief stay in the prison, leaving a hazy evening light hovering over us that guarantees to cloak us in darkness. We slink into the darkened stable. Dull light filters through the wooden slats as Faburth directs us to the first stall.

"You'll need to share," he whispers. "I am sorry, Lady Grace." With a gentle nudge, a midnight black horse moved forward, hooves barely making a sound on the straw-littered ground. Unlike the last time I snuck into the stables, silence is imperative this time.

Faburth secures the bridle on the horse, his movements deliberate to avoid any clinking of metal. Leyden heaves himself on the horse's back first and holds out his hand for me. I swallow down any immediate complaints at having to cling to him during the entire ride. The snide thoughts aren't real and only keep me from panicking at what will happen if we're caught by a less-than-sympathetic guard. Leyden pats my hand where it rests around his chest.

"Feel free to snuggle," he whispers, loud enough for only me to hear. I squeeze tight, thankful he understands my need for the distraction.

After we're settled, Faburth quickly selects a second horse. At my raised eyebrows, he smirks. "A distraction," he mouths silently.

When we're both tacked and seated, he leans forward and clasps me on the shoulder again. "I'll create a ruckus and head towards Helne. The guard presence is heavier there, closer to the wall. You go towards Arcove."

"Thank you again, Faburth," I whisper.

"Take heed, Gracel. I am sure we will meet again." And with a loud smack to his horse's backside, he takes off, whooping loudly. The guards' chatter in the distance stops and a flurry of movement replaces it. Leyden directs the horse away from the training grounds. We can just feel the ground shaking as a contingent of guards chase in Faburth's direction.

And we secretly steal away.

Beneath the moonlit sky, we spur on our stolen horse. His hooves drum a desperate rhythm against the dirt, gravel cracking under our weight in a discordant symphony. It sounds deafening in our silent escape, but each thump carries us farther from the looming castle and closer to that ephemeral boundary where Leyden's magic will reawaken.

But Faburth's distraction doesn't protect us long. As the castle shrinks behind us, the thundering gallop of hooves echoes from behind us. Clutching Leyden's tunic, I crane my neck to catch a glimpse of our pursuers.

A stream of soldiers chases after us, all on horseback. Kórol leads the charge, his ice-blue eyes aflame in a tempest of rage and desperation. He holds a bow and arrow, determination etched across his face. Tans is almost neck-and-neck, spurring on his own horse but weaponless. Some of the dozens of soldiers behind him brandish swords. Others have notched arrows, each surging forward at Kórol's shouted commands.

Leyden jerks the horse to the right, steering off the path and towards the Hallard Mountains that run perpendicular to Raddare's Pass. My temple collides with his shoulder blade, igniting a surge of pain and a kaleidoscope of white spots that hinder my vision. I wrench my neck back forward and press closer to Leyden's sweat-soaked back, willing the throbbing pain to recede.

Arrows soar above us, a deadly cascade from our pursuers. I tighten my grip on Leyden, and he grunts from the strain. But each one misses its mark, embedding themselves harmlessly into the loamy earth, a trail of potential violence in our wake.

A small grove of trees appears before us, and Leyden urges the horse towards it. We surge through it, the stolen horse leaping over roots and dodging between trees, its breath forming clouds in the brisk air. Shadows dance at the edges of our vision, the moon's silver glow casting eerie shapes among the branches. We're hidden from sight, but only just, as the guards relentlessly press forward. Arrows graze the trees, but still they miss us. Kórol's furious shouts fill the night, his desperation growing as the distance between us narrows. I cling to Leyden as he clings to the horse.

"Are we far enough away yet?" My voice is almost lost to the night air whipping past us.

"Almost," Leyden shouts. "Hold on for a bit longer."

My breath hitches with fear, gaze darting between the rocky ground and glint of moonlight between the trees. The landscape will be against us soon enough, when the trees disappear and there's only open air until the mountains or the sea.

All too quickly, our hideout empties into a clearing, illuminated by the silver glow of the moon and exposing us for our pursuers. Whatever magic, poor aim, or willing blunders that kept us safe from the arrows' path falters. A shaft zings near my ear, rustling my hair, too close for comfort. I press closer to Leyden's back and chance another look behind me.

Tans' and Kórol's horses are running side by side, their reins twisted together. They're grappling for Kórol's bow, which is still notched and ready for release. Tans wrestles the limb away, but Kórol elbows him in the nose. Tans' grip falters and Kórol yanks the bow from his grasp. With a manic grin, Kórol re-aims the bow even as Tans' scrabbles for it in the air. As Kórol releases the shaft, Tans grabs hold of their knotted reins. The shaft veers towards us just as the two horses collide and Tans and Kórol are thrown off their saddles.

"Duck," I screech, bending low in my seat. My heart clenches in my chest in terror, for Leyden and myself, for Tans who might not survive another fall from a horse, even for Kórol.

Leyden folds in half, but it's too late. The arrow flies overhead and embeds in his shoulder. He lets out a howl, his hands yanking hard on the reins before releasing them. The horse rears, his long antlers almost striking us as his neck arcs backward, and we tumble to the ground.

Leyden lands on top of me, knocking the breath from me as I hit the grass with a hard thump. Leyden keeps rolling, spinning until he stops a few feet away and lands on his front. The horse keeps running. Leyden's head slammed into my cheekbone, and it feels like it snapped in half. But there's no time to consider the pain; we must get away from Kórol and his men. I crawl towards Leyden's still form, my palms splitting open, leaving a trail of blood that joins Leyden's. Grass and rock embed themselves in the scratches.

Behind me, I can hear the horses slowing. My hair covers my face but between the matted clumps, I see Tans and Kórol grappling. Relief mixes with the pain, that they aren't hurt, but I can't think about it for long. I shuffle forward faster. There's no telling when Kórol will break free or one of his guards will fulfill his whims.

When I reach Leyden, the shaft of the arrow is sticking out of his left shoulder. My hands flutter over his broken skin, trying and failing to pull up any knowledge on what to do. But there's no time to second guess myself. I snap the arrow in half, the shaft barely protruding from his skin, and shove him onto his back. His face looks as bruised as mine feels. I pray to the Fates, to *whomever* that he hasn't broken his neck. His hands press hard against his shoulder, wrapped around the remains of the arrowhead, blood dribbling between his fingers.

"You...really...should...have...taken...those...trainee...tests," he gasps raggedly.

My heartbeat thumps in my head like a booming drum, too loud to even hear myself think. "Keep pressure on it," I scream.

"No...need...to...yell," Leyden says. His eyes widen as he looks behind us.

I spin, my fists up as ineffective shields. Kórol has thrown off Tans and is running towards us. But two guards leap at him, grasping his arms and trying to hold him back. Tans stands and races towards him.

"We need to get out of here!" I clutch his shirt and pull him to sit. He nods woozily. One hand raises in the air, bloodstained and dripping. I press my hands around the arrow shaft. *Goddamnit, I should have taken those tests,* I think mirthlessly. Leyden could bleed out and this would be all for naught, just more guilt to add to my ledger.

Leyden rips a jagged line in the air, four disjointed slashes that wobble weakly, but it's enough to get through. Each keeping one hand on his wound, together we get on our knees and fall through the opening. My back hits against the side of the tear and I swallow down the sick that arises. With Leyden's upper half leaning against me, I shove him to the side and yank his waist through the opening as it seals itself up, closing right as his feet clear the opening. The last thing I see is Kórol's inhuman snarl and Tans' grim face above him.

Leyden's opening brought us beneath the sheltering canopy of a colossal tree. He grunts with each shuffle forward, still on his knees. As we stumble into the shadowy refuge, he drags himself to lean against the trunk, one hand still pressed firmly against the arrow lodged in his shoulder. My gaze trails over his shaking body, his skin looking paler.

"We need help," I say, my voice trembling. It feels like I'm yelling.

"No...allies...here...for me...but maybe...you," he eeks out between strained breaths, his words hanging heavily in the crisp air.

"What? Where did you bring us?" I demand, my eyes wide with a mixture of fear and anticipation. I'd thought Dànna was our destination, but maybe he brought us closer to Samsen.

In the dim light filtering through the leaves overhead, he gestures weakly behind us.

With shaking limbs, I spin around, my gaze locking on a construction unlike any I've seen in Dalner. In front of us is a concrete structure in a honeycomb shape, with an asphalt path leading through it. Beyond it, the Chicago skyline sprawls against the moonlit sky.

He's brought us to Earth.

AUTHOR'S NOTE

Thank you for reading *When Walls Rise*, the second in The Ascend Trials and sequel to *If the Walls Fall*.

If you're interested in more expanded and bonus content, check out my website (**kmalady.com**). You can find other fun information there, including the **free prequel novella** told from the point of view of the Great Matron (when she was known only as Bittállí), focusing on her reason for revenge and providing more history on Sekai and the War that led to the wall.

I've also got several other books upcoming, including a genderbent Theseus and the Minotaur tale (Threaded Secrets), the third book in The Ascend Trials, and more fantasy romance and romantic fantasy adventure stories.

SNEAK PEEK OF BOOK THREE

G race and her friends will return for Book Three. Check out a short sneak peek of part of chapter 1.

"All these books have similarities, including a border between the mortal world and the magical." He snags my spiral bound notebook holding our notes, flipping through each repeated mention. "There must be something similar here. A place where there's a thinning between our world, or a portal. The question is simply *where*."

I'm tempted to be skeptical of the claim, but Sekai exists, and Leyden is living proof of 'fairies.' The books have a multitude of differences, but enough parallels to prove the prior visitors on Earth left breadcrumbs about the Eósy. The inability to lie, the importance of promises (or 'deals'). Even some of the creatures are somewhat similar: the dobhà (called dobhar-chhú here) and the sàchenda (called an ellen trechend here). "Do you have any ideas?"

He nods. "The false version of us, the *Aos Si*, are Celtic. We should check there."

"As good a place as any," I say, shrugging and pulling up a search engine.

'Fairy portals in Ireland' give few results, but we cobble together a half dozen locations, of fairy trees and rocks, of mountains and rock formations. Some of the pictures, where the emerald-green pastures stretch into rugged mountains that meet the sky, even look like the landscape of Dalner. *This might work.* "Any of them sound familiar?"

Leyden smirks as he flaps a long-fingered hand at the computer. "Pull up a map of the country on the interwebs."

"You stalked humans for decades," I say, downloading an illustrated map. "You know it's called the internet."

He sniffs and doesn't respond. Together we stare at the map of Ireland until he leans in close, almost touching the screen and pointing. A zip of static flies from the screen to his finger and he squeaks. Sticking his finger inside his mouth, he gestures with an elbow. "Flip it upside down."

"Of course, my liege."